To DeeDee with gratitude

Juanula DaCosta

OH MY BELOVED

✦ BOOK TWO *of The* HAWK ISLAND SERIES ✦

MANUELA DACOSTA

ARCHWAY PUBLISHING

Copyright © 2020 Manuela DaCosta.

All rights reserved. No part of this book may be used or reproduced by any means, graphic, electronic, or mechanical, including photocopying, recording, taping or by any information storage retrieval system without the written permission of the author except in the case of brief quotations embodied in critical articles and reviews.

This is a work of fiction. All of the characters, names, incidents, organizations, and dialogue in this novel are either the products of the author's imagination or are used fictitiously.

Archway Publishing books may be ordered through booksellers or by contacting:

Archway Publishing
1663 Liberty Drive
Bloomington, IN 47403
www.archwaypublishing.com
844-669-3957

Because of the dynamic nature of the Internet, any web addresses or links contained in this book may have changed since publication and may no longer be valid. The views expressed in this work are solely those of the author and do not necessarily reflect the views of the publisher, and the publisher hereby disclaims any responsibility for them.

Any people depicted in stock imagery provided by Getty Images are models, and such images are being used for illustrative purposes only. Certain stock imagery © Getty Images.

ISBN: 978-1-4808-9588-1 (sc)
ISBN: 978-1-4808-9589-8 (e)

Library of Congress Control Number: 2020917592

Print information available on the last page.

Archway Publishing rev. date: 10/16/2020

To Lhalh with all my love
(And we still don't know if we see the same green…)

Oh my beloved if you go away,
As I've heard rumors say,
For me, engrave your name,
On a pebble of the quay

1

The Stranger

Long, long ago, when animals could talk and men could listen, Angela lived in a village of a remote island. One could live a lifetime on Hawk Island and never go to Two Brooks, the most far north and high-up village. So, if a stranger went there, it was for a very specific reason or the same old excuse.

Then one day a stranger with wild hair and a hooded smile knocked at Angela's door and asked for the fastest route to the city. Angela knew she was looking at a liar.

> *Yes, my lying heart,*
> *have you seen the roads*
> *to get you there?*

But he didn't quote poetry—he asked for water.

The summer was being particularly cruel with drought. To ask for water, even just a bit, was to ask for too much. Would this lying stranger know of her sacrifice? Angela stepped aside to let him enter her kitchen. She called for her dog, Viriato.

The man drank his water looking at Angela. She saw his teeth magnified by the bottom of the glass. Although all were waiting for rain, the morning was full of light, the garden was green and the hydrangeas mantling the boundary stone walls were full of bloom.

Angela looked out the window to the backyard. Hercules the cat was sitting on the wall where the hydrangeas had a bald spot. Hercules was big and gray. He could be a cross between a cat and a cow.

The man followed her gaze and pointed to the cat. "You should put a saddle on that thing."

This man was the cloud on their horizon. They were prepared for him as one prepares for a storm. Monsignor Inocente had brought this stranger to them as he did with Angus Pomba. Would this man be as brutal? They would have another stranger looking at their secrets and assessing their sins. Every so often they were visited by mainlanders with excuses. And they stayed around, observing, looking for unrest.

"What do you want?" she asked.

Viriato growled. The stranger kept an eye on the dog. "I want to rent a room. I was told that you have rooms for rent."

"So, you're not lost. I thought you wanted the fastest road to the city." She filled one of the glasses with water.

He hesitated, but finally said, "I wasn't sure if I wanted to rent a room from you. I was told that you are a witch." He smiled.

Almost anything could make Angela laugh. But that was before the tragedy in Two Brooks. Now and then, she momentarily forgot that life was no longer simple, and that look of laughter was no longer second nature to her.

"I'm working on the Night Justice incidents across the island, not just Two Brooks," he said. "But most importantly I'm working on the case of the disappearances of the young men from this village."

"Ah!" she said and closed her eyes for a second. How much pain was he bringing with that smile? One of the young men who disappeared was her husband and the other one was a kind and beautiful creature with a body for loving—Manuel, beautiful, tragic Manuel who loved Madalena as if he couldn't do anything else. There was another who also had disappeared—Saul, Madalena's husband. They didn't know what to think of Saul. For so long they thought he was one man and then, like a miracle, he seemed to be revealed as another, transformed by love or simply looked at with kindness.

"I'm a police detective. I came from the mainland specifically to look into these…acts of aggression and disappearances."

Acts of aggression. Angela pondered on the way he put it. If he was not a stranger, she would talk to him about aggression. He had no idea about the aggression they suffered and the aggression they delivered. But, again, hearing a stranger speak of her man disappearing was comforting. Everyone believed he had died, swallowed by that furious sea of roar and foam. Only Lazarus' wristwatch had been retrieved from the sea cliffs where he had disappeared— recovered by his father. A Timex sent by Filomena Lucia, a gentle godmother in Canada, for Lazarus' confirmation. Oh, how Lazarus loved that small, kind, beautiful woman who left like so many others and never came back, not even to visit.

The wristwatch was in the pocket of her dress—she always had it with her. It was the last thing that Lazarus touched. Sometimes when she couldn't sleep, she imagined the wristwatch slipping off his wrist, while his body scraped and battered was swept out to sea, leaving a shiny memento jammed in the rocks.

The village was divided about Angela—some thought that she grew strong with her loss and others thought that she went crazy. There were times when the truth about losing Lazarus was so heavy that she buckled under it, and other times it was so unreal that she treated it as if it was a lie. This was one of those times when the truth got too heavy. She softly hummed a mournful tune and then whispered the words as if easing away from the sharp pain.

> *She was my beautiful boat*
> *With the colors of the sea*
> *Deceitful like a lover*
> *Sailed away far from me*

She closed her eyes, tired. She was so tired of everything—of fighting, of being always on guard, of pretending she was strong. She didn't care if this man saw her raw sorrow. He believed that Lazarus disappeared, and that was a thousand ways better than to presume that he had died. To hope was infinitely better than to just accept. And she was hoping in front of this man, in her kitchen smelling of soup, fresh bread, and other good things. She was hoping that this man would tell her that Lazarus didn't die. Viriato whimpered because he knew of this complete sadness that assailed her unexpectedly and made her surrender to a heaving sorrow. Hercules the cat had been all along witnessing the interaction, but only now he got interested. Viriato was whimpering, and there was a stranger in the kitchen. The cat slowly approached the man, sniffed him, bit him on the ankle, and ran away. The man screamed, Viriato howled, Hercules hissed, the ducks and chickens clucked and fanned their wings in disapproval. The glasses on the table fell on their sides and water ran across the table into her lap, down her legs, and onto the floor. Sitting in water pooled in the seat of her chair, she looked down at a polished black shoe, a navy-blue sock with little white horses, and a naked ankle punctured red by Hercules' fangs.

She caught herself digressing into foolish things. She did that often, in the middle of something sad. She was invaded by thoughts that seemed to have nothing to do with anything. Sometimes these thoughts were ridiculous and she wanted to laugh, like now, about this man's socks with little white horses... *unleash those horses and let them trample you up to your balls,* she thought.

The man had a look of amazement, and he thought he saw a grin on her face. Was he hurt? A cat the size of a cow had just bitten him. He exclaimed, "That cat should be shot!"

She fixed him a cold stare. She heard that before. Hercules was the target of more death wishes than a war criminal. Suddenly she felt the urge to throw this mainlander out on the road.

"He doesn't like strangers," she said. "But if the cat is a problem, you don't have to rent from me. There's always the city." Her voice went down an octave. If he knew her, he would have recognized this as a warning.

"I'm sorry," he said. "I don't hate animals. I was just taken by surprise... I've never been bitten by a cat... by a dog, yes, but never by a cat." He looked down at Viriato with suspicion.

Viriato was panting, his tongue out, looking at the man with kindness. The man thought about his conversation with the monsignor, the village priest. The monsignor said that Angela was unpredictable, even crazy. She confused animals with people and she would disconcert him when he least expected.

The monsignor kept the village on a path of rectitude and redemption, never giving up on the villagers, while never letting them rest. Suffering was his favorite virtue. And those who he didn't count among his sheep, like the poor detective from the mainland, he unleashed hell, profanity and bodily harm.

The man was staring and Angela returned his stare.

"The monsignor thought that you needed the business and I am willing to pay well." He added after a long pause, "I'm assuming that you trust the monsignor?"

"He scares the devil out of us... literally. We avoid sinning just not to go to confession."

She is making fun of me, he thought. He smiled, showing white beautiful teeth. His smile illuminated his dark eyes, which conveyed a hint of wickedness. His hair was dark and wild, his skin tanned and smooth.

He looks like a gypsy, she thought. *With that raspy voice, he could sing one of those romantic wails...* She stopped herself.

They didn't like mainlanders in the archipelago of Atlantis. Mainlanders had come and gone, always leaving damaged people behind. Mainlanders were pretentious, liars, spies, exploitive, and always ready to cause pain.

The man looked so intensely at Angela that she held her breath.

He was measuring her up, assessing, deep in the resolve to find out everything there was to know about them—who was foe and who was just trouble. After all, that was his job... This girl dying of grief would be no problem. She was too transparent.

"Don't make that mistake," she warned. "Don't underestimate us. There was a time that half of the village went to jail and the detective in charge couldn't find out anything."

The man was surprised. She read his mind.

Then she added, "Other people from the mainland came here too, like you, and they weren't able to succeed in what they came to do." She stared. "They were co-opted…left after failing miserably or…they died. In the end, one of these things usually happens."

He grew serious now. Did this woman just threaten him? He knew about the other detectives. He heard the stories and the warning from the chief of police.

"This should be interesting," he said in a measured tone.

"I want you to find out what happened to Lazarus, Manuel, and Saul. But you'll fail if you go into the Night Justice and other things…" she said.

"This Night Justice business may be connected with the disappearance of these men," he said.

"No, they're not connected. The Night Justice is not anyone's business but our own. Have you ever thought that maybe there is no justice for the crimes the Night Justice punishes? Do you think that the almighty law of the country cares about us here?"

"They cared enough to send me over."

"Please, Detective, don't insult my intelligence. They sent you over because the motherland is nervous about something. They send people to keep an eye on us. They don't care about justice, especially justice for us."

"That's quite a cynical view," he said quietly.

They stared at each other. He was thinking that Angela was a lot more than strange. There was a force about her. He had been warned.

"You want a room in my house…be my guest…literally." Then she added, "If you are brave enough."

They looked at each other for a moment. "You will fail," she said. "You are so out of your element!"

"We will see, won't we?" he retorted.

His name was Emanuel Santos.

Angela took Mr. Santos up to the second floor to show him the room. Her house was big and airy, with wide windows and freshly painted stucco walls.

The opened windows let in the hot murmuring summer. A gentle breeze stirred the curtains and the peach tree planted in the middle of the garden filtered the sun into dancing soft shadows. The bed wide and low to the floor seemed like a lover in perpetual invitation—white cotton sheets, light blanket comforting for a summer's night. There was a dresser, an armoire, a desk, a bookcase full of books and an armchair reliable and sturdy like an old servant.

"This is perfect," he said surprised. "I couldn't ask for anything better!" He walked around the room, opening the armoire, the drawers, laughing softly, satisfied with his situation and himself. He looked out of the window onto a terrace. Beyond the terrace, the generous garden sloped down to a bed of flowers. Far in the back, there was a high stone wall, shrouded with hydrangeas. Mr. Santos abruptly retreated from the window. "He's looking up at me!" he said in disbelief.

Angela went to the window, and there he was, sitting on the wall where the hydrangeas had a bald spot. Hercules was looking up, narrowing his eyes at the poor man.

Angela would do for the police investigator what she did for the others: provide three meals per day, clean rooms, clean clothes, and get paid weekly in advance.

Angela's house was one of a handful of houses in the village that had indoor plumbing. Such niceties existed in the city, though not in the villages. During a drought, however, indoor plumbing didn't help—everyone had to go to the public fountain. Needless to say, taking in lodgers during drought was no easy feat.

The meals would be served at the same time every day—morning, midday, and evening. If they weren't home when the meals were served, well, they were out of luck. If they didn't like the meals, they were free to find food somewhere else.

Angela was in the kitchen preparing lunch when Mr. Santos returned.

Before he put his bags down, Angela said, "There are a few things you need to know before you settle in."

He looked at her with a doubtful expression.

"Viriato the dog, Hercules the cat, Dalia the duck, and Nixon the pig, who you haven't met, eat with us and sleep in the house. They are family. And another thing, during drought season, no one takes showers, you can take a bath but you must save the water for the garden."

No wonder the garden looked so fresh and green in drought season—at the expense of her lodgers' hygiene, he thought. He folded his shoulders inward in resignation. He had just noticed Dalia under the table pecking corn.

Dalia jumped and quacked, scaring Nixon who was coming through the door. Nixon was a running pig; he rarely walked. Viriato and Hercules entered side by side as if having a private conversation. Hercules looked around in his perpetual scowl, then blinked when he saw the detective. *Fresh scratching posts*, the cat thought looking fixedly at Mr. Santos' legs.

Dona Mafalda, the teacher and one of Angela's lodgers, was also from the mainland. Mafalda Maria de Lourdes Dias Santos Sampaio do Monte da Cruz was her name. She came from one of the last kings of the country's noble lineage. She was not from the lineage of a mistress like so many important people were. She was from Queen Mafalda's line.

Dona Mafalda was short and round with white velvety skin. She was very proud of her skin—just like Queen Mafalda's—she was told. It was impossible not to notice that Dona Mafalda had fallen in love with another lodger, Dom Carlos, who continued to interact with her as if she didn't confess her love. He was kind, helpful, and annoying at times with his gentle teasing. Dona Mafalda, in the face of unrequited love, suffered from bouts of resentment and fault-finding.

Dona Mafalda could hardly contain her curiosity about the new lodger and compatriot. This new man could be her ally. Maybe he was also from royal lineage, maybe cousins since they both had Santos in their names. She came through the door running almost as fast as Nixon, with similar small steps and similar sounds.

Angela had lunch on the table: vegetable soup, freshly baked bread and salad. Dom Carlos was already sitting in his usual place, next to Viriato, deliberately avoiding Hercules, and feeding Nixon under the table.

Dom Carlos was a tall, distinguished man who always dressed impeccably. He had the classic look of a movie star—tall, green eyes, fair skin, and light brown hair with shining curls. His smile was disarming and produced two perfect dimples, complementing a large generous mouth. When he smiled, he showed slightly overlapping incisors. Those incisors were the only thing that weren't straight with Dom Carlos, and they fit him perfectly. There was great disagreement about his age. Younger women said that he was in his late twenties, while older women swore that he was in his late forties. It could be said that Dom Carlos was the dream of every woman on the island—old and young alike. The stories about him were abundant. Although he had an apartment in the city, he spent most of his time in Two Brooks. People saw him as a rich and mysterious man. Some believed that Angela Matias knew his secrets, while others doubted that even Angela knew all there was to know. Dom Carlos was tight-lipped about his private life, although he was generous with his thoughts about life in general. He was kind, liked to laugh, and was always looking for a funny angle about everything. His name was not Dom Carlos, but António. He became Dom Carlos when Angela looked at him for the first time and thought that he looked like Dom Carlos, the last king. And so, he became Dom Carlos to all.

When he arrived on Hawk Island, he came to Two Brooks looking for a place to stay. He became Angela's first lodger, with the determination of a pest—to stay. Most people were curious. Such a sophisticated man in Two Brooks, and with an apartment in the city. Some said that it was Monsignor Inocente who recommended Angela's home, but according to the monsignor, he had not. He didn't even like the man, making the monsignor virtually the only person who didn't.

Dom Carlos, a businessman from the mainland, established himself on the island as a distributor of agricultural machinery. Angela and Lazarus were partners in this business venture, "The Cooperative."

Dom Carlos didn't know about the new lodger until he got home. He, along with Dona Mafalda, didn't like other lodgers. They had in the past paid off traveling salesmen to stay somewhere else, much to Angela's distress.

"The monsignor recommended the new police detective to come here and…" Angela explained.

"Ahhh!" Dom Carlos muttered. "That man! That…that…" and he couldn't think of anything else to call the monsignor. Dom Carlos was a gentle man who rarely got angry, but the simple mention of the monsignor was sure to annoy him.

Angela smiled.

"He is the one, the promised detective to look at the…Night Justice incidents and the disappearances," she said quietly.

"How many incidents have we had in the last few years?" Dom Carlos asked regarding the Night Justice attacks that sporadically beset the island.

"I don't know…a few," Angela answered vaguely.

"How about the new detective?" Dona Mafalda asked, full of anticipation.

"He's here, finally..." Angela said.

They all knew that this day would come. The previous detective, Angus Pomba, had died, and it was just a matter of time before another detective would arrive. The general sense was that the motherland was interested in something, and not necessarily on the Night Justice or the disappearing men. At times, the islanders felt that the motherland was circling them like a shark, while they waited for the awful bite. Other times they thought that something was going to be snatched away from them, but they didn't know what, so they couldn't even hide whatever was being coveted.

The sea, according to the villagers, in the last year had swallowed three men and one of them was Lazarus. The sea—that murderer that surrounded everything—it was always peering in, ready to pounce, ready to swallow them.

The village men were wrapping up their day and coming down from the fields. "Lover...Diamond...Brilliance...Star..." they called out, their cattle answering with lazy moos.

Walking up to the monsignor's house, Dom Carlos mused that if the men were half as kind to their wives as they were to their cattle, they would get a lot more loving.

He was bracing himself to knock when the door opened in a flash as if the intent was to yank it by the hinges. The monsignor, austere and trembling like a reed, ushered him in.

"The new detective is here. What are you going to do about it? Where is all that influence that you brag about?"

Dom Carlos, with his arms crossed over his chest, said in the same flat tone, "*You* are responsible for this whole mess, Monsignor. Don't ask me to fix it! You messed up by calling the dogs from the mainland!"

The stress on *you* set the monsignor on a higher level of fury. "*You* too are mainland trash with no place to rest your ass! If you can't help us, then leave!" he barked, pointing a finger in Dom Carlos' face.

Dom Carlos said quietly. "And as far as mainland trash, so are you." He took a deep breath and said in the same quiet voice, "Take your finger out of my face or I'll break it. I will *not* leave Angela's home and I will not be responsible for fixing your meddling, fucked up messes. You own this one."

The men stared at each other, measuring the power of their words.

"Damn you!" the monsignor whispered.

"You are a bit too late," Dom Carlos retorted.

Dom Carlos didn't go to church and when the monsignor, with pulpit-punching enthusiasm, denounced him as a non-believer—without ever saying his name—the villagers knew that the monsignor was talking about Dom Carlos. "There are those who don't even believe that Jesus is the Lord!" the monsignor screamed from the pulpit.

But …was that true? Dom Carlos didn't believe that Jesus was the Lord?

How could that be? They liked Dom Carlos. If there ever was a kind soul in this world, it was Dom Carlos. The monsignor must be talking about someone else or he was just wrong.

Of course, the monsignor was right. Dom Carlos didn't believe Jesus was the Lord. Jesus was something, but not the Lord. He was a prophet, an exceedingly smart Jew, a rebel, a political figure, a demagogue. This was what Dom Carlos said at the table that night when faced with the question if he believed in Jesus. Yes, he believed in Jesus, but not that he was the Lord. Dom Carlos was not even sure there was a Lord.

So, again, the monsignor didn't lie. They should have known that the monsignor never, ever lied.

The villagers didn't know what to do with the accusations monsignor hurled against Dom Carlos. And what was a demagogue anyway? He was so kind, always. Wasn't that what Jesus wanted? Kindness above all? António Dores, the deacon, believed that Jesus was the Lord and yet he was a tyrant to his wife and kids. So what was the point?

Dona Mafalda, who was not a fan of the monsignor, silently enjoyed the fact that Dom Carlos antagonized the priest mercilessly. She had had a few unfortunate run-ins with the monsignor's authority. Most serious, and the final straw for Dona Mafalda, was the slap that the monsignor planted on her face—an open-handed slap that left the mark of his four long, thin fingers, like claws, turning red on Dona Mafalda's royal skin.

Maria Gomes had witnessed the whole thing and she was the first to assist Dona Mafalda after this humiliating incident. This window into Dona Mafalda's humiliation gave Maria the freedom to get close to that snobbish woman and explain to her some of the village politics, and at the same time make excuses for the monsignor's inexcusable behavior.

"As you may know, some people don't like the bishop because he is trying to control the village by stealing the Holy Ghost from us," Maria said.

Dona Mafalda's superior mind started immediately organizing an argument as well as a teaching moment for this poor woman.

"A slap wasn't that bad," Maria continued, interrupting Dona Mafalda's rebuttal. "You can't imagine how much harder it is to be hit by a missal."

"A missal?" Dona Mafalda asked.

"Yes, a missal," said Maria Gomes. "That big black book of prayers he carries all the time. He hit me with that. Someone commented about the monsignor looking in the direction of Mercedes Graça's bedroom window and he thought it was me. The monsignor called me over, right here where we stand, and hit me so hard on the side of the head that I went running sideways all across the church finally ending up against Saint Pedro over there." She pointed to a lugubrious Saint Pedro. "He could have killed me if he fell on me!"

Dona Mafalda looked bewildered. Imagine having to live here all your life, with these crazy people. One ends up crazy too… Too often she had forgotten who she used to be and slipped into a foreign skin, as if she was possessed. *I need to be careful*, she thought. *Otherwise, I will end up mired in their insidious ignorance or fall prey to their cunning.*

This was a village of incredibly kind and violent people, all at once. Teaching their children, she could make a difference. But she felt the pull grow stronger each day to become like them—childlike almost, courageous and fearful, transparent and deviant. And that madman of the monsignor right in the middle of everything, confusing principles, exploiting divided loyalties, coddling the villagers, and encouraging them to believe that he knew the reason and the path to everything. He was their brain, their will and redemption.

Dona Mafalda, while waiting for the detective to show up, was musing about what relationship he may have had with the monsignor or with Dom Carlos. Were they connected somehow or was he another madman like Angus Pomba, sent over by the motherland?

Dom Carlos, also waiting for the new lodger, was completely engrossed in his thoughts. He had a distant and vague look, like a dreamer. He fell into these moods often—his lips slightly parted as if about to form a revealing word or receive a kiss.

When Emanuel Santos came downstairs, everyone stared in his direction, including Hercules who rose ever so slowly.

If cats could smirk, Hercules was doing it.

When Emanuel Santos reached the bottom of the stairs, he stopped, slightly taken aback. Everyone was staring open-mouthed, even the pig, sitting in the corner of the kitchen with a bowl of soup in front of him.

The cat was the first to move. He stepped down from his chair and went to Emanuel and sniffed his shoes. The cat looked up at the man and hissed. It sounded more like a guffaw than a hiss, but Emanuel didn't move and looked at Angela in a silent plea.

Silently she picked the cat up and sat him again on his chair.

The introductions were brief—they already knew of each other. They ate in awkward silence, conscious of the chewing sounds and the silverware ringing like bells on their plates.

"I'm sure you already know why I'm here," Emanuel broke the silence. "I would like to talk with each of you at some point this week."

Dona Mafalda had a dreamy look on her face. She had a roaming, large and thirsty heart, and she found this new man not only interesting but beautiful and refined… like her.

Emanuel said, addressing no one in particular, "I came to investigate the mystery of the missing men… According to my boss, your own priest made the request. And I was also charged with the responsibility to look into the Night Justice incidents going on around the island."

Emanuel remembered the last conversation he had had with his boss before coming to Hawk Island. According to the police superintendent, it was unlike the monsignor to request outside help. The monsignor knew everything—who lived and who died, who ran away on the midnight ship and who lay low for a few days to wait out a disgrace. But these events, these three disappearances, the monsignor couldn't explain.

Previous attempts to deal with the people from Two Brooks had ended in disaster. Two Brooks was suspicious of authority and with good reason. The injuries caused by Angus Pomba, a police detective from the mainland, were all too fresh.

Emanuel had been surprised when the superintendent informed him that he was being assigned to go to Atlantis because he fit the desired profile. The superintendent declined to elaborate on what he meant by that.

2

The Sacristy

The women were now sitting, thinking about that time eighteen months earlier, around Christmas and before Nascimento got married. They had promised each other not to talk about the missing men because they didn't know what to do. But life was hijacked by the devil and it was time to start thinking about those events because a new detective had just arrived.

Since they were children, Angela, Nascimento, Madalena, and Ascendida were summoned to the sacristy almost after every confession. The villagers, between worry and amusement, labeled them as the "Sacristy." Most of their trespasses, according to the monsignor, seemed so conspiratorial that simple penances individually delivered from the confessional did not suffice. Their sins were collective and consequently so should be their punishment.

Now the four women sat in front of the fire looking at its gentle destruction. The huge clay oven was a dome of heat at the back of the chimney room, a small stone room at the back of the kitchen where fires roared, and where the cooking was done. They felt baked by the heat but comforted by each other. The linguiça slowly dripped fat, making a hissing sound on the hot mouth of the oven.

They liked to meet on "baking bread day" to talk about little and big secrets because no one wanted to be in the kitchen during that time—not the children, the men, the dogs, distracted chickens, or even the cats. But the secret that got them huddled together that day in Ascendida's chimney room was too big for words and too much of a foe that had been avoided for over a year.

"I'm glad we finally are going to talk about this," Nascimento said. "We pride ourselves on being brave and we've been avoiding this for such a long time."

Nascimento was referring to one of her nights of voyeurism, more than one year ago, when she saw two men dragging another up the road, and Nascimento was convinced that the man had been dead.

"Well, how do you know that the man was dead?" Ascendida asked.

The others looked at Ascendida and saw the little girl of many years ago who had always been unreasonably determined about everything. She walked straight ahead, never responding when they nicknamed her *Ass*. Ass didn't stick because Ascendida was one thing above all—stubborn. And now she didn't want an unknown dead man in the already complicated picture of Two Brooks.

Nascimento was wringing her hands under her apron.

Ascendida continued, "He was probably drunk, and the other men were bringing him home."

That was very possible. Men were often falling-down drunk and before they got home to their wives and mothers, other men sobered them up. This was a way of keeping women truthful when they proudly stated that their sons or husbands never came home drunk. No, they didn't, and that was one of their ways to love their women—never go home drunk.

Nascimento persisted quietly that the man she saw was dead. Two men passed her by in the night supporting another man dragging his legs in the mud, bobbing his head and looking lifeless.

"It was too dark and the moon hid precisely when they came near. I couldn't see who they were," she said, as she had maintained a thousand times before.

Nascimento was a strange woman. She was fearful of everyday things—the monsignor's wrath, her husband's sadness, the cunning of the fishmonger, but she roamed woods and hills, crossed brooks and bridges and sat on the cemetery wall at midnight to spy on the darkness of her village. When she got home wet and cold from her nighttime outings, her husband would think she was sleepwalking again. He would dry her hair and change her clothes and tuck her in, terrified of what could have happened. He had the whole village on alert for her. But when no one ever saw her at night, they forgot about his fears. Sleepwalkers sooner or later were caught, according to the monsignor, and no one had ever seen Nascimento sleepwalking. When Jaime went to the Carpentry or the Music Club House, he was always apprehensive that one of the men would say, "Hey, Jaime, I saw your wife last night." But no one ever did.

Nascimento was initially remorseful about the pain and worry she was causing her husband, and to atone for her strange nocturnal meandering, she was a truly loving wife. She loved him completely and thoroughly almost every night and Jaime fell asleep satisfied.

Nascimento had roamed the streets at night since she had been a little girl.

She fell in love with Jaime when she saw him at night, in his mother's kitchen, washing her tired feet. Such tenderness could only be good husband material.

She also saw things too ugly to divulge—not even to the monsignor—when she went to confession. It was during her nights of voyeurism that Nascimento learned about sex, love, and perversity. She became the encyclopedia for all behaviors in the village—everything bizarre and everything wonderful.

For a while, the women quietly ruminated on the promise they had made to each other eighteen months ago—that they would refrain from talking about the dead man. They should wait and see what or who was different. If someone died, the body would show up, someone would be missed, someone would be crying. They had a history of waiting for difficult things to take care of themselves. They should do now what they did when they were kids—wait and see. If a man was killed, the body would show up. Nascimento said the men came up from the landward side of the village, not down from the cliffs and the sea.

Angela sighed heavily. She tried not to think about that time in her life. She had such a brave heart and was afraid of nothing except unkindness, malice, veiled hearts and careful words. She was fearless in her loving, but things she could not explain held her by the throat like a vice. The monsignor had told her once that she was a dangerous woman because she was not afraid. "Women who don't fear do not recognize sin!" he had declared.

Angela thought about that night. She waited for Lazarus to come home from the shop. He came in quietly. It was later than usual, and Angela was almost asleep. She was surprised by his silence. He always came in singing, *"She was my beautiful boat..."*

The night that Nascimento saw the dead man, Lazarus had made a new pair of sabots for Angela, but only one was sitting on the kitchen table. The other one was nowhere to be found. The following morning Lazarus looked for it around the house and in the garden, but still couldn't find it. Maybe Viriato had played with it and lost it.

Lazarus made a replacement the next day. Angela remembered going into the woodshop and there he was making one sabot. "I've never made just one sabot," he said, "my one-legged angel." But he was so sad. Why?

In his woodshop, Lazarus made things for journeys: sabots and coffins.

Madalena rested one hand on her chest as if trying to settle her heart.

Angela closed her eyes tightly. She didn't want to think about those awful times, when she lost Lazarus and Madalena lost Saul and Manuel. Three men gone, just like that and no one had heard a word from them, no explanation.

If at least Manuel had written a letter...

Ah, they should have been more vigilant about happiness, Angela thought.

Nascimento went home later than she expected. Being with her friends and talking about the past was exhausting. At times, she felt that God had forgotten about her—in a good sense. Nothing terrible had happened in her life. Ascendida lost Mario, Angela lost Lazarus, Madalena lost Saul and she was coming home to her precious Jaime. He was already home, sitting outside with a bruised expression, waiting for her.

Jaime had a terrible suspicion that Nascimento was somewhat off, not like other women, but he couldn't tell what it was. She was sweet, funny, and reflective, she was so sure about people and things, and at the same time she was immature, almost childish. Most men wouldn't accept waiting outside for their supper, while their wife was roaming around the village.

When she walked through the gate, there was no apology in her demeanor. She looked at him and smiled. She went into the kitchen and lit the fire.

"I'll warm up supper in no time," she said. "Meanwhile, let me love you." And as the range warmed up his supper, Nascimento pulled down his pants and in the middle of the kitchen knelt at his feet and took him in her mouth with deliberate delight. Jaime forgot that he was upset about supper. Nascimento was like that: generous and inventive in her lovemaking. She knew things that he sometimes wondered how and where she had learned them. So when Nascimento was a little remiss on the domestic front, Jaime knew he would be getting something exciting. Perversely, he almost wanted her to mess up and he was perpetually expectant.

As night fell, Emanuel went to the living room, a spacious and quiet place with wide doors opening onto the terrace. Dom Carlos was sitting on the terrace looking at the night slowly transforming everything from brilliance to shadows. He was so deep in thought that he didn't hear Emanuel.

"What keeps you in such a place as this, Dom Carlos?"

Dom Carlos was startled. "And what place is that, Detective?" he asked.

"Well...I could say Atlantis, this group of nine islands sticking out of the Atlantic like thorns on a stem...or this village, these people. What keeps a man like you here?"

"A man like me…" he gave a short laugh. "What do you know about me?"

"More than you think…"

Dom Carlos looked at Emanuel for a long time, got up and bid him a good night. At the door, he turned around and asked, "Am I a suspect of some kind?"

"But, of course, everybody is," Emanuel answered.

Emanuel looked up and saw the curtain fluttering out the open window over the terrace. He smiled happily. He felt that he had landed precisely in the right place. He was still thinking about his brief exchange with Dom Carlos when Hercules in one jump perched himself on the railing of the terrace. The cat was like a demon, materializing out of thin air. Hercules licked his whiskers and lowered his head just a fraction. Emanuel struggled to his feet ready to retreat when Angela's gentle voice sounded behind him, "Get down, you bully, and leave the poor man alone."

Later, you poor excuse of a detective, Hercules seemed to say, blinking at Angela and then staring at Emanuel.

"Of all the foes I thought I could encounter in this assignment, a cat was not one of them," Emanuel said, visibly relieved that Hercules was gone.

Angela sat at the small table facing Emanuel. It was getting dark and the shadows of the trees were growing onto the terrace. Weak moonlight filtered through the overcast sky. Emanuel was bathed by the light spilling from Dom Carlos' window.

He strained to make out her face. "Can we talk about Lazarus?" he asked.

There was a long silence. She didn't move. Then she asked, "What do you want to know?"

"The truth."

"Which one?"

"The truth is only one."

"Impossible, the story of my life is full of little stories—all of them true. Which one do you want?"

"Tell me about the day Lazarus died."

"I thought you said he disappeared," she said.

"What do you think? Do you think he disappeared?"

"Yes, like Dom Sebastião, the lost king."

Was she laughing at him? He persisted, "Tell me about the day Lazarus disappeared."

"It's late. Can we talk some other time?" She got up to leave, but before moving from the table, she reached across and placed her hand on his resting on the notebook. He felt a shudder of surprise and something else unexpected.

"Detective," she said, "be kind to us. There has been much sorrow." Her touch was cool and gentle. He stayed seated in the same spot for a long time.

The light went off in Dom Carlos' room, the crickets started singing, there was laughter transported by the wind and somewhere in the village, a guitar moaned a love song.

Dona Mafalda had positioned herself to peek through the curtains without being seen, so she could spy on Emanuel. She came out to the terrace as Emanuel was going into the house.

"Detective Santos, you are still up I see," she said casually.

"Ah, Dona Mafalda," he answered bowing his head slightly as a salute.

"Do you care for a stroll in the garden? The moonlight is dim but it's still a beautiful night."

They walked slowly up and down the garden paths, talking about innocuous things such as the comforting sound of the crickets. The roses were in full bloom and here and there Dona Mafalda's robe got stuck on the thorns. While she giggled in amusement, he helped disentangle her. Dona Mafalda and the detective bumped into each other on the narrow paths.

She had so many things to say and he wanted to listen.

"For instance," she said, "have you not observed that Lazarus' pictures are nowhere to be found in the house?"

Yes, he had noticed that.

"Or," continued Dona Mafalda happy with the initial success of her observations, "that wristwatch Angela carries with her, Lazarus' watch, still has water inside from…you know…but it isn't scratched. Wouldn't it be scratched if it was found on the cliffs?"

A good point.

"Who found the wristwatch?" he asked, already knowing the answer.

"His father," she said in a confidential tone. "It stopped at 2:30. Odd, don't you think? What was he doing at 2:30 on the cliffs? The boy didn't swim, He didn't go for limpets, according to Angela. But that night he was there with his father. What was he doing at 2:30 in the morning on the cliffs with a father who brutalized him?"

Emanuel pondered while Dona Mafalda pontificated.

"Angela's mother said that a few weeks before Lazarus died, he was home a lot in his woodshop, instead of going to the Carpentry Shop. One of those times she saw him making a coffin, but no one had died—not that she knew of."

Emanuel was about to ask a question when they heard a voice coming from a corner of the garden. "Well, well, well, my fellow lodgers, on a midnight stroll," causing Dona Mafalda and Emanuel to start.

"Well, Detective Santos," Dom Carlos said in a congenial tone, "have you been trained in the Gestapo fashion?"

Dom Carlos was settled on a bench further into the garden, against the stone wall. He probably had been there all along, just eavesdropping on their conversation, and, at the opportune moment, he pounced. Emanuel faced the voice coming from the bench.

"I beg your pardon?" Emanuel said.

"The Gestapo interviewed their suspects when they were exhausted and their guard was down. Many well-intentioned people talked too much and many innocent ones were persecuted. You must know that, Detective."

Dona Mafalda was upset. Dom Carlos in that deep melodious voice was insinuating that she was a suspect who talked too much. And now with the understanding that the police investigator appreciated her observations, she felt emboldened to take on Dom Carlos. "Dom Carlos, I'm not a suspect and I don't talk too much. How dare you…"

She was interrupted by Dom Carlos, he who never interrupted anyone, "Dona Mafalda, you are a sweet, gullible, meddling woman. I know you mean no harm to Angela, but this story is not yours to tell."

Dona Mafalda was taken aback.

"And, yes, you are a suspect," he continued serenely. "Haven't you told her that, Detective? Aren't we all suspects?"

Emanuel didn't rise to the bait. "Dona Mafalda was not here when the men disappeared. She is not a suspect," Emanuel answered evenly.

"Ahhh!" Dom Carlos sounded amused.

"Dona Mafalda," Emanuel said bending his head slightly in her direction, "thank you for a delightful evening. You are indeed pleasant company."

More ecstatic than she'd been in a long time, she turned around and left, pulling her robe off the brier roses. The men watched her disappear into the house.

Emanuel heard Dom Carlos drink something. He had been sitting in the garden drinking alone.

"Whiskey," Dom Carlos said, as if guessing Emanuel's thoughts.

"A man should never drink alone," Emanuel said.

"We are never alone, Detective. Haven't you noticed?" Another gulp of whiskey. "In this village, you are never alone. Even if you lock yourself in your room, you feel the people seeping through the walls, with their joys, their sorrows, even their ruminations."

Emanuel sat next to Dom Carlos. The bench was still warm from the sun, smooth and comforting. Dom Carlos passed him the bottle. "That's quite a haunting thought," Emanuel said, taking the bottle but not partaking.

"Sorry, I only have one glass," Dom Carlos said. Then he murmured, "Haunting... how appropriate." He let out a big sigh and asked, "Have you been visited by Lazarus' ghost yet?"

Emanuel relented and took a sip from the bottle. "Good whiskey," he said, choosing to ignore Dom Carlos' provocation about ghosts.

"I tend to like only good things." They were quiet for a while, and then Dom Carlos said, "Was Dona Mafalda talking about Lazarus' ghost?"

"She mentioned it. She said that some people had seen him..."

"But you don't believe in ghosts either..." Dom Carlos said.

"Not really. But I guess these people must have seen something..."

Dom Carlos gave a short laugh, "But certainly not a ghost."

"I wonder what it was then," Emanuel said.

"You will find out that these people have a fertile imagination. You wouldn't believe the things they come up with." And after a long pause, he said, "Can you see the cat's burning orbs fixed on you? Look over there."

"Give me that glass!" Emanuel said, plucking the tumbler from Dom Carlos' hand, spilling whiskey on them both. And in a flash, he threw it in the direction of the burning eyes. They heard a soft *thump* and a howl. Hercules ran out of the bushes like a demon.

"That was an antique crystal tumbler," Dom Carlos said.

"Sorry," Emanuel answered. He took the bottle from Dom Carlos and drank.

"By God, that was worth it!" Dom Carlos said. "That cat is the bane of my existence here."

And both men broke into companionable laughter.

Dom Carlos said, "Do you know that Angela and I have a son?

Emanuel turned to him as if he suddenly had grown two heads. "What?"

"We have a son," Dom Carlos repeated. "If to give life is to become a parent, Angela and I have a son. His name is Nixon"

"The pig?" Emanuel exclaimed.

"Now, now, don't call him names. He is my son," Dom Carlos mocked.

"It's because of him that I met Angela. Eventually, I would have anyway. Angela is kind of inevitable."

Emanuel was not sure if Dom Carlos was drunk.

"Pedro Matias took the pig to the city to sell it at the market," Dom Carlos continued. "This was her pig. He had given her that pig when it was a tiny thing about to die. But he grew strong and smart. So, one day Pedro, that ass, took it to the city to the market. Well…long story…anyway, I bought the pig and gave it back to Angela."

Emanuel had read that story on Angus' notes, along with startling comments about Dom Carlos' intentions toward Angela. "Is this why you are sticking around…to share parental responsibilities?" Emanuel asked.

Dom Carlos laughed.

Emanuel's first few weeks in Two Brooks flew by. Between going to the city to examine records, traipsing across the island to follow leads, trying to catch people to talk to, and avoiding Hercules—at the end of the day, he was exhausted. Today had been one of those days. He had just missed dinner. The bus had stopped at every village to unload all kinds of things—chickens, cheese, eggs, and people. The foul diesel smell and the constant stop and go of the bus had made him nauseous.

Emanuel hurried up the road, hoping that the dinner table conversation had extended the meal. But as he approached the house, Nixon was running out of the kitchen, followed by Dalia, and Hercules was already sitting on the wall facing the window of his room. Viriato came down the road wagging his tail and licked his hands. Emanuel let out a disappointed grunt. He was hungry and tired and he had missed dinner. Absently he scratched Viriato's head and slowly entered the house.

The aroma of dinner was still in the air: beans and fresh bread. Today was bake bread day. The meals on bake bread day were served in the dining room owing to the heat in the kitchen. Emanuel entered the front door as silently as he could. He was not in the mood to see anyone. The after-dinner sounds followed him up the stairs.

In his room, Emanuel organized his notes until the house went to sleep. Quietly he went to the bathroom. Washing in a bathroom used by other people was a challenge, and having to carry out the dirty water to a wooden vat outside the kitchen door was a nuisance—but there was a drought, and water was like gold. He usually waited in his room for everyone to go to bed before his last ablutions of the day. As he washed up, the cold water distracted him from the hunger he felt. He was thinking about the manipulations of the heart. How easy it was to be taken in by a person like Angela. If she came across as duplicitous or bitter, he could deal with that. But to witness her bouncing between sadness and hope was unsettling, troubling. Emanuel wondered if Angus Pomba had felt disconcerted as he did.

Angus Pomba—the menace.

"Detective Santos." The call from the dark garden startled him.

He let out a soft scream. *Like a girl*, he thought, *startled like a little girl*. He heard a pleasant murmur of laughter and smelled a calming blend of mint and lavender.

It was Angela.

He felt exposed in his pajamas as if he had stepped naked onto a stage. The lamp in one hand, the soap and towel on the other, and the nagging thought that maybe his pajamas were transparent or the fly was unbuttoned. His hair was spilling onto his forehead, unruly and wet.

Angela was quiet, but Emanuel heard the menagerie. He could feel the eyes of the cat, smirking with laughter, *your balls are hanging.*

She emerged into the light, followed by the animals. "Are you hungry?"

"I've missed dinner…I tried…" he said.

She took the lamp from his hand, lightly brushing his fingers, and placed it on the kitchen table. "Come. You look like you had a hard day. Your dinner is waiting for you."

He sat down, feeling wet and vulnerable. His stomach started to growl, and Angela gave him an amused look as she placed dinner in front of him.

"I know you tried your best to get home on time," she said.

He was famished. He ate, without haste while he thought about kindness.

"You took a bath in cold water," she added. "I heated water for you, it was on the range. Next time check—it should always be there."

He vaguely remembered that she had told him something like that on the first day. But on that day she told him a host of startling things, such as a pig and a duck ate at the table with them, and she had denounced him as a spy for the mainland. So, the protocols of hot water had escaped him.

"While you eat, Detective Santos, I can tell you one of my truths," she said, noticing that his eyes narrowed almost imperceptibly.

He is confused again, she thought. *He is feeling ridiculous.* "I thought you wanted to talk, but if you are too tired… "

"No, no," he quickly interrupted, "please…stay."

She got up and poured wine for both of them. Hercules was sleeping next to Viriato on the floor at her feet. The pig and the duck were making soft noises in the chimney room where they slept.

And so she talked. She told him a mesmerizing story—one of her many truths.

"I've known Madalena all my life," she started as if telling a child a bedtime story. And she told him about Madalena and her twin brother, Lazarus, and her husband, Saul.

Angela paused for a long moment. Finally, she said, "Madalena's father is a tyrant and a bully, a brute of a man…everything that is nefarious, dishonest or evil in this village has to do with him. Of all the things I'm telling you, this is the most important."

He looked at her over the rim of the glass.

Angela poured more wine for both of them.

"We don't get along. If he dies, I should be your first thought." She smiled at his serious face. "Don't worry. I believe that thou shall not kill."

He knew what he had in his notes about Angela and Lazarus. She was only sixteen when she married Lazarus and, according to his notes, it was because she feared Pedro would eventually kill Lazarus if he didn't leave his father's home.

"Pedro Matias was going to kill Lazarus," she affirmed. She stopped for a second as if to assess how much she was going to tell him, then continued, "The older Lazarus became, the more vicious his father got. He was infuriated by Lazarus' lack of backbone, as he called it. So, he provoked him, expecting at any moment that Lazarus would rebel. But Lazarus would never defy his father and Pedro was going to kill him, I was sure. When Madalena got married and left the house, Pedro's directed all his maliciousness at his wife and Lazarus."

Emanuel didn't hear confessions of love and passion.

"I know what you're thinking," she said. "You're thinking that I married Lazarus out of a sense of protection, for his safety."

"Didn't you?"

"Yes, but because I loved him. I couldn't live with the fact that he was being beaten every day. I love him. Lazarus came to this world to be mine and I was born to be his. I've always known this truth." She paused and leaned forward, "Have you ever loved someone, Detective Santos?"

"Yes, I have," he answered, quietly remembering all the women he had loved. But had he ever loved so furiously as Angela? What passion drove a sixteen-year-old to shoulder the responsibilities of an adult and become the protector of a soft-hearted husband? Joan of Arc and why she defeated the English came to mind—a foolish thought, no doubt. "I was thinking of Joan of Arc," he confessed.

She laughed. "I don't know what to make of your answer...but...that doesn't bode well for me."

He couldn't see her face. The weak flicker of the lamp played with shadows and her silhouette contrasted with the white stucco of the dim kitchen.

"I have a theory why she defeated the English," he said.

"She was a nut," she answered.

Now he was the one who laughed. He feigned surprise. "You don't think she was a saint?"

"At the end of the day, we are all saints and sinners." She paused and then asked with sincere curiosity, "Why did she defeat the English?"

"Because she changed the rules of the game. All those experienced generals were playing by the same rules of war, but not Joan of Arc—she was going by her heart."

Viriato whimpered a little. Emanuel's senses were so keen that he could hear the thumping of his own heart and Angela's soft breathing.

"All her courage," she said almost dreamily, "came to naught in the end, because she listened to her heart."

After that surprising conversation with Angela, the oil lamp flickered out, they said goodnight, and Emanuel went upstairs in the dark. Before going to sleep, he wondered what would have happened if he had given in to the urge to plant a kiss on her mouth—a foolish and dangerous thought. He knew it was the wine, the moonlight, the intoxicating smells, a haunting story, and a sense of gratitude for the food. What would she have done if he had leaned across the table, had taken her face in his hands and had just rested his mouth on hers? He could imagine her mouth tasting like sage, her lips cool and soft under his, just for a moment. And after the kiss, would she have said, "Goodnight, Detective," as if it was nothing? He could imagine her kissing him back. He could see Dalia suddenly flying around the kitchen, and Nixon running out the door in alarm. Viriato would yawn, but no doubt that Hercules would leap and bite his balls, rip his flimsy pajamas off his ass. But tonight he had not been afraid of the cat. Hercules had slept at Angela's feet, motionless, like a disarmed dragon.

The next morning Emanuel had dark circles under his eyes and his head hurt. He was the last one coming down for breakfast and he could hear the noise downstairs. When he entered the kitchen, the laughing and talking stopped and everyone looked at him curiously.

He looked at Angela, suspiciously fresh and untouched.

"Good morning, Detective," she said congenially.

Dom Carlos, with a tilt of his head and a faint smile playing in his eyes, asked, "Did you have a tough night, Detective?" And then those detestable dimples showed up.

"I have a slight headache, that's all," Emanuel grunted.

"Not a good thing if you are going to meet with the monsignor," Dona Mafalda said, "because you most certainly will have another headache when you're finished."

He looked at the plump, happy, eager woman sitting across from him. How did she know he was meeting with the monsignor?

"Is there something wrong, Detective Santos? You look bereft," Angela offered.

"I have a headache," he said annoyed.

She came around the table and placed a cool hand on his forehead, measuring his temperature. Emanuel tensed with her touch and then relaxed when her other hand cradled the back of his head while she waited to have a better feel. Her hand was strong and cool on his forehead.

Dom Carlos said, "She is never wrong, not even by a degree. She is better than a thermometer."

Depends on the thermometer, Angela thought, and then she chastised herself for thinking of absurdities. It crossed her mind the time she told Lazarus that if he was hospitalized, they would use a rectal thermometer on him—and he believed her.

"You are a bit warm," Angela said. "I think you should take it easy at least today. I'll prepare a tonic for you before you go to bed."

"Oh, my dear!" wailed Dona Mafalda. "You're not talking about that foul tonic of garlic, moonshine and God knows what?"

"It works," Angela said evenly. She looked at Emanuel again. "And don't try to escape. I'll find you. If you get sick, we all get sick."

And right before bedtime, like a punishment, a terrible odor of garlic and moonshine permeated the house. Dona Mafalda retreated to her room pinching her nostrils, letting out a loud nasal complaint. Reading in the living room, Dom Carlos laughed softly. Emanuel, getting ready for bed, was completely unprepared for Angela's tonic. The menagerie left the house—someone was going to suffer and they didn't like suffering, except for Hercules who accompanied Angela.

3

Free Falling Like Alice

When Angela knocked at Emanuel's door, he had forgotten about the tonic. He peered at the mug.

"That smells terrible," he said weakly. "What's in it?"

"Poison," she said. She looked at him steadily and added, "Garlic, moonshine, lemon, honey, ginger, and a few other things..." And she handed him the mug. "Drink it while it's hot."

Hercules was looking up, sitting next to Angela's feet, as if prepared for a show.

"Drink it!" she said again.

And he did, all at once, without breathing between gulps. And when he was finished, he yelled in disgust. He heard someone laugh. It must have been the cat or Dom Carlos.

Angela extended her hand waiting to receive the mug back. "Get in bed," she ordered. He sat down on his bed.

"Under the covers!" she insisted.

"It's too hot!"

"Too bad, you need to sweat it out."

Angela pulled the covers up to his chin and knelt at the side of the bed looking at him closely as if studying his face. Emanuel noticed that her eyes had little specks of honey in the deep brown. *That must be what gives off that light when she looks at people,* he thought.

"What is it?" she asked.

"Nothing," he mumbled. "I think the poison is starting to work..."

"Tomorrow you will be fine, but if you're not, you will stay in bed." Then she got up and closed the door softly.

After the garlic tonic, he slept for two days, as if he had been drugged. He vaguely remembered drinking other brews that left him weak and sleepy. He submitted to Angela's orders to stay in bed like an invalid while she cared for him with the attention of a nurse. "Aren't you afraid that you'll get sick too?" he asked when she blew out the light.

"I never get sick," she said. "That's why I'm taking care of you."

"I thought it was because you cared," he answered feebly.

"We can't have another detective dying on us. What would the motherland say?" she said. She pressed an open hand to his forehead, measuring his temperature. He stared at her and she smiled. "Your fever is gone," she said. "I also can see in the dark, so don't stare."

In a few days, he was feeling better but those days of seclusion left a permanent impression on him, a feeling of something otherworldly. He felt branded, sucked in as if he was Alice falling into the rabbit hole. He constantly checked himself to see if he had strayed into the wonderland of these strange people and was irreparably touched. He rarely dreamt, but during that week he had vivid dreams—erotic and unreal. One day he dreamt that Angela was kissing him on the mouth, sweet wet kisses that turned into exploding desire, covering every inch of his face. Her tongue parted his lips and entered his mouth. He woke up with a startle and she was looking down at him.

She said apologetically, "I'm sorry, I don't know how Viriato got into your room. He loves to lick people…"

Emanuel walked up the street to the monsignor's house.

The women were waiting in a single file at the public fountain, making sure that no one cut the line. The water dribbled into a wooden bucket. They stared—these people stared unabashedly. He was a distraction in that otherwise hot and boring task. A woman took her now-full bucket and perched it on her hip. She smiled at him and said, "You look pale, Detective."

Did they know, like Dona Mafalda, that he was going to see the monsignor? Of course, they did, judging by their faces—a mixture of curiosity, pity, and amusement. He felt like a specimen under a microscope.

The monsignor was waiting for him at the door. Stern-faced and rigid, he ushered Emanuel in. They sat in the monsignor's study, a large room facing east.

Catarina, who worked for the monsignor, brought in tea. She was a spinster who cared for her aging parents and catered to her younger brother who had been a priest in the nearby village, but only for a short time because the bishop sent him away due to something secret and terrible. All her life she took care of people, and then life passed her by, hurtling on fast and indifferent. When she noticed, her youth was gone and it was too late.

"How is the investigation going?" the monsignor asked, sipping his tea. "Give me an update."

"Monsignor, with all due respect, I'm not here to give you an update. I'm not working for you," Emanuel said.

"Why are you here then, man?" the monsignor yelled, agitated.

"I'm here to ask you a few questions."

"I am not a suspect to be questioned! I'm the one who asked your superintendent to open an investigation on these disappeared young men and on these...these... shameless acts of violence in the name of justice. And what did we get, Detective? Incompetence and abuse from the mainland. I'm going to be highly involved with this, whether you like it or not!"

"Monsignor," Emanuel said quietly, "I know you terrorize everyone in this village. You bully them, and you even strike them at times, but those antics won't work with me." He waited for a comeback, but none came. The monsignor, sitting on the edge of his chair, was speechless and trembling with rage.

"Now," Emanuel said, taking the notebook out of his pocket, "please talk to me. I am not Angus Pomba, and I will not be paying for the sins that preceded me. But I need your help."

This seemed to appease the monsignor.

"Why do these young men in particular worry you? Why not all the others who disappeared in the past?"

"The others just went away," said the monsignor slowly. "They didn't disappear." He cleared his throat. "Before they went away, I was informed, either by them or by their parents. Sometimes I helped with money. I've always known when one of them would leave us." He paused, looking at his hands.

"And where did they go?"

"At first, we didn't know. They wait for the ship to come around the cliffs and they jump on board. They don't know where the ship is going. Sometimes America, other times Canada, Brazil, and even Australia."

"The ship comes to the cliffs of Two Brooks?"

"Yes, Detective Santos, this is Atlantis! Haven't you noticed that we are in the middle of the Atlantic?" He sounded impatient. He waited a moment and added in a more subdued tone, "They would wait on the cliffs and wave a white flag. The ship would send a small boat to the cliffs and they would jump in. Now they go to the city and board the ship or leave as stowaways."

"It is illegal what you do—helping them to escape the war."

The monsignor looked at the detective sharply and said, "Those who don't want to fight the war in Africa, those who want a better future and have no way out, those who have nothing to lose, those who are tired of hunger and dirt, yes, they leave and I help. So, arrest me, Detective!"

That confession was not in Angus Pomba's notes. Emanuel wondered what Angus would have done with that information. Knowing Angus, he would have taken the monsignor to jail. They were silent for a long while. They both looked out the window. A woman across the village circle opened a window. She spread her arms to push out the shutters. For a second, she looked like a Madonna, with her arms extended and her face tilted up to the sun bathing her white skin and long black hair. Then she disappeared into the house.

"You see," said the monsignor, "if they had gone away like the others, even if they didn't inform me, they would have written by now. It has been eighteen months."

Emanuel pondered. What would have made three men disappear in short order without anyone knowing where? And why not send word back to appease the hearts of loved ones? He looked at the monsignor, who was looking at the open window across the circle. The monsignor looked sad and old, like a defanged tiger.

"Do you believe that Lazarus fell into the ocean?"

"Ah!" said the monsignor in disbelief. "That boy hated the sea. He didn't know how to swim. Why was he catching limpets? That's hogwash!"

"Tell me Monsignor, what do you think happened to him?"

"I wish I knew," he said quietly. "I feel that something is terribly wrong and I don't know how to make it right."

"What made you call the mainland for help?"

He looked at Emanuel, his eyes calm and certain. "It was Saul."

They were silent. Emanuel waited—the lazy sounds of summer filling the void. An ox cart clattered down the street, dogs barked, children laughed, a woman was singing a love song, *Love is like a prayer...a given grace...* her words came clear and then far away, lost in the breeze.

"Saul was in love with his wife. He was living the life of his dreams with the woman he had loved all his life... So why would he leave? Unless he did something terrible and ran way..."

"What, for instance?" Emanuel persisted.

"Don't really know," the monsignor mumbled, plunging his hands into the pockets of his cassock.

"Kill a man?"

"I don't know, Detective!" he said in frustration. "I think of things, of horrible things! But I know nothing! Some say that his father killed a man. Of course, Saul's father is dead now, but some say that he had killed a man."

"The sins of the father?" Emanuel asked.

"Something like that. Saul was a big man, strong and uncommonly quiet. Some say that he was dangerous when he got angry because he didn't know his strength. However, he was a truly gentle soul and misunderstood by many." The monsignor raised his arms in exasperation and exclaimed, "Nothing makes sense! Nothing!"

Emanuel checked his notes. He still needed to confirm a few points, compare stories and clarify understandings. "Why did Lazarus marry Angela? What is it about Angela?"

"Pedro is a brute, a violent man," the monsignor said, waving his hand in a dismissive gesture. "He likes to make people miserable. He beat those children without pity, especially Lazarus." He let out a deep sigh. "He beat the spirit out of them—his wife, his boys—but he could not beat down Madalena. Angela, on the other hand, was loved like no child in this village," he continued. "Those parents loved that girl, like every child should be loved. Angela grew up knowing things, people's souls and dreams. She knew how to read at the age of four. She is bright, insightful…and a bit off, as you probably can tell. When she was a child, at the end of the day, her father tired from work would come by my house to get books for her to read. Poor child, she knew the story of every saint who has ever lived. Joan of Arc was her favorite."

Joan of Arc. Emanuel felt a surge of something rise from his belly and sit on his chest.

"I think that Angela is an illuminated soul," the monsignor said, surprising Emanuel. "She is wise beyond her age and she knows things that only a lifetime can teach."

"Is she a healer?" Emanuel asked.

The monsignor was silent for a few seconds and then said, "She heals people by using herbs and common sense. Most think that she is, but she denies it. If you ask her, she will tell you that she reads medical books and likes to experiment…She detests being called a healer."

"But people go to her to be healed?"

"Yes, they do, but Ascendida is the official nurse for the village. She dispenses pills and gives injections, but they go to Angela for healing"

"It's against the law," Emanuel said.

The monsignor looked at him for a long moment. Then he said, "Only if she was being compensated for her work. But she never accepts anything, not even praise."

Emanuel remembered Angus Pomba's notes. He was going to arrest Angela for healing people. And then everything went belly up with his investigation. Emanuel reflected on his recent flu episode—how she healed him with strange potions...that left him bewitched.

"Have lunch with me, Detective Santos," the monsignor said. "I want to tell you about the scourge of my life—the Sacristy."

Emanuel accepted the invitation. There was a brief lilt in the monsignor's voice when he called Catarina to let her know that there would be two for lunch.

"Let me tell you about the burning barn," the monsignor said. "These four girls—the so-called Sacristy—set fire to a barn because they wanted to create a hell for the teacher, Dona Lidia. It was a terrible thing... the flames, the screams, the parents' despair...When night came, we resigned ourselves that they were all dead. The villagers looked for them everywhere and they were nowhere to be found. I had a young priest working for me at the time, Father Tiago, and he went to look at the burned barn. The four kids, who had been hiding all along, came around the building arm in arm, still dressed in their school white smocks. When they approached Father Tiago, the poor man almost died of fright. He thought he was looking at their little souls. I never saw a grown man scream so loudly."

The monsignor grimaced and continued, "There are stories that connect the people of Two Brooks like links in a chain, but the burning barn is the grandest. After all, Angela and her friends had died and been resurrected together. They are part of each other like limbs are part of one's body. One of them is not complete without the others."

The monsignor looked pointedly at Emanuel. It was important for the new detective to understand the connection that these four women had kept up all their lives.

Emanuel was going to follow the monsignor's recommendation and interview the four women, the so-called Sacristy. He was sure that such a talk promised to be interesting if not revealing. But it could be close to impossible unless the monsignor helped him with the arrangements. He had tried going it alone before and had been thwarted, always.

Of course, the village had enough reason to fear him. He was the replacement for Angus Pomba. However, his methods were not the same. But Two Brooks knew only that the police were not to be trusted.

After this initial visit, Emanuel and the monsignor had lunch together regularly, and more often than not they didn't talk about the investigation. Emanuel was certain that the monsignor was full of secrets, and secrets eventually reveal themselves, providing information, if one was patient and paid attention. The monsignor talked about the village and the deep love he had for its people, about the changes taking place, about progress.

"Progress replaces irreplaceable things," the monsignor said sadly. "We no longer hear the sound of the longhorn. The men stayed overnight in their barns protecting their wheat before the cleaning. They blew on a bull's horn, to let other men know that they were guarding their wheat. And after a while, those mournful sounds echoed all through the village—the men guarding their wheat."

While the monsignor talked, Emanuel was thinking about Angela's property. It had that circular threshing-floor—it was big with a smooth dirt floor the color of soft light sand. Would she cover it with grass? Did she dance there with Lazarus? There was also a windmill, looming big and desolate on the top of a hill. Its sails were torn like those of an outgunned, overpowered man-of-war.

Angela had told him a few days earlier, "We've been terribly hurt by this investigation…I don't want history to repeat itself."

"Sooner or later, with you or without you, I will find out what happened," he had answered her.

She had said calmly," You have no idea what you are promising."

Emanuel felt like the English must have felt when they fought Joan of Arc—different rules of war.

"Do you know, Detective Santos, I was never mistreated by anyone, except by my teacher, Dona Lidia?"

He had had no idea why she volunteered that. But he waited.

"I've been loved all my life. One cannot understand love if we have nothing to compare it with," she continued. "Dona Lidia, in a mean and nasty way, taught me about love, because she was its opposite." She had turned to Emanuel with amusement and continued, "She beat me to a pulp because I couldn't say *abominable*."

There had been a suspended laugh on her face.

"And why did she want you to say *abominable*?" he had asked astonished.

"I don't know," she said. "But that cost her a broken leg. My mother looked for her all over the village and when she found her, she went after her with a pitchfork. She chased her down the road and Dona Lidia slipped in bullshit and broke her leg. She has walked with a limp ever since."

When their laugher had died down, they were surrounded by the quiet sounds of the afternoon. Angela said after a long silence, "While my mother was looking for Dona Lidia, my father taught me a trick for remembering how to say that word: *a-bomb-in-a-bull*."

"That's abominable," Emanuel said.

"Easy for you to say."

They laughed again, and Emanuel thought that laughter had brought them a bit closer into that special intimacy that only humor can offer.

After a long silence, she had said, "The comparison I wanted to make with Dona Lidia being the opposite of love…is the same about you and Angus and your kindness. Because Angus was so terrible, we appreciate your being kind. I don't want you to think that we don't notice."

The monsignor looked at Emanuel and knew that he was far away, daydreaming. To regain Emanuel's attention, he broke the silence with, "You asked me about Dom Carlos before. Here is what I know," and he started as if he was reading from a business profile, "He came here to set up ventures across the island. He owns the Cooperative that pasteurizes the milk and makes cheese. He also brought farm machinery to the island to clean the wheat and sack it for retail and export. He established the motorized mill to grind the wheat and the corn. That is also part of the Cooperative. He is Angela's and Lazarus' business partner." There was a heavy silence. "He killed a way of life that was remarkably pure," the monsignor added with resentment. "People in this village, on this island, use work to socialize, to break down isolation. If we give way to machines, it will kill a way of life. One must know people to love them. They help each other with the harvest, they eat together and sing together while they work and…love together. Work is a noble reason to know our neighbors." The monsignor looked sad. He was playing with a bit of bread on the table. "All the threshing-floors will eventually disappear. They won't be needed to clean the wheat. On those specially flattened outdoor surfaces, where they beat the wheat out of the chaff, is also where people sing and dance after the work is done. The abandoned windmills have fallen into disrepair, like defeated giants. At the end of the day, every man, woman, and child came to the threshing-floor to celebrate their work. They ate and sang and danced together. The singing circles were the start of many marriages in this village.

The children also had tasks and they worked and celebrated like everybody else. The machines are marginalizing the old and the children as useless members of society. There is nothing for them to do other than to be cared for."

"You can't stop progress, Monsignor," Emanuel said.

The monsignor looked at him and said in a tired voice, "Not every change is progress, Detective. What I know is that progress isolates people." The monsignor was silent for a few moments and then said, "When there was just one radio in the village, almost everybody got together around that radio to listen to the broadcast. So every afternoon, after work, people got together. Now almost everyone has a radio and they no longer congregate to listen to the broadcast. You see? Affluence creates isolation."

Emanuel understood the monsignor's sadness. Most people would not be fully aware of the profound change that machines and progress would bring to their lives—and not all good.

"Why here, Monsignor? Why is he here?" Emanuel kept on Dom Carlos.

The monsignor looked amused. "Don't tell me that the motherland is worried about Dom Carlos."

"He is affluent, he is a heretic, and some say he is a communist. Would you be surprised if the motherland was worried?" Emanuel asked.

The monsignor icily responded, "If you came here to inform the mainland of our political activities, tell them that we are too poor to worry about politics!" Then with a thin smile, he added, "Also tell them that when people have nothing else to lose, they should worry. But we still have our pride and we want to preserve that."

"Do people like Dom Carlos?" Emanuel asked.

"They love him, as if he is the second coming of Christ," the monsignor said with transparent resentment.

"Well, he is luckier than I am. They can't stand me," he sighed. "Dom Carlos had vision—coming to a place like this," Emanuel said pensively, "A man like him could be anywhere in the world. Why here?"

"Why don't you ask him?" the monsignor snapped.

"I did."

The monsignor lifted his head suddenly. What was that light in the monsignor's eyes? Was that anxiety?

"And what did he say?" the monsignor asked.

"Something vague and non-committal. As always, he was poking fun at everything. He said that the motherland was stuck in the past, still paranoid about the Bolsheviks, Fátima apparitions and little shepherds predicting political unrest. He said that the Virgin Maria should have gone to the United Nations and talked to those powerful men and left little shepherds out of it," Emanuel answered somewhat amused.

Both jocular and serious, the monsignor said, "That heretic!"

On one of his visits to the monsignor, Emanuel returned to the subject of the Sacristy. "The bonds created in childhood are almost impossible to break," said the monsignor. "Angela was almost sent to a correctional school because of her loyalty to the others."

Emanuel didn't know that. His interest piqued, he asked, "What happened?"

"Dona Lidia, the teacher at the time, a vile woman, was hitting Ascendida and Nascimento at the same time. She had picked the two up by the collars of their smocks and was banging them together like cymbals in a philharmonic. Nascimento was always a slow learner. Mind you, she's not stupid, but she learns differently and at her own pace. She is lefthanded and that brought her many spankings. At the end of the second grade, she still didn't know how to read. Ascendida sat behind her and fed her the lines when it was Nascimento's time to read. The system worked well because they were sitting in the back of the room and Dona Lidia was sitting in front of the class only half-listening. But one day she came silently down and caught them. You've heard about Nascimento's nickname, haven't you?" asked the monsignor.

"White Goat?" Emanuel answered. Everyone had a nickname—it was hard to keep up.

"Little White Lamb," corrected the monsignor. "That was the assigned reading, or in Ascendida's and Nascimento's case, the lesson they were cheating on."

The monsignor continued, "When Dona Lidia was not letting up in beating them, Angela got up and attacked her. She kicked her and pulled her hair until she fell. And the rest of the class got up yelling and screaming. It seemed they were going to kill Dona Lidia. If it wasn't for the lunch lady, they would have."

"Was this before or after the burning barn and pitch-fork incident?" Emanuel asked.

"It was the following year…right before the summer vacation. When Dona

Lidia submitted an official request to send Angela to a correctional school, I got involved."

"What happened to Dona Lidia?"

"Well, when I got involved, I had two routes: Angela or Dona Lidia. The choice was clear. Dona Lidia didn't lose her job, but had to work without pay for a whole year and, most importantly, was forbidden to use corporal punishment on any child. She died a few years later. I think it was her poison turned within—no children to spew it on."

"What did she die of?" He knew what Angus Pomba had in his notes—Dona Lidia had been murdered.

"Well…it was her heart. Of course, people don't believe it because she didn't have a heart." The monsignor was very still. Then he said, "I am the coroner of this village, most of the time. The old, the sick, I let the authorities know what happened, I write the death certificates and they sign them. No questions asked."

"Was Dona Lidia's death a natural one?" Emanuel asked quietly.

The monsignor responded evenly, "Of course it was. I said so."

Angela's hands trembled when she unlocked the workshop door. The space was neat and larger than it appeared from the outside. The curls of wood were still in the rubbish bin and the clean smell of cedar permeated everything. The door and window were painted sky blue, and there was a flower box below the window.

They stepped in. Angela took a deep breath—Lazarus, the smell of Lazarus. The tools were cleaned and oiled. The coffins were stacked against the wall in different stages of completion. And at the end, Isaac Lima's finished coffin.

The walls of the shop were lined with shelves and tools. On the bottom shelves, the lining for the coffins was neatly stacked by the color—black, dark blue, light blue, pink and white.

"The first coffin he made," Angela said, rearranging the stacks of fabric, "was for a woman who died in childbirth. Lazarus cried throughout, soaking the lining. She was buried in a coffin washed by his tears."

Emanuel stood at the door and looked around uncomfortably. His request to see the woodshop now seemed invasive and unnecessary.

"I'm so sorry," he said.

She crossed her arms and stood rigid. "Sometimes I forget his face," she said. "I remember parts of him, but not the whole Lazarus. I took down all his pictures because I must remember with my heart. How can I forget?" She lowered her head to hide her tears. "There are times that I'm positive he's still alive. And then I think, how? How in the world can he be alive? If he was alive, he would come to me." Her eyes were fastened on Emanuel, seeking affirmation. "He's at the bottom of the sea and I think that Pedro is at fault," she concluded.

"That would be murder," he said quietly.

"I know, and I can't prove it. He is an ignorant bastard. He can't even read, but he is no fool..." she said.

"I would like to use this space for my office...but if it is too taxing on you, I can use my room," he said.

She waved her hand dismissively. "It is time that I let go. I come here sometimes to feel closer to him...his things, his smell..."

"Plenty of space, I don't need to move anything," he added. "I can even use that coffin for sitting." He pointed at Isaac Lima's coffin. "I will move some of my stuff tomorrow. Today I'm having dinner with Regina Sales."

Angela looked at him for a long time to gauge how aware he was of what he was in for. He held her gaze and frowned.

"You do know about Regina, don't you?" she asked.

"Of course, I do. I know of her reputation."

"She will have you for dessert," Angela said with a serious face.

He laughed. "I have no intention of being her prey."

"You don't know how good a hunter she is."

Steak. How he loved steak. He only had it when he went to the city. Angela's home was mostly meat-free. On only rare occasions did they have meat, and she refused to prepare it. "How would you like to be slaughtered for someone's pleasure?" she asked savagely, her eyes emitting ire, the first time he mentioned his craving for meat.

And now he was looking at a big juicy steak salted and ready to be broiled. Emanuel sat in Regina's kitchen and watched her prepare lunch. She set the table while they talked about many things, but above all, they talked about Angela.

"She is not all there, you know," Regina said pointing to her head. "All her animals die of old age, even the chickens. She has more chickens that don't lay eggs than chickens that do. She is different, like…" Regina was unable to come up with a full description of Angela. After a long silence, she said, "I'm sure that she sleeps with Dom Carlos."

Angus Pomba's notes said that Dom Carlos and Angela were lovers. But even Angus had a question mark after this statement. He had comments about Dom Carlos' intentions toward Angela, but Regina sounded sure.

"And how do you know that?" he asked.

Regina looked at him and smiled, "Her mother is my best friend. But if you want to know more, you have to do something for me."

Emanuel was measuring the worth of the information. "What do I have to do?" he asked suspiciously.

"Actually nothing," she answered. "I'll do everything. I'm an expert on prostate massages."

"Certain things must be left alone. My prostate is one of them."

"Dom Carlos also resisted, at first," she said guiding him to the bedroom, "I had a hard time waking up his poor thing. And when I did, he kept on saying no. I told him to think of Angela. No sooner had I said that he came with a terrible cry, he cried for God, he who says God doesn't exist! And he had tears in his eyes. I think he is in love with her."

Regina was looking intently at Emanuel's face, "Some say that Dom Carlos is here for something that no one knows what, that he is a spy. And others say that he is involved with piracy on the coast of the archipelago, sunken ships from long ago, hidden treasures. The man is a mystery, that much I know."

Regina Sales was massaging his back with almond oil. She was telling him interesting things about the villagers. Emanuel surrendered to Regina and listened, closing his eyes and imagining the touch of someone else. He didn't cry like Dom Carlos when Regina had her way. He was tied to the bed and didn't fight much against her betrayal. She laughed when he said weakly, "I thought we had an agreement, Regina, you liar."

His body ached in that peculiar way when one is sexually satisfied. He felt relieved from the tension that had gripped him since he had come to Angela's. He was vaguely aware that he smelled of almonds. Probably Viriato or even Nixon would sniff him as soon as he got home and cast suspicion on his lunch with Regina.

But when he got home, it was not Viriato or Nixon who went to smell him—it was Dona Mafalda who put her nose up in the air and asked, "What is that smell?"

Angela looked at Emanuel. She knew where he had been. He felt his face burn and his groin oily. He desperately wanted to take a bath. Angela returned to the kitchen, while Dom Carlos tried to hide a smirk in his book.

Dona Mafalda was still sniffing, trying to locate the smell of almonds.

4

The Bullfight

Later, when the household finished their ablutions and went to bed, Emanuel sat in a tub of hot water, despite the heat, scrubbing away. Afterward, he drifted into the garden because he couldn't sleep. He didn't expect Dom Carlos to be in the garden, in the dark, quiet as a mouse. As soon as he realized that Dom Carlos was there, Emanuel did an about-face to retreat inside when Dom Carlos said, "I was waiting for you."

"How did you know that I was coming to the garden?"

"I had a feeling."

Emanuel and Dom Carlos sat silently for a while.

"So, Regina had her way with you," Dom Carlos said.

"Yes, she did."

"And Angela knows," Dom Carlos said.

"Angela is not my keeper. And does she know about you?" Emanuel returned.

"Who said that I've been there?" Dom Carlos asked.

"Regina did. And she said that you cried for God," Emanuel said.

Dom Carlos gasped in disbelief. "I didn't cry and much less for God!" he vehemently denied.

"She said you did. She also said many interesting things about the village, about you being a pirate... hunting treasures, that you are a spy, and other stories."

"She makes me sound so romantic," Dom Carlos said. "Was it worth the sacrifice?"

"It was no sacrifice. I like sex. She said you are a pirate and a spy. She also said that you sleep with Angela."

Dom Carlos received this last claim with complete calmness.

"Pedro Matias," Dom Carlos said. "He broadcasted that all over the island. No one believes him because it isn't true." Dom Carlos turned to Emanuel and quipped, "Don't tell me, Detective, that you submitted yourself to Regina to learn what everyone already knows." Dom Carlos laughed. "What else did she say?"

"She said that you were a novice..."

Dom Carlos sat quietly for some time. "She certainly surprised me with her methods," he quietly replied.

"What did she do to you?" Emanuel asked, trying to hide a smirk.

"Probably the same thing she did to you," Dom Carlos answered.

Dom Carlos remembered Regina putting her hand inside his pants and squeezing his penis until it brought tears of pleasure. He still remembered her whisper in his ear, "Say yes, say yes."

He had never been with a prostitute. His knowledge of women was sweet and loving. There was affection with the women he had had in his bed. Regina was so out of his realm that he felt embarrassed for being caught unaware. But the worst was being rescued by Angela. She had knocked at Regina's door and demanded to see him, waiting with her arms crossed over her chest in Regina's kitchen.

Emanuel sat at the big oval table at the library, near the church. The smell of books evoked memories of school days and childhood—something sweet and painful, all at once. That smell reminded him of wonder and dreams. It also reminded him of loss and sorrow.

By now the whole village knew about the new detective's planned interview with the Sacristy. People found a reason to run errands past the library, where they ambled by while peering in.

The four, as Emanuel had expected, arrived together, like a block of defiance. As they sat down, they looked at him with a scowl.

What could they say to this man? they thought. *What truths could wipe out the little lies in their lives? And weren't they entitled to their secrets?*

Emanuel fixed his eyes on Angela. He had had moments of intimacy with Angela that only laughter and sorrow can create. Her hands, now so still resting on the table, were the same that so gently touched his brow when he was sick. Now she sat there distant, looking at him from the other side, in solidarity with the other women. As if reading his mind, she held his gaze and smiled—that open beautiful smile of hers. Instantly, he felt his muscles relax and he returned her look of familiarity, that light in his eyes.

Nascimento had been worried since she learned that the detective wanted to interview them. Jaime, her husband, asked full of surprise, "Why you? I didn't disappear?" She knew that if someone like a police detective from the mainland started to ask questions about the things they'd done, there was a good chance one of them would reveal something compromising. She didn't believe that this police investigator would grab her by one finger and break it as Angus Pomba had done, but nevertheless, she, unlike her compatriots, was not a skilled liar. How was she going to keep secret that she saw what she thought was a dead man being dragged by two other men? "And when was that, Mrs. Nobre?" she imagined the police detective asking, and she would say, "At midnight, when I go out for a stroll." No, she had to keep her mouth shut. Let the others speak—they usually did a better job at keeping lies straight. She gingerly caressed the finger that Angus Pomba had broken. Beads of perspiration started to form on her upper lip as she remembered Angus Pomba holding her index finger and twisting it until it snapped.

It seemed that everything hinged on that night, the night she saw the dead man.

Emanuel was sitting at the table, leaning back with a relaxed look about him.

He is deceiving, thought Ascendida. *He looks like we are about to have a casual conversation. But he is no Angus Pomba. This one will not hurt us like that. No, the monsignor would not have called us to meet with him if he was like Angus Pomba.*

He smiled—a hooded smile of unshared thoughts.

Madalena was very still, hardly moving her head. She was thinking about Saul and why he was gone. She wanted to know for sure, but she didn't want to give anything away to this stranger. They, the villagers, would deal with their dead and their missing. Was this man like Angus Pomba? No, Angela liked him, so he must be somewhat decent.

Emanuel said after a while, "I need your help. I need to hear your thoughts about what happened to the three men who just vanished in the last eighteen months."

They were quiet. He waited. He could wait out anyone. He never rushed an investigation or an interview. But if he could wait, so could they. And they sat stony eyed, saying nothing.

"Well?" he asked.

"Well what?" Ascendida snapped, quite annoyed.

He zeroed in on her. "Let's start with you, Mrs. Costa," he said pleasantly. "What is your opinion about these missing men?"

"You think I have time for opinions about other women's men?" she leaned in and looked at him with open dislike. "I have five children and a loving man, God knows he is loving, and you think I have time for this nonsense?"

"Missing men are not nonsense, especially if they are your friends and neighbors," he briefly glanced at the others, and right back at her.

"They're not missing," she said in the same belligerent tone.

"So, you do have an opinion after all," he said. She had fallen into her own trap. "Why do you think they're not missing? And if they are not missing, where are they?" he continued.

"Lazarus fell in the ocean and the other two ran way afraid of being drafted to fight in the African war or something." Ascendida snapped.

Angela paled at Ascendida's brutal words.

"Saul wouldn't have been drafted," Emanuel said. "He was caring for his mother. He would be exempt. So, why did he run away?"

Madalena was fidgeting with her wedding ring.

"Do you think, Mrs. Amora, that your husband would do that? Just pick up and leave?"

Madalena was shaking now, a faint tremor. "Yes," she said. He did leave—that was a fact. She breathed in deeply and held Angela's hand resting on the table.

"Why, Mrs. Amora?" he asked softly.

"I wish I knew," she murmured. "He left because I broke his heart, or because somewhere there are things and people that I never knew about... things stronger than his love for me."

Yes, he thought. He was also thinking that he had never seen a woman so beautiful as Madalena. Lazarus must have been that beautiful—like a baby Jesus.

"And you, Mrs. Nobre," he turned suddenly on Nascimento, "What do you think?"

Nascimento didn't expect him to turn to her that fast.

"Nothing," she said, "My husband didn't disappear. What do you want me to tell you?"

Emanuel contained a chuckle. This was the little white lamb who almost landed Angela in a correctional school.

Ascendida crossed her arms over her abundant chest. "Go home, Detective," she said. "And let us mourn our own."

Home. He had never felt that he had a home anywhere, except now living at Angela's. Since he was a little boy, he looked for that sweetness of place. *I am home*, he thought. *This crazy place is home—the sweet smell of bread, the fragrances drifting through open doors and windows from the garden, the fire burning on the range, and the soft quiet bed at night with the moon peering in, and, yes, even the cat biting my ankles.*

Angela smiled—a brief, stolen smile, hidden from her friends. And, again, she saw his face light up. He could smile without moving a muscle.

"Do you think that the disappearing men have anything to do with the Night Justice incidents?" Emanuel asked.

"You're the detective," Ascendida said. "Why don't you figure it out?"

"That's what I am trying to do," he answered evenly.

"You're not welcome here!" Ascendida said.

"Are you speaking for all of you?" he asked.

"Yes, I am."

"Well," he said and leaned in. "Get used to me. I'll be around for a while. I like it here."

Ascendida turned to Angela and hissed, "Kick his sorry ass out the door!"

"I think this Night Justice gang is a gang of women and not men," he said in a smooth, matter-of-fact kind of way that took the women a few moments to absorb. Emanuel thought he saw them blush. He stared at Angela. She was pale, Nascimento was blushing and Madalena lowered her eyes. He was going to try something different.

"Have you interviewed the victims of Night Justice?" Ascendida asked with a frown.

"Yes, I have."

"And what did they tell you?" she asked.

"That five or six men attacked them."

"Then why do you want to turn this on women? Don't we have enough shit we are blamed for? Do we have to be the Eve of this story also? You eat the apple and it is our fault, to carry for eternity?" Ascendida was getting angry. Her voice rose, "Go to hell, Detective!"

Emanuel looked at her for a long time and she held his gaze.

I can stare with the best of you! Ascendida thought.

"Thanks for coming," he said to the women. I just need to talk a little further with Mrs. Amora. You may go," he said.

"Madalena is coming with us," Ascendida said, putting a protective arm around Madalena's shoulders. "She had enough of your kind! Do you think for a moment that we would leave her alone with a police detective?"

Emanuel stepped in front of Ascendida, "Mrs. Costa, I think you have the wrong idea here. I call the shots, not you. You go wherever you need to go, but Mrs. Amora is staying here with me. Do you understand?"

Without warning, Ascendida gave Emanuel an open-handed slap. It sounded strangely as if someone had clapped.

The other women shrank and covered their mouths to not cry out. But Ascendida looked like a bull, with flaring nostrils and huffing bosom. Nascimento didn't wait for more drama—she took off running out the door and down the street. She wasn't waiting to have another finger broken.

Emanuel touched his lower lip with the tip of his tongue. A thin drip of blood dribbled down his chin. And before they could say anything else Ascendida left taking Madalena by the arm.

Angela was rooted on the spot where she was standing. "I'm sorry," she said finally. "Ascendida can be such a cow, but we are justified when it comes to Madalena." She seated him on a chair, took the tip of her handkerchief and dabbed gingerly at the cut on his lip. She said, "I didn't save you from the flu to have you killed by Ascendida."

But he was not amused.

She shook her head and added, "Forgive us, Detective Santos. We are all nervous…and very protective of Madalena." Her hands were slightly shaking as she touched his face to clean the cut. He could smell the faint odor of smoke in her hair. She was concentrating on his mouth, but she could see the steeliness in his eyes. Angela was worried that Ascendida's outburst would make things so much worse.

"You're not responsible for the actions of others, nor am I," he said.

He took her by the wrist and made her sit in front of him. He said, "You are the rescuer, Madalena is the damsel in distress, Nascimento is the screwup, and Ascendida the bully, the dragon that guards your secrets. Am I right?" His voice sounded cold.

"Make up your mind," she said calmly. "I thought I was a witch, or a warrior."

"Sooner or later you'll have to trust me," he said. "Make it sooner, because I'm losing my patience."

This sounded like a vague threat. "Or what? What are you going to do if *you lose your patience*?" she asked somewhat irritated.

"Angela," he said in a contained voice, "God knows I want to do right by this damn village, but it's not easy."

They stared at each other for a moment.

"Let's go home," he said in an exasperated tone.

They walked home, side by side, quiet, looking straight ahead. People stared openly at them. By now, half of the village knew that Ascendida had slapped the police detective.

When they got home, Rosa was already serving lunch to Dona Mafalda and Dom Carlos. Hercules was sitting at the kitchen door waiting for Angela. Viriato and Nixon came running, but Dalia was not around. Angela had not seen Dalia since last night.

The silence of the knowing, thought Emanuel. They all knew that he could send Ascendida to jail—she had assaulted a policeman. They were curious and expectant. The silence persisted, except for Nixon who made noises near Dom Carlos.

Everyone was waiting for Emanuel to say something. "Don't worry," he said impatiently. "I will not send a mother of five to jail because of a slap."

Angela let out a sigh of relief. "God bless you, Detective.Santos."

Emanuel harrumphed but smiled back at her.

The bullfight was going to be formidable. One of the most famous bulls on the island, Ninety-nine, was going to be at Two Brooks. Ninety-nine was a star. Ninety-nine was lethal.

People across the island put on their most flattering clothes to go to the bullfight.

The energy of the village was palpable. The open windows were decorated with bed covers of brilliant hues that swayed in the late morning breeze. The horse wagons were going by, full of children and women from the neighboring villages. The street vendors advertised their wares, while people walked briskly to the center of the village and surrounding streets, looking for a good spot. The more fearful looked for high and out-of-the-way places where the bull could never reach. But those less afraid, or less knowledgeable of what a bull could do, were sitting on low walls or other less protected perches. Some were even foolish enough to remain on the street.

The streets were closed off—no cars, motorcycles, bicycles, horses, horse carriages or other forms of transportation. The doors and shops were boarded up for protection against the rage of the bull, women and children started to populate verandas, windows, and high walls, while men, old and young, pranced gaily up and down the streets, looking up at the women.

If a bull hurt someone, it was an outsider—usually, someone from the mainland, an emigrant who never before saw a bullfight or an American military man. In a perverse way, if the bull had to hurt someone, an outsider was always the best victim.

Emanuel was coming from the city that morning. The bullfight of the year was not something he wanted to miss. Besides, he could talk to a few people, unofficially, of course, because they would not be going anywhere with the bull rampaging in the street.

Emanuel was closing the gate ready to leave when he saw Angela running down from the windmill place. She had apples gathered in her apron from the orchard nearby. Running alongside her was Nixon and Viriato, as if in a race. He heard her call out, "Emanuel!"

He went up the road to meet her halfway, a bit surprised by her urgency.

"Thank God I caught you," she said out of breath, taking a seat on a low roadside wall. "I thought you were in the city."

He waited for her to catch her breath.

"Don't go to the bullfight," she said.

"Why?" he asked surprised.

"Because they are too dangerous." Her face was tilted up to him. Her skin was covered with sweat, making her shine like precious metal. She dropped the apples at his feet and Nixon immediately started on them. She wiped her face and neck with the corner of her apron.

"You told me that already," he said.

"No, I didn't. I told you to be careful in general. I didn't tell you to be careful *today*."

"What is this about?" he asked. He sat next to her, peering into her face curiously.

Their faces were close enough that she could see the small cut on his lip. Would he not go to the bullfight if she told him that she had a dream in which he died?

He held her gaze.

"Just don't go," she said. "Not everyone here likes you, Detective Santos. Don't go to a place where you are surrounded by people who could hurt you. You could be gored to death...like Angus Pomba."

He frowned. "I promise to be careful," he said with mild amusement. "Are you worried about me?"

"Of course, I am. How can we explain two detectives being gored to death?"

"Ah, so you don't care about me particularly," he said with a slanted smile.

"Detective Santos, please be serious. Don't go into the streets while the bull is out," she said with some frustration.

He took her hand in his and didn't want to let her go. He was vaguely aware that Nixon was sniffing his shoes looking for more apples. Then she pulled her hand away and they walked down to the gate of the house. Angela looked at him as if waiting for an answer.

"I'll be fine," he said. "I promise to be careful. I always keep my promises."

"I hold you to that, Detective Santos," she said, "I won't forgive you if you die."

"Your potions would bring me back to life," he said.

"See? You're not taking me seriously."

He laughed.

They stared at each other for a moment as if to clarify their understandings—he was going to the bullfight and Angela knew that something terrible was going to happen.

And so he turned around slowly and went to the biggest bullfight of his life.

When Angela got home, she drank water as if she was on fire. She couldn't stand her dreams. This dream sat on her chest and she couldn't shake it off. She quietly listened as the gusts of wind carrying the sounds of the bullfight: shouts, laughter, and the singsong of the street vendors. She was like an antenna picking up every sound.

Yesterday while they had sat drinking tea at Ascendida's, she had told her friends about a dream. "I was hanging clothes on a clothesline in the churchyard. It was for a funeral. Then I saw the detective sitting naked on the church steps waiting for his clothes to dry for his funeral. I opened my mouth to scream and all my teeth fell out."

They had been utterly silent until Nascimento had asked, "Did you spit the teeth out before you screamed?"

Angela had slapped her arm in irritation. "I was terrified, you jerk!"

"It matters!" Nascimento had said defensively. "Spitting teeth on the ground means certain death."

Angela had continued, "I don't remember what I did with the teeth... What I remember next was the monsignor coming out of the church with an enormous envelope with red and blue borders, an envelope the size of a coffin, and he asked in a high-pitched voice, 'Who will cry for this man? Who will pray for his soul?'" She had tried to imitate the monsignor.

Ascendida's nostrils had flared as if moved by disturbing thoughts. "You have no business dreaming about the detective," she had accused Angela. "He is a police investigator just like Angus Pomba. Don't forget that!"

"I can't control my dreams!" she had answered angrily.

After that interview in the library fiasco, Angela felt that Emanuel was a good man, especially when he let Ascendida's slap go, but she couldn't say it to her friends. It would have been like surrender.

The villagers hated the detective, and they felt more unified rallying against a common enemy. While he was around, they almost forgot the bishop and the Holy Ghost mess. Even António Dores forgot his campaign against sin and hedonism and left the Holy Ghost in peace to hate the new detective.

Of course, to say that the villagers hated the detective was not true. The women liked Emanuel and he counted on that rapport to advance his investigations. And the women talked. Regina Sales had a bag of stories about the village to entice Emanuel to visit her. Luciana, smiling like Mona Lisa, answered his questions in monosyllables. Emanuel couldn't leave the house without Elvira heading in the same direction for some reason. She had stories about the Night Justice—her uncle was among the victims.

As Emanuel walked up to the center of the village, he was aware of the stares, occasional jeers and name-calling directed at him. He was used to it.

The villagers weren't afraid of him, at least not as much as they had been afraid of other police investigators. They knew he had the same authority to hurt them like the others, but he had a different heart or a smarter strategy. He was more like a thief who picked their locks than a pirate who broke down their doors.

Emanuel was still charged by Angela's nervous energy. He had never been so challenged to read a transparent mind. But there it was—this contradiction of a woman wanting to know the truth and hiding facts that could bring her there. Oh, yes, she was hiding things, that much he knew.

The sun was bright and brutally oppressive. The breeze died down as the afternoon approached and a haze of heat lifted from the ground. Emanuel was surrounded by men, many whom he didn't know, from the surrounding villages. He paid close attention to their behavior and imitated them: If they ran, so would he. If they stopped, he stopped too. He was trying to be careful. As the bull approached, the men started to run and raised their arms to the windows, verandas, and walls. And those already perched on the walls pulled these running fools up to safety. Emanuel tried to do the same, but no arms stretched down to him as he kept on running and trying to find a safe perch. When he jumped up to a wall, he failed to find a place to hang on to or he was kicked down by other men trying to flee. Again and again, he tried until he fell on his back and hit his head on the ground. He got up feeling dizzy and heard screams. He looked back and saw the world in double. He realized that there was a wall of terrified people watching him fall. Emanuel looked up at a high veranda and women were covering their faces, while others were praying. He fell again. He got up again and started to run. The road was almost empty and when Emanuel looked back he saw a huge animal running after him. He vaguely saw arms stretched out as if looking for redemption, but he couldn't stop for fear of being overtaken. People were screaming, anxious voices urging, "Fall down! Fall to the side!" Emanuel didn't understand what they meant. Some people were calling out to the running bull and throwing jackets at the animal to distract it. But this was Ninety-nine, the bull that relentlessly hunted its target until it got it.

The screams became horrified shrieks and Emanuel felt a swoosh of warm air on his back and then a barge of sheer strength hit him from behind and he flew up in the air, high as a bird, and then he fell on something before he hit the ground.

Before everything went dark, two things crossed his mind: He was going to die and Angela's laughing face saying *a-bomb-in-a-bull*.

Dom Carlos tried to be away from the village every time there was a bullfight. They were both boring and gruesome. As much as he loved the island culture, he abhorred bullfights—a bull with a rope around the neck being taunted by foolish men, while other men, called shepherds, pulled and manipulated the animal, directing or inciting it.

Dom Carlos sat at the Café by the Sea, looking at the shimmering water, waiting for the day to be over. He would have dinner and go up later to Two

Brooks, or maybe go up tomorrow morning and have lunch with Angela and Dona Mafalda to hear all about the bullfight. He patted the pocket of his blazer where a letter from France, with news that he didn't want to know, awaited to be open.

The streets smelled of freshly brewed coffee and good food. He walked up Cathedral Street and from where he was standing he could see the veranda of his apartment. The carnations were beautiful and in full bloom. Dona Gloria had been watering them well.

The traffic guard waved him across the street. As he entered the vestibule, the neighbors' umbrellas had a forlorn look, as if saying: *here we are desperate for rain.* He went up the stairs and as he opened the door to his apartment, the familiar odor of books and food wafted out from the other apartments in the building. They were pleasant, familiar smells. Dom Carlos walked to the veranda to look at the carnations. He let out a sigh. It would be a matter of seconds before Dona Gloria would show up.

Dona Gloria was a young and pretty widow of a gentle and boring city man, Arturo Montes. Married at only sixteen, she felt that she'd been rescued from a life of hard labor in her nearby village of Four Brooks. She rarely visited her village, but hosted her family often, showing them with pride the good life she had. She gave them money and her old clothes, and her family thought of her as magnanimous and treated her as a person of great importance. In the city, she grew into a beautiful woman of leisure. She ate chocolates, listened to the radio, read fashion magazines and romance novels, and had great expectations about marriage and love.

Soon she realized that her husband, although gentle, was not a creative man, and every day he made love to her the same way as he had their first night: she bent over the kitchen table, grabbed the edges, and waited for her husband to finish.

One day Dona Gloria found him in bed, cold and stiff. He had died as he had lived—quietly. Arturo had worked hard and saved every cent he could— he lived poor to die rich. He had bought a generous life insurance policy, just in case, since he was much older than his wife. He left Dona Gloria with a supermarket, located on the outskirts of the city, and quite a bit of money. He had worked day and night into an early grave.

Life without Arturo continued to be good to Dona Gloria. Her business was successful and she enjoyed the money it generated. She bought pretty things, went out to dinner, the theatre and the movies. She had treated her husband as a gentle obligation when he was alive and as a sweet memory now that he was gone. Every night she prayed for his soul and thanked God for her lucky stars—for having married Arturo and for having lost him because her heart belonged to another man.

She'd been in love with Dom Carlos since she first saw him and secretly pictured his face in every romance she'd read, in every thought she had, in every dream and desire. He became the light of her days. For a brief period, they had been lovers, but it ended because of love, and she was left with an ache that dimmed her smile and shadowed her eyes. She missed his touch as one misses the touch of the sun.

She spent her days listening to the sounds on the other side of the wall. Dom Carlos was a quiet neighbor, but there were sounds that she strained to hear—a chair being pulled, the keys being placed in a porcelain bowl, the door of the armoire being opened and closed, the radio being turned on, and most of all, she listened for visitors.

Today Dona Gloria heard the familiar sounds. But she was in no hurry to see him because she was dealing with a problem of conscience. She had done something and now she couldn't look him in the eye. He was always so gentle and caring. How could she have done that?

There was only one thing to do. Go to him and confess.

He would, of course, no longer look at her with kindness. He would find another neighbor to water the carnations. This thought made her so sad, so sad, that the last time she remembered being this sad was when she looked at Arturo laid out in their living room, receiving the last goodbyes from family and neighbors. He looked so vulnerable and gone. His pants forever fastened around his waist. She would never again see those kind brown eyes look at her with such devotion. She had lost the person who loved her the most. Now she would lose the person she loved above all others. *How sad*, she thought. She got up slowly, picked up the little bundle on the table, and went to Dom Carlos' apartment.

She knocked. He opened the door. He invited her in, sensing that something was off. He put a hand on her back as she sat down. He leaned forward placing his elbows on his knees. This was such a familiar gesture. Then he noticed the bundle of letters she was holding and sat up straight.

"These are yours," she said, handing him the letters.

They had been opened. He took them almost in slow motion and looked at them frowning a little, and understanding everything. He waited for her to talk.

"Forgive me," she said. "I violated your trust."

And after a moment of complete silence, she said, "If it makes any difference, I didn't read them—I don't know French...I tried, even bought a dictionary... but I couldn't continue with my wickedness."

The sun was streaming through the veranda doors, along with the sounds and smells of the city. The bell of the cathedral rang the half-hour and Dona Gloria stirred in her chair. She was crestfallen, defeated. Women instinctively knew things of the heart.

Facing Dona Gloria's misery, Dom Carlos thought about his behavior. How cavalier he'd been with other people's feelings. He had sex with her and then told her, "I'm in love with someone else."

Intensely ashamed, he looked at Dona Gloria, wishing for her forgiveness. He said, "It doesn't matter." And he got up and took her in his arms, hugging her head to his chest.

And she said what she had felt for the last three years, "I love you"—just a whisper loosened out of her chest by his kindness.

"I know," he said, and he thought of love. Love and courage to embrace it, and love and fear to risk rejection. He was the latter. He thought that Dona Gloria and Dona Mafalda in their infinitely lonely hearts were braver and truer to themselves than he would ever be. Sadly, he admitted to himself, he wasn't a daring man—at least not when it came to love.

5

Looking for Home

It was the sudden change in the afternoon that alarmed Angela. The faraway noises carried down in the breeze suddenly changed into a tumult of terrified screams. Hundreds of voices—men, women, children, animals in their pastures, became a roar of distress that bore down the street, passing houses and fields to come to rest at her gate.

The bull killed someone, she thought. *I've heard this fear before.*

She knew it. Pedro Matias had boasted about it. He was the chief shepherd and he gave the commands to the other shepherds when to pull the bull's rope and when to let it go. Angela waited for someone to come down the road and let her know what was going on.

"It was an outsider," said one man dismissively. And he moved down the road to get to his own village.

"It was a mainlander," said the next man. And he walked by like the other.

And no one from Two Brooks came by because everyone was witnessing something familiar—someone dying while running with the bulls because they didn't understand how dangerous it was.

When Dona Mafalda got to Angela, she already knew it was Emanuel. Her heart told her so.

"Is he dead?" she asked, tears already running down her pale face.

Dona Mafalda encircled Angela with her round plump arms and cried softly while whispering in her ear, "Most probably, my dear. They don't know yet. He was taken to the city."

I should have kissed him this afternoon, Angela thought. *His face was so close to mine and I could have just leaned forward and kissed him.*

"If you want to go to the city, I will manage things around here," Dona Mafalda said. "I will call your mother. We will manage." And with a sob, "You probably need to start the funeral arrangements, contact his family...I don't even know if he has a family. Oh, my dear! What a terrible thing!" Dona Mafalda wept openly now.

Both women cried inconsolably in each other's embrace, thinking about that terrible and strange loss.

Emanuel was dead.

Dom Carlos stood still looking at the letters on the table. What did they say? Did they talk about love and forgiveness, like the one in his pocket? What more did beautiful Vivienne want from him?

Vivienne's letter left him unsettled. Why all these letters in just two months? He wondered if Dona Gloria would have given him the letters back if they were not in French. *Mon amour*—she knew that much French.

His reveries of love, unkindness, and cunning were interrupted by the sound of the doorbell. Who would be calling on him on a Monday afternoon? He pressed the lever that unlocked the massive door downstairs and went to the door of the apartment to meet his visitor. As he looked down the corridor, he saw a familiar head emerge up the stairs.

For a second, Dom Carlos was speechless. What in the world was she doing here? When she saw Dom Carlos coming down the corridor to meet her, she almost ran into his arms. In a few quick steps, she bridged the distance and rested her body against his, her head resting on his chest, her arms around his waist. Instinctively, Dom Carlos embraced her and thought, *this is where you belong, in my arms.*

"Thank God you're here," Angela said. "I was afraid you were gone."

Inside, sitting at the veranda, Angela told him about Emanuel. She had gone to the hospital, but he was being stabilized. At least he hadn't died, as she had feared. They wouldn't allow her to see him because she was not family. She waited around and when he was taken to his room and the nurse left, she snuck in. He was either asleep or unconscious. She had only time to call out his name when an enormous nurse with the flanks, nostrils, and teeth of a horse came in and threw her out.

"I didn't know they had a nurse that looked as horrible as that," Dom Carlos said, knowing how she tended to exaggerate to make a point.

"The damn woman is quite pretty, but she is tall…and when I looked up, I only saw nostrils and teeth," Angela explained. "To me, she will be always the Horse because she kicked me out without mercy!" She was silent for a moment and finally added in a whisper, "Emanuel was so beat up."

"But not dead," Dom Carlos said. "Think of it that way." He touched her cheek in a brief caress. "Don't go to a dark place, not yet," he added.

The city was dying down—the sounds, the smells, the light. There was a calmness about that time of day. There was the reassurance of love and shelter with loved ones when people hurried home at the end of the day. The setting sun gave way to a bruised blue sky that turned into night.

They sat on the veranda. The street below was almost deserted, with only a soldier on leave who had no home to go to, no money, waiting out his last few hours of freedom.

Angela was unusually quiet.

"Hawk?" he asked. When they were alone, he called her *Hawk*. She became Hawk when Lazarus died. Dom Carlos told her that she would endure because she was tough like her island—resilient like a hawk.

"What is it?" he insisted, leaning forward and placing his elbows on his knees. Their faces were inches apart. Angela looked into his clear green eyes. Such peace and reassurance she found in this man!

"I had a dream," she said finally. "And in that dream, Emanuel died. He was mauled by a bull and killed."

Dom Carlos knew about her dreams and how much importance she attached to them. When she told him the details of the dream, she saw him trying not to smirk.

"You are dying to make a joke about it," she accused.

"Well…I didn't, did I?" He got up as if to receive a trophy for his self-control. Let's go out to dinner and we will strategize how you can visit Emanuel tomorrow," he added.

"Call the hospital now!" she said, "They will listen to you."

He made the call and after a few connections, waits, and clicks, Dom Carlos was talking to someone in the hospital. He was using his influence well, giving his full name for effect. As he talked on the phone, he was looking steadily at Angela, who in turn was staring back trying to discern the outcome.

"His wife?" Dom Carlos said into the phone, but still looking at Angela.

"Wife?" she mouthed.

Dom Carlos was making "hem, hem" sounds on the phone, apparently in agreement with what was being said. He looked around for the means to write something down. Angela grabbed a pad and a pencil and gave it to him.

"Where is she?" he asked prepared for the information. More "hem, hem" and suddenly the pencil stopped poised over the paper. He finally wrote *Monsignor Inocente*. He put down the phone and looked at her.

"He has a wife?" she asked in disbelief. "He never once told us about her!"

"Well…" said Dom Carlos, "he asked to see *his* wife and that Monsignor Inocente would know. He asked for a police officer to go and see the monsignor about locating his wife." Dom Carlos crossed his arms over his chest. He was staring at her.

"How come we didn't know about her?" Angela asked, feeling dejected. She saw her lodgers like family, and someone as important as a wife should be someone that she should know about. She was almost disappointed with the news.

"Especially *you* should know," said Dom Carlos.

"Not that I have to know the private lives of my lodgers, but if one has a wife I should know! Who is she?" she asked, changing from feeling indignant to being curious.

"Angela Matias," he said flatly.

It took her a second to understand. She started to laugh. Dom Carlos was not amused.

"Why didn't I think of that when the Horse threw me out of his room?" she asked.

"Because you aren't devious," Dom Carlos said.

"Imagine the monsignor's face when a cop knocks at his door looking for the detective's wife." Angela made a serious face trying to imitate the monsignor, "Officer, you are sorely mistaken. That poor bastard has nothing! Not even a wife." She laughed.

Dom Carlos didn't think it was that funny and expressionless waited for her hilarity to abate.

During dinner, Dom Carlos was quieter than usual. While serving their meals, Bernardo kept an eye on Dom Carlos, his most generous customer. *This man,* thought the waiter, *was always laughing, but not today because of the girl with intense eyes. I think she will hurt him.* Angela smiled at the waiter with the droopy mustache. He bowed his head slightly in acknowledgment. She shifted her gaze back to Dom Carlos and leaned over the table. "You're jealous," she said.

"Jealous?" he asked dismissively, "Of whom and why?"

"Of Emanuel, because he said I was his wife."

"You're not his wife. So why would I be jealous?" He studied her for a long time.

"Dom Carlos," she said, "if Emanuel had a wife somewhere, so what? But if you did, I would kill you." She laughed and held his hand over the table. He grasped her fingers in his, but he was less moved to laughter.

They left the restaurant to go to the hospital. Suddenly, Angela stopped and turned to look up at him. "You are so good to me," she said, full of emotion. She got on her tiptoes and placed a kiss on his cheek. His clean smell of soap lingered on her lips. *If he had turned his face just a fraction, I would have kissed his mouth,* she considered.

Dom Carlos was very quiet.

"Why are you grumpy?" she asked.

"I don't even know what grumpy is," he retorted.

"Well, grumpy is a businessman going to see a detective in the hospital, against his will, because his landlady made him do it."

"No, I'm not grumpy because of that," he said quietly. As soon as he said it, he repented but it was too late.

Angela stopped on the street and faced him. "What is it then?" she asked.

"Mind your business!" he said.

"You are my business," she answered unfazed.

A streetlamp illuminated her face turned up to him, waiting for a reply. He touched her cheek and said, "Don't be a bully. We all have secrets."

"Yes, but you have too many. You remain full of mystery, while you know everything about me, everything. There is no balance in this relationship. I think you never invited me to your apartment because you're hiding something. It's like you lead a double life." She laughed at her outlandish statement.

Dom Carlos was thinking about truth—how impractical it could be. What would Angela say if he told her that he had had sex with Dona Gloria? "Do I know everything about you?" he asked.

Angela lowered her eyes. No, he didn't know everything. He didn't know about Night Justice. She had no business looking innocent and angelic. She had put a candle up someone's ass…she had undressed men and flogged them. She had fried a man's genitalia. She was a fraud.

"You know the important things," she said quietly and ceased talking about secrets.

When they got to the hospital, Angela was praying for the Horse not to be there. But she was and when she saw Angela, she icily exclaimed, "You again?"

"I came to visit my husband, Detective Emanuel Santos," she stated simply.

"How interesting! A few hours ago you didn't know he was your husband, did you, dear?" Nurse Santiago said with feigned surprise.

Angela didn't want to bicker with the nurse—she wanted to see Emanuel. She felt emboldened by the good news that he wasn't dead and took off down the corridor straight into Emanuel's room. The nurse chased after her, but Dom Carlos braked her progress by engaging her with his charm.

Emanuel was propped on pillows, naked from the waist up and seemingly asleep. His upper body was full of bruises and cuts being dressed by a nurse.

Angela gasped at the sight, and Emanuel opened his eyes. The nurse turned around and was going to send her out of the room when he said, "Please, let her stay. She's my wife."

"Visiting hours are way over, missy!" said the nurse disapprovingly.

"I just want to see him for a second," she said to the nurse.

"Five minutes the most!" warned the nurse. "This man could be dead now with the type of injuries he suffered. He could have perforated lungs."

"God forbid!" Angela said in a whisper.

Angela smiled at Emanuel and walked slowly over to his bed. She leaned over as if she was going to kiss him. She placed her mouth on his ear and whispered, "When did we get married?"

He smiled. Nurse Santiago stood by the door like a disapproving sentinel.

"You promised to be careful," Angela said, sitting on the edge of the bed.

He extended a bandaged hand to her and she held it gingerly. "It was a-bomb-in-a-bull," he said and they both started to laugh. He gasped with pain. Angela held her breath, helplessly, watching him fight for control.

"He can't laugh!" said the nurse. "He has multiple rib fractures that are causing breathing problems!"

Angela looked at his pale face, his mouth open, in an attempt to control the pain. Then very deliberately she caressed his face as if to smooth away the stress. His short takes of breath became slow and steady.

Emanuel looked at her almost without blinking, and then she lowered her face to his and kissed him on the cheek. He sought her mouth and they kissed— a long, sweet, unhurried kiss. When Angela lifted her mouth from his, their eyes locked for a moment.

This was what Dom Carlos and the Horse saw. Emanuel was hoping that the kiss would never end, Angela was grateful that he was alive, and Dom Carlos wanted to murder him. Finally, the Horse queried Dom Carlos, "And who are you? Her father?"

Emanuel chuckled, and then reeled in pain again.

"Kissing is a lot easier on the ribs than laughing, Detective," nurse Santiago said. "No laughing or moving about. No lovemaking for a while either! And you have five minutes to visit, *five*!"

"When will you be coming home?" Angela asked Emanuel.

"Soon I hope," he answered. "I don't have internal injuries, only fractured ribs and a lot of bruises."

Angela said, "I was so worried about you and you didn't listen. You were in the street after I told you to stay away."

"I'm sorry," he answered just as quietly.

Dom Carlos gave him a fake smile and said, "Very touching. While you're healing here from your injuries, Angela will be healing with me from the pain you caused her. She needs a vacation from you, Detective." Dom Carlos sat down and picked up the newspaper as if his interest in the detective had expired.

Angela said softly, "I'm so sorry, Emanuel, so sorry."

Emanuel forgot all about Dom Carlos, hidden behind the newspaper, spying.

"It wasn't your fault. Short of locking me in the house, you tried to stop me," Emanuel said.

Dom Carlos cleared his throat, "Did he know about the dream?" he asked from behind the newspaper.

"What dream?" Emanuel asked.

Angela gave Dom Carlos a warning look, but he was purposely avoiding her eyes. He lowered the paper and said without looking at Angela, "She had a dream, an omen to your demise. Now she's blaming herself for not letting you know about it. She thinks that if she had, you would have stayed home, terrified."

For a split second, Emanuel thought that Dom Carlos was joking.

"I don't believe in dreams, Angela," he said. "That wouldn't have stopped me."

"Well, I don't either, but this one was a powerful dream," goaded Dom Carlos.

The nurse appeared—the five minutes were up. "Say your goodbyes, my dear. This man needs to rest."

Emanuel reluctantly let go of her hand.

"Well, give him a kiss, girl, and go home!" the nurse said impatiently.

"You've heard the nurse," Emanuel said. She sat again on the edge of the bed and kissed him on the lips, a sweet, lingering kiss. This time Emanuel was not panting with pain or caught by surprise. He received her kiss, holding her close and not letting go.

Dom Carlos was watching. He saw Emanuel's hand with bruised knuckles, on the back of Angela's head, holding her face to his, as they kissed.

On the way to the apartment, Dom Carlos was very quiet. The moon big and bright seemed closer—as if curious and trying to listen in.

"You didn't have to kiss him to convince the nurses that you were his wife," Dom Carlos said finally. "That was my job."

"To kiss him?" she chuckled.

She was amused. Then she said, "That's not why I kissed him."

"Why did you?" he asked.

She said after a long pause, "He looked lost, like a person without a home. He broke my heart—so alone and no one to care for him."

Dom Carlos harrumphed. Angela looked up at him to understand his meaning.

"He is an arrogant bastard," Dom Carlos said moodily. "He may not be as lethal as Angus Pomba, but he is just as arrogant. I'm surprised that you and your friends, including Regina, embraced him so readily. I think he is a fraud."

"Oh, Dom Carlos," she reprimanded, "Why don't you like him? He is a nice man. You are so good to everybody."

"I am not good to everybody," he said as if warding off an insult.

"Yes, you are. You are the kindest and sweetest person I know."

"Sweet? You make me sound like a cup of tea!"

"There is nothing more attractive than kindness, and you are kind and good to everyone. Tell me a person who you're not good to. Tell me!" she insisted.

"The monsignor," he said.

"The monsignor doesn't count," she said dismissively.

"Since when did you grow sympathetic to the police, mainlanders, authority, and so on?" Dom Carlos asked impatiently.

"There is something about Emanuel that…is kind, well-meaning. I feel it in my heart. They could have sent someone else altogether," she said, quietly remembering how terrible the last police investigator had been.

"Have you ever thought that it is just a different strategy that he's using?" They were at the vestibule outside the door of the apartment. Dom Carlos placed his hands on her shoulders and peered down at her. He said, "Be careful. His methods are different, but it doesn't mean that he won't hurt you any less."

When they got to the apartment, it was late. All the nervous energy and worry over Emanuel had left them spent and immediately they got ready for bed. Angela plopped on the sofa and said a tired goodnight.

Dom Carlos performed his ablutions without his usual whistling or turning on the radio, and when he went by the living room he looked at Angela already curled up on the sofa.

"I'm staying there tonight," he said, "and you take the bed."

"Not tonight," she said turning her back to him. "Good night."

When Angela said goodnight, she was thinking about the softness of Emanuel's mouth and how his tongue had caressed her lips. She felt her heart flutter and like an assault, Lazarus came to mind. He didn't seem real any longer. Lazarus was like a dream that belonged to someone with a fantastical imagination. How could this be? Lazarus, the man she loved all her life, was slowly evaporating, like a mere thought, like an inconsequential memory. She felt wicked and this feeling persisted like a tormenting devil.

Dom Carlos lay in bed, his hands clasped behind his head, staring at the ceiling. He looked for the familiar horse on the plaster created by moonlight hitting the mirror. But all he could see, seared in his mind, was Angela kissing Emanuel.

He had just finished reading Vivienne's letters, full of remorse and love. He couldn't even remember now how he had loved her. When she left him for another man, he had been stunned—having had no idea that she was unhappy. After he signed the divorce papers, he left France. "I don't love you as a wife should, Antoine," she had said. And it was over like that.

He heard Angela shift around. She couldn't sleep either. He remembered when Lazarus died—nights full of tossing and turning, nightmares, and crying out. He got up and walked to the sofa. The moon was sending a silver strip across the apartment.

"I'm sorry I woke you," she said.

"I was awake," he said sitting at her feet. "Why can't you sleep?"

"Remorse, I think," she said. "I was dreaming that Lazarus was running away from a bull. He came running toward me and I didn't pull him up, my arms were too heavy."

"Do you want me to stay with you?" he asked.

She let out a sigh and said, "I broke that terrible habit...no!"

"It's not so terrible. Most people don't like to sleep alone," he said.

"I take it to extremes. I take everything to extremes," she said with a rueful smile.

He waited for a few seconds and said, "Come."

On the other side of the wall, Dona Gloria was imagining *her* Dom Carlos going to bed with this woman who showed up at his door. So, this was *the* French woman. After all those letters and *Mon Amoures*, she had finally arrived.

"Vivienne," Dona Gloria said softly. How she wished she was Vivienne. She sat on the floor, with her face pressed on the wall that separated her home from Dom Carlos' and cried. She imagined him making love to Vivienne, looking into her eyes, caressing her face, as he had done to her before. And then she felt a tremendous longing for Arturo who had loved her so completely, if not creatively. She spent the night sitting against the wall dozing in and out of cruel dreams.

The next morning Dom Carlos and Angela woke up with someone knocking insistently at the door. As soon as he opened the door, Dona Gloria came in glancing in every direction. He put an index finger to his lips for silence and guided Angela to the kitchen. Dona Gloria had brought bread, goat's cheese, olives, and the knowledge that Dom Carlos had a woman somewhere in the apartment.

She stopped when she saw Angela—a petite woman, unfashionably tanned, with big eyes and a big mouth, messy hair, wearing men's pajamas. This woman was not pretty. This poor thing in his kitchen couldn't compete with her own loveliness. This poor girl looked like a cat left out in a thunderstorm. She felt a huge sense of relief.

"Bonjour!" Dona Gloria said to Angela, "Je m'apelle Glorrria."

Dom Carlos, behind Dona Gloria, signaled for silence. Angela was confused but had the presence of mind to say, "Bonjour" to this very pretty woman and stopped at that. And because Dona Gloria didn't know any more French, she too didn't say anything more. They were both staring at each other, with pleasant smiles plastered on their faces. Dom Carlos coaxed Dona Gloria out the door, thanking her for the thoughtful gifts.

He came into the kitchen.

"Who's Glorrria?" Angela asked.

Dom Carlos let out the laugh he had suppressed minutes before. His head was thrown back showing a long strong neck rippled with laughter.

"What was that about?" Angela insisted.

"It's a long story," he said finally.

"She has a crush on you," Angela said.

"Adults don't have crushes," he answered, turning around to make the coffee.

"What is it then?"

He didn't know what to say. What he felt for Angela was not a crush. He'd been in love with her even before Lazarus died. It was an impossible love, but love nonetheless. He was unwilling to trivialize Dona Gloria's love, so his own wouldn't suffer the same fate.

"What?" she asked again, looking at his back.

After a long moment, he said, "I'll tell you tonight."

I will not sleep with you tonight, she thought. *A decent woman wouldn't do that! I'm walking on the edge of sin. One stumble and I could fall and be irreparably broken. I will not sleep with you tonight!*

If only she could pay to have hours of profound sleep. She would hoard it and stack it, and every night she would take ten hours, knowing that she had a room full of it. Her thoughts swung to Dom Carlos. He was a package of profound sleep. Why did it have to be a person? Why not Viriato or Hercules? Why not a cow or even a horse? To sleep with a horse would be strange, no doubt, but it wouldn't be a sin...or almost a sin...perhaps only a sin of self-indulgence...

She remembered when Lazarus was gone, and Dom Carlos kept her company on the nights she couldn't sleep. As soon as Dom Carlos settled for the night next to her, she slept like a baby. Since then, he offered to be her soporific. And she took it as much as she dared.

In the village, the rumor started that she was sleeping with Dom Carlos. The monsignor ordered him out of the house, but Angela didn't allow the monsignor to tell her who could or couldn't live in her house. The monsignor cast about for another strategy—the new teacher should be a woman. If another woman was living in the house, people's tongues would stop wagging.

In the city, Dom Carlos seemed different than when he was in Two Brooks. Maybe it was this subtle difference that made her think of sin. It was something she couldn't name. She noticed things about him that she hadn't before, like his strong hands and the beauty of his neck. It must have been Dona Gloria's love and its transforming powers that lent Dom Carlos that sexual, guarded nuance.

"Is there something between you and Dona Gloria?" she asked.

"No," he answered simply, "we are only neighbors." He had his eyes fastened on his plate.

"I had the feeling that…she was upset to see me."

He held her gaze for a moment and then got up from the table, leaving his food unfinished.

Angela suddenly understood that she touched something that she shouldn't have. "Are you in love with her?" she asked crestfallen.

He turned to face her. He was extremely serious as if he was about to tell her something important, but he only said, "No, I'm not."

"I'm so used to having you all to myself…I've been very selfish." And all of a sudden, she felt vulnerable.

He turned around and left the room.

Angela arrived at the hospital in mid-morning. She came in looking rested and happy. Emanuel had never seen her look that rested. Dom Carlos' vacation was working well.

"Hello, wife," he said, touching her hand. "What took you so long?"

"Hello, Emanuel, you are looking much better." She sat on the edge of the bed.

"So much so that I'm leaving tomorrow," he said.

"I thought you had to stay a few more days." She was surprised.

"Not if I have a nurse to help me out at home."

She asked with concern, "Are you sure you will be alright if you come home?"

They were quiet, each one assessing the other. "Imagine what Hercules will do to you if you can't even laugh," she broke the silence.

"Or scream," he added. "I'm hoping that he will focus on Dom Carlos."

She laughed and the nurse yelled from the nurse's station, "Do I hear laughing?"

"That Horse!" Angela said with annoyance.

"She is very kind. Her name is Margarida, not Horse." He smiled amused and then frowned because Angela seemed nervous.

"Emanuel," she said gravely, "I live in a strange and beautiful place that you, with all your worldly knowledge, cannot understand." She measured her words. "What happened to you was not an accident. They wanted you to be caught by the bull and for you to die."

His brow furrowed. He held her hand as if afraid she would get up and leave.

"Who are *they*?" he asked.

"Two Brooks," she said. "They are poisoned against you, against what you represent. We all drink from the same water. Even those who have no reason to hate you, they do because they get caught up with the sentiment of the majority. We have a collective conscience. We are weak and strong that way. We have survived for centuries because of it."

"You think they were trying to have me killed, like Angus Pomba?" he asked, still unconvinced.

"It looks that way, doesn't it? You were pushed time and time again onto the street in front of the bull until you were caught. You were luckier than Angus Pomba, that's all," she said.

"Angus had an accident," he stated, his voice a degree colder.

"What I know is that he was hated to no end and he died here in Two Brooks, gored by a bull. And now you?" she said impatiently.

"This is different...Angus Pomba was alone with the bull. I was with hundreds of people at that bullfight..." his voice trailed into a murmur and he stared at her.

She shook her head, convinced of her truth. "Stop staring at me," she said disconcertedly. "I don't want you to be hurt! Don't be a fool thinking that you know everything, because you don't!"

"Would you have cried if I had died?" he asked.

"I cried for you and you didn't even die—a waste of my tears...and so did Dona Mafalda and every woman in that miserable village," Angela said, annoyed with the drift in the conversation.

"Dona Mafalda cried?" he asked pleasantly surprised.

"Like a baby," she answered.

Emanuel closed his eyes for a moment, delighted with the idea that they had cried for him. It was such a strange feeling to be cared for by more than one person at a time, by a community. Since he'd been injured, he received letters and small gifts—mostly chocolates and sugar-covered almonds—from these weeping women, young and old, who just wanted him to be well. This left him with a feeling of elation and a hint of something else—like a new responsibility for someone else's affliction. When was the last time he did something just for love? He couldn't remember. When was the last time someone cried for him? That he remembered well, although it was such a long time ago when he was a young boy.

"Open that drawer," he said to Angela and pointed to the side table. He gave her a smug look.

Angela opened a drawer full of gifts. "The nurses will think that you are a philanderer," she said, "receiving gifts from women…"

"I told them they were from you," he said.

"No wonder they asked me what I was bringing you today," she answered. "Enjoy all of this attention while it lasts, Detective Santos, because when you get home we will return to mistreating you."

"You never mistreated me," he said.

"I'll fix that then," she answered.

Nurse Santiago came in and pointed to the door, as Moses pointed to the Red Sea, "Go away!" she said.

6

The Edge of Sin

Angela scanned the crowd for Dom Carlos. The plaza was busy, full of people going somewhere in a hurry, weaving in and out through the maze of people who were enjoying their leisure and taking in the sun. The taxi drivers waited around their cars, some playing cards, others just looking at passersby. The sidewalks were crowded with café tables with white, crisp tablecloths rippling in the gentle breeze.

Angela caught Dom Carlos' wave and quickly crossed the square to sit at his sidewalk table under an umbrella. "He is coming home tomorrow," she said.

"He isn't going to die then," he said, looking out onto the square.

"Stop making jokes! I think they threw him to the bull on purpose, so your jokes about him dying aren't funny," she snapped.

"Come on, Hawk!" he said in disbelief.

"Yes, they did. He wanted to blend in, to be like everybody else, not realizing that they were watching and waiting for him to trip over his ignorance." She continued, "What do you think happened at the bullfight? Can you imagine a whole village closing ranks, leaving a man out to die? Can you imagine such a cold thing? I can't forget Angus Pomba!"

He reasoned, "Angus was an accident—he was alone in a pasture and he was gored by a bull. It happens! Hundreds of people get hurt at the bullfights because they're stupid, not because people want to kill them. The detective was stupid and arrogant. You warned him, didn't you?"

"I have a feeling about this that I can't dismiss!" she insisted.

"We will take care of him, all of us. No bull, cow or goat will have a chance to touch him, ever!" he said, letting out a frustrated sigh. And then with a wicked grin, he added, "We will sign up Dona Mafalda to do the kissing. Nurse Santiago said he couldn't laugh, but he could kiss."

They laughed at the thought of Emanuel being kissed every three hours, like a medicine, like cough syrup.

Dom Carlos and Angela walked down the street toward the Café by the

Sea, where Bernardo bowed slightly before serving them. *This girl is going to do some damage to this man,* the waiter thought again.

After a leisurely dinner, they headed back to Dom Carlos' apartment, walking slowly, until they reached it and settled on the veranda enjoying the evening turn into night. Angela stayed on the veranda long after Dom Carlos went to bed. She couldn't sleep. She felt unsettled, anxious, and still battling with her resolve not to seek companionship for the night.

She peered into Dom Carlos' bedroom, where he was sleeping peacefully. Stealthily she walked in and sat on his bed. If she was careful, maybe he wouldn't wake up.

"You are having dark thoughts, I can tell," he said.

"I thought you were asleep."

He sat up in bed and said, "You don't have to sneak in, Hawk. The bed is big enough for both of us." He put a pillow between the two of them and made a gesture as if exhibiting an idea worthy of an award.

She harrumphed. This for her was the same thing as wine offered to a drunk. "I know!" she said ill humoredly.

She laid down with her back to him. After a long pause, she asked, "Would you cry if Emanuel died?"

"What an astonishing question," he said.

"Well, would you?" she pressed.

"I have no idea, Hawk. I can always push him under a bus and see..."

The soft light of the streetlamp came through the open veranda door. She was oddly alert and fighting startling thoughts. She was thinking about death, how close Emanuel came to dying, and how mundane it was to lose people one loved...she was distressed with the possibility that Dom Carlos could die, just like Lazarus. If Dom Carlos died, she would die too. Lazarus used up all her tolerance for grief. Instead of being stronger for having survived such a loss, she felt fragile and exposed.

"I didn't know I cared for Emanuel as much as I do until I thought he had died..." she said.

"Why are you thinking about death?" he asked.

"I think about it often. Sometimes I even cry with the thought of losing someone I love. Life is very cruel to those who love much because sooner or later loved ones leave us. I used to think *who will cry first, Lazarus or me?* And it was me..."

"Hey, why are you so gloomy?" he asked.

"Emanuel's accident jarred my soul. I should have known that happiness is measured only when we lose it, and, yet, I was complacent about joy."

"Go to sleep, Hawk. Tonight, think only of beautiful things," he said, touching her shoulder.

When Emanuel got home that afternoon, after four days in the hospital, the village was abuzz with the news. People came by with gifts and plenty of curiosity, and Dona Mafalda, who was given the task to look after him, was making sure that the nurse's instructions were followed to the letter. Angela had shared with Dona Mafalda her paranoia about the village wanting to hurt the detective and Dona Mafalda didn't need any help for drama and paranoia.

He was temporarily moved to the first floor, a room near the kitchen. A wide window opened to the garden where the morning sun was generous and bright. Anyone coming into the garden and curious enough could look in on the bedridden police detective. Rosa told Angela that she should charge admission for people to come in and peer through the window. "You would make a fortune. When I go out, you can't imagine how many people ask me about him…mostly women, of course." Angela couldn't help thinking about the spectacle: Heavy curtains over the window, people outside waiting, and Dona Mafalda, with a theatrical yank at the curtains, announcing "Behold!"

Even as Emanuel remained unconvinced that the village wanted to kill him, he was elated with their attention and especially with Dona Mafalda's dedication to his healing. She was devoted to his care and was unbending regarding restrictions on visitation, especially from women. When Emanuel told her about Rosa's proposal, she didn't even find it funny. He was allowed to read, write, eat, and sleep and generally rest, but no women, not even Angela.

With all this time on his hands, Emanuel organized his notes on the investigation and got bored often. When Dona Mafalda was not around, Angela snuck in like a bad deed, allowing visitors. They came running every time they saw Dona Mafalda on the street—Elvira, Ema, Fatima, poor Olivia with tape on her glasses. Regina came with steak in hand. Luciana sat by him and sang beautiful soothing tunes that made him sleep and gave him erotic dreams.

One afternoon, when Dona Mafalda was organizing his room, Emanuel asked, "Dona Mafalda, do you really think that the villagers wish me dead?"

She looked back at him. "I was at the bullfight, Detective Santos. I saw what happened."

They were silent, and the sounds outside streamed in, amplified by the silence in the room—dogs barking, someone singing, chickens clucking, men talking to their cattle. She sighed and came to sit down in the chair near his bed. "They wanted to hurt you, or at the very least, scare you. I saw them as if with one mind, leaving you out exposed, at the mercy of a bull. I don't know if they believed that their wish was becoming reality— moments before, they seemed to repent all at once and wanted to save you, but it was too late." Her eyes were moist with tears. "I was there, screaming with the others. When you came by running, I didn't stretch my arms to you. I felt paralyzed. I felt that one pair of arms would be useless—just one pair of arms, and you wouldn't see me. I simply screamed until my throat hurt. I was right there when the bull caught you and tossed you up in the air. You flew high up like a rag doll and landed on a veranda full of women. That's what saved you—the women. If you had veered one inch outwards you would have fallen on the hard stone pavement and would have died…like Mario did, so many years ago." She paused. "You broke Olivia's glasses with your shoe when you fell on us…"

One pair of arms…That would have been enough to save me, he thought. Tears ran down Dona Mafalda's face. He reached for her hand and held it to his lips. "Don't cry," he said. Emanuel let go of Dona Mafalda's hand and she wiped her eyes and face, and loudly blew her nose. She had imagined so many situations, little romantic scenes while taking care of the detective. She never imagined sitting next to him, crying, tears and mucus running down her face and making trumpet sounds with her nose. Her eyes were swollen and her marvelous clear skin was blotchy red, but she felt light as if a heavy blanket had been lifted from her heart.

Emanuel was closing his eyes as if to go to sleep.

Angela came to the door. Lucas, the mechanic, was asking to see Dona Mafalda. Lucas often met with Dom Carlos regarding the operation and repair of the pasteurizing machines. Probably he called on Dom Carlos more often than he had to, hoping to catch a glimpse of Dona Mafalda, who he had fallen for since he had first seen her.

Dona Mafalda gave Angela an inquisitive look but went out to meet Lucas Pires, who was in the garden, looking cleaner than usual. When he heard footsteps, he looked up and smiled at Dona Mafalda, his adoration showing as well as his nervousness.

"I just wanted to say hello," he said timidly.

"Thank you for the courtesy," she said primly and eyed him with coldness.

"I also wanted to let you know that the new nurse is coming tonight, to take care of the detective. She is Mother's goddaughter and will be staying with us tonight."

Dona Mafalda felt like kicking Lucas. She wasn't sure why. Maybe because he brought news about a nurse who was going to interfere with her patient or because this man had the nerve to think that she would be interested in him.

"Dona Mafalda," he said almost trembling, "I know you like dark chocolate. I got a bar from the American base. I would like you to have it." He offered the chocolate to Dona Mafalda, who was rooted on the spot, looking at that marvelous thing resting on the palm of his hand.

If she picks up the chocolate now, Lucas thought, *she will love me.*

"It isn't proper for me to receive gifts from gentlemen who I don't have a relationship with," she said coldly.

"We could try," he said terrified but said it. Now the cat was out of the bag and he was going to finish what he started.

She took a step closer to him and in a measured cold voice she said, "Don't you think that you are above your station addressing me in that fashion?"

He was not surprised by her response, but what he thought was that she was talking fancy about something that only required a yes or a no. However, what she said sounded like a no. He looked down at his boots, clean and polished. He had polished his boots to come there and hear this. He hated boots. They hurt and pinched the feet. He much preferred wearing sandals made from old car tires. Now he felt ridiculous in shining boots, with chocolate melting in his hand.

"I'm sorry, Dona Mafalda. I didn't mean to offend you." He blushed like a little boy and got angry with himself. Damn it! He was going to finish this shit! "Dona Mafalda," he said looking her straight in the eyes. "I am in love with you and I want to marry you. There! I think this is plain talking and I would appreciate if you did the same with me—plain talking."

She opened her mouth to speak, but she was too surprised to say anything. Lucas saw the opportunity to suggest something else. He couldn't take a rejection right there and then. It would hurt too much—it would hurt more than wearing the boots. "Don't say anything now," he said. "Think about it and let me know by Sunday. I'll look for you then." He turned around wincing and walked away.

Emanuel opened his eyes and stared at the ceiling. He seemed momentarily confused. Then he looked at Angela sitting next to him.

"You came to kill me," he said.

"It crossed my mind," she answered.

"Where is my dragon?" he asked, looking around for Dona Mafalda.

"Your dragon is in her room. Something happened in the garden with the mechanic." Angela lifted her hand to stop the questions he was going to ask. "Lucas has been in love with her since the first time he saw her. And because he is a simple mechanic, too young, she says, and not of pedigree, she thinks he is audacious for even thinking about her. She is royalty, don't forget."

"She should marry Dom Carlos then," Emanuel said. "They are about the same age and both of royal blood." After a long pause, he added, "Thank you for all you've done for me."

"I didn't do much," she protested truthfully.

"More than anyone had in a very long time," he answered.

"Life has not been that kind to you then," she said jokingly.

He didn't say anything.

Curious, she said, "You never talk about your family. Who will I call if you die again?" She grinned.

"No one."

"Who raised you, wolves?" she chuckled.

"I was raised by Catholic nuns...in an orphanage." He smiled at her embarrassment.

"I'm so sorry," she said, regretting her flippant demeanor.

"They were good to us," he said. "The priests were a different matter, but the nuns who took care of us were good."

She felt that pang in the bottom of her stomach—the same feeling that prompted her to kiss him in the hospital. "No one..." she said.

"I have a wife," he smiled.

She returned his smile. "Some wife. She couldn't even keep you home with her—you preferred to go to the bullfight. You're such a typical man."

"I can't fall for you," he murmured.

This was such a startling statement, almost out of context. She frowned and straightened on her chair.

"What?" she scrutinized his face, searching for a laugh, a joke, or something less dangerous than what she thought he had said.

"I don't want to love you," he said quietly, closing his eyes to evade her gaze.

"What you are feeling is gratitude," she said. "Gratitude is a wonderful feeling. It is love, joy, and thankfulness all wrapped into one." She touched his hand gingerly. "It's only gratitude, Detective Santos. Don't complicate things."

"I'll take it. I'll take anything except loving you." Maybe she was right. He had fallen in love so many times, but this felt different. It was heavier, deeper, enveloping, and ever-present. "When did you fall in love with Lazarus?" he asked.

She thought for a minute and then said, "I didn't fall in love with Lazarus. I simply loved him. I've loved him all my life—I don't remember falling in love. When I became aware of my existence, Lazarus was already a part of me."

"So, you don't know how it feels to fall in love," he said.

"I guess not," she admitted. "It sounds perilous, like stumbling and crashing. It implies hurt and distress."

"I suppose it's all of those things."

"Then it can't be love if it hurts that much."

"How would you know if you never fell in love?"

She was reflecting on his words. He was waiting for an explanation on certainties about love, about falling for someone. But she was trying to collect her thoughts and put everything she knew into one sentence. "I suppose I don't know much." It sounded almost like an apology.

They were both silent, looking at Viriato sleeping peacefully. She asked, "If you fall in love with me, how will I know?"

Emanuel gazed at her for a long moment. There was no guile in Angela. She wanted to know the signs of someone falling, like a tree in a forest or a glass jar breaking on the floor—physical, irrefutable signs that something had been forever changed. He touched her lips lightly, remembering the kiss. He said, "Love is self-evident."

Angela was not so sure of that. There were so many forms of love. She loved so many people. What was the subtlety that made the romantic love between two people distinct? Was it the falling, the hazardous way that people connected, like an accident? Falling in love didn't promise to be everlasting. If you fall, you get up, and it's over. Angela straightened up in her chair. This conversation was making her unsure of what love should feel like. Look at Dona Mafalda brooding in her room and Lucas aching with love for her—he fell, and she was unmoved. "I'll take you to the garden. It might rain finally," she said hurriedly and helped him out of bed, not aware that Hercules had entered the room.

"Angela," Emanuel said, "I can't even scream if this thing attacks me."
She picked up the cat, which hissed at Emanuel, *imbecile.*

Angela didn't want Emanuel to talk about love. Once she was so sure what it was, it was so clear. Love was what Lazarus and she had. Love was that joy to be with the other and care for the other for no reason at all. It was to look at him and say from your heart, I love you. Love was to find yourself smiling with the thought of the other. It was like nothing else and forever, single-minded and overwhelming, completing—not leaving a sliver of space in one's heart for someone else to get in. And then she lost Lazarus and she was left only with sorrow—so strong that at times she could hardly breathe. And as the sorrow abated, that wisdom about love was gone. Lazarus became thin in her heart, one-dimensional—only a story she could tell. She was like an empty room with open doors in every wall and she didn't know what to do with the flood of thoughts and emotions surging in. She sighed with relief when Emanuel veered the conversation to the investigation.

"Pedro Matias said that he went to get limpets with his son and that Lazarus fell into the ocean. The only thing left behind was his wristwatch. I would like to test it."

"Do you know that this wristwatch was a miracle?" she asked after a heavy silence.

How could a Timex be a miracle? A Rolex, maybe... but Emanuel was getting used to Angela's way of looking at the world, and he waited for the explanation.

"The thing that Lazarus wanted most was a wristwatch. He was eleven years old when he received it from his godmother in Canada. She sent it for his confirmation. One day I found him in church kneeling in front of Jesus crucified. He was praying fervently about something. I wanted to know what he was so keenly praying for. And he told me that he had been praying for a wristwatch. He was on his last day of a novena. I remembered looking at his beautiful brown eyes, full of faith, and I told him that I would also pray for his wristwatch. Surprised by my offer, he said, 'But you don't like to pray.' He left the church, truly believing that he would get that wristwatch. I looked at Jesus crucified and prayed. I remember saying, 'Come on Jesus. He isn't asking for a car!' Then I told Jesus that if He didn't find a wristwatch for Lazarus,

I would never look at Him again. Imagine, threatening Jesus on the cross... When Lazarus got home he had a beautiful shining Timex from Canada."

"Was it the novena or your threats that moved Jesus?" Emanuel asked.

"Have you ever received a miracle, Emanuel?" she asked joining in the mirth.

"No, I never did. I prayed once for a miracle, but it didn't happen." Sometimes miracles were like dreams or secrets—they could not be revealed.

"What was your unanswered miracle?" she whispered.

"It was about a woman, who I loved more than anything and anyone," he said.

"What happened?"

"She died. My miracle was for her to be alive, for her to come back to me."

"I'm so sorry," Angela said. "Sometimes love can be a terrible thing, especially if it is taken from you. It is like receiving a grace long enough to feel blessed and then be condemned without it. If one doesn't love, one doesn't hurt. Memories... no matter how sweet are hardly enough."

"I remember the love, though. I remember, and I know that it can transform a person," he said as if talking to himself.

In her room, Dona Mafalda was making decisions about Lucas. No, she was not going to wait until Sunday and then have that brute come to her and demand answers. Who did he think he was? Her inkwell was always full—her being a teacher—and she had an elegantly monogrammed stationery set. She put pen to paper:

> *Dear Mr. Pires,*
>
> *Today, much to my chagrin, you proposed marriage. You don't have to wait until Sunday for my answer. I am, if nothing else, a decisive woman. I don't want to marry you or have any interactions with you of any nature. Your insolence and lack of proportion in your assumptions were astounding. Your nerve to think that a woman of my station would entertain such a preposterous idea leaves me speechless.*
>
> *Respectfully,*
> *Dona Mafalda Maria de Lourdes Dias*
> *Santos Sampaio do Monte da Cruz*

Dona Mafalda called Rosa and asked her to deliver the letter to Lucas. It was about a bicycle she wanted to buy. So, she need not wait for a response, because Lucas would have to find the bicycle first. Dona Mafalda thought that this would satisfy Rosa's curiosity.

When Rosa gave Lucas the letter, he opened it with trembling hands. He knew that handwriting.

"It's about the bicycle," Rosa said.

"What bicycle?" he asked.

"The bicycle Dona Mafalda wants you to find for her," she said.

The girl was waiting for a reaction. But what she saw was sadness on his face and two fat tears running down his cheeks. His tears fell on Dona Mafalda's note and the ink ran down the paper onto his feet.

"Tell Dona Mafalda that I got the message," he said, looking for composure.

Rosa ran all the way home to Dona Mafalda. She had never seen the matter of a bicycle cause a man to cry. When she got to Angela's house, she found Emanuel reading in the garden surrounded by the menagerie, minus Hercules. Angela was inside.

"Dona Mafalda sent a letter to Lucas," Rosa said to Angela.

Angela looked surprised.

"And he cried," Rosa said. By now she suspected that the letter had nothing to do with a bicycle.

Angela peered into the garden. Emanuel was reading, and she left the house quietly. She found Lucas with his head inside a machine, looking for problems.

"I understand that Dona Mafalda wrote you a letter," Angela said.

"She told you?" he asked.

"No, she didn't. May I see it?"

He hesitated but took a folded piece of paper from his shirt pocket and handed it to Angela. She unfolded the letter and could hardly read it with the ink smears.

She sighed. What a mean-hearted letter!

"What are you going to do?" she asked Lucas.

"I wish I could write her a fancy letter. I can't write fancy as she does." Lucas was feeling terribly out of place in his own garage. He was so sorry that he didn't like books. He had no business falling in love with a teacher when he didn't even like school.

"And what would you say?" she asked.

He thought for a while and then said, "I would tell her that she broke my heart twice: She didn't want to be my wife and she didn't care if she hurt my feelings."

"I can help you write that," Angela said.

"I understand fancy. I just don't know how to do it myself," he said hopelessly.

Lucas found a pencil and a paper. He didn't have ink, but a pencil was good enough. Angela dictated the letter and helped with the spelling:

> Dear Dona Mafalda,
>
> I just received your letter. It was with great sadness that I've read the content of your missive. Needless to say, I will respect your wishes and stop any attempt to interact with you. I will cross to the other side of the street if I see you—I don't wish to cause you any further anguish.
>
> Permit me to say just one last thing. Unworthy of you was the cruelty and the disregard that you had for my feelings. If my proposal of marriage was offensive, I ask for your forgiveness. To love is not a crime, but to hurt those who do is indeed sinful. I wish you happiness.
>
> Respectfully,
> Lucas Pires

Lucas was very happy with the letter. He smiled albeit sadly and put the letter in an envelope. Angela took the letter home and discreetly slipped it under Dona Mafalda's door.

It didn't take long before Dona Mafalda marched down the garden path with the letter in hand. She looked at Emanuel and Angela and said irately, "Look at this, Angela! Look, a letter from Lucas, the mechanic. He didn't write this letter. He doesn't speak like this."

Angela took the letter and reread it. She gave it to Emanuel, who read it with interest.

"It doesn't sound like Lucas..." Emanuel started to say, but Angela gave him a murderous look and he fell quiet.

"Someone else wrote it for him!" Dona Mafalda exclaimed.

"Maybe there is more to Lucas and your unkindness doesn't allow you to see it," Angela said quietly.

"He's a mechanic!" Dona Mafalda said offended as if unkindness to mechanics was allowed.

Rosa showed up with wine and bread, placed them on the table, and said looking at Dona Mafalda, "Lucas cried when he read the note about the bicycle."

"What bicycle?" Emanuel and Angela asked in unison.

"Oh dear," Dona Mafalda said softly, "Oh, dear lord! I am a cruel cow."

The following morning, bright and cheerful, the new nurse knocked at Angela's door. The hospital had sent the youngest and most beautiful nurse they had. When Angela ushered her in, everyone was at the kitchen table having breakfast.

Angela was holding Dalia as if she was a baby. The duck had been brought home after disappearing for a while. The nurse looked at the duck first and then at Angela. There was a slight look of distaste on the nurse's face. She was invited to have breakfast and was introduced to everybody. Dona Mafalda thought that the nurse was too young and consequently too inexperienced and she would have to call and complain.

While Rosa was cleaning the lunch table and Dona Mafalda was explaining everything about Emanuel's care to the young nurse, Angela grabbed Dom Carlos by the arm and took him into the garden. Angela placed Dalia on the patio. The duck, with a bandaged wing, cooed and pecked at the ground. Dom Carlos and Angela sat on a bench in the shade of the peach tree, the breeze played with the leaves, shards of sunlight snuck into the shade to bathe their faces.

This is where my heart is, thought Dom Carlos, his arm extended on the back of the bench. The breeze blew a strand of Angela's hair onto his hand. It stayed there like a ribbon of silk, and Dom Carlos took it and wrapped it around his finger, lightly pulling at it.

Angela looked at him for a long while.

"Dom Carlos, we have to talk about Pedro."

"I know," he answered. "We have no proof that he took Dalia. Dona Amelia won't tell the police he did it, and even if he did? It's just a duck in the eyes of the law. He will say that the duck got into his property, and he thought the duck was his."

Dona Amelia knew her fowl—and Pedro. She sent a note to Angela to come and get Dalia before Pedro did anything to the duck. But it was not Angela who showed up at her door. It was Dom Carlos in his impeccable attire. And it was Dom Carlos who jumped into the chicken shit and picked up the duck while the rooster was flying at him with extended talons. Dona Amelia picked up a broom and knocked the rooster out. The bird fell on its side, motionless.

Dom Carlos came home with Dalia, cleaned her up, fixed her wing, and had her tethered by a string in the garden. And now he was sitting with Angela recapping the day's events.

Again, there was a long silence.

"Can you imagine me coming up the village, in my Italian shoes, covered with chicken shit and a duck under my arm?"

He laughed, but Angela was nervous. She was afraid of what Pedro Matias could do. He was getting bolder and nastier every day, forgetting that he was inviting Night Justice to reactivate and swoop down on him.

"I have a story for you about a man and a duck," Dom Carlos said, trying to take her mind off Pedro Matias. "A man went to a bar with a duck under his arm. The bartender said, 'Some pig you got there,' and the man said to the bartender, 'Are you blind? Can't you see it's a duck?' And the bartender said to the man, 'I was talking to the duck.'"

With their heads together and eyes teared with mirth, they laughed, not seeing Dona Mafalda planted in front of them emanating disapproval.

"I can't believe you two,' she said offended. "With all the things that had gone wrong lately, your levity is offensive!" She put a hand on her forehead as if to forestall imminent fainting.

Dom Carlos looked up at her and asked in surprise, "What in the world have we done?"

"You," she said pointing at both, "you are laughing as if the world is sane. The world is far from sane!" she shrieked.

"Sit here, Dona Mafalda," Angela said, making room for her on the bench.

Dona Mafalda sat down, all her anger expended with nothing to rekindle it. Usually, kindness had that effect on her. Angela patted her hand and left.

7

The Unkindness of Love

"What in the world do you have so much to laugh about?" Dona Mafalda asked after Angela was out of earshot.

Dom Carlos thought for a moment. "Angela is very much in tune with my humor and I appreciate it."

Dona Mafalda gave him a righteous look. "A woman who lost her husband shouldn't feel that cheerful! She should be overwhelmed by sadness and loss."

"There is room for all of those things—sadness and laughter. That's life. If you had seen Angela as sad as I have, you would have done anything in your power to make her laugh, I'm sure. There was a time that we all thought sadness was going to kill her."

Dona Mafalda harrumphed and crossed her arms over her round bosom. She remembered Angela losing her mind with grief, not being able to sleep, to have joy or peace.

Dom Carlos got closer to her and put his arm around her shoulders. She stiffened. "Let it be, Dona Mafalda," he said. "Let others find joy in the small things that come across their lives." And looking into her red, rigid face, he said, "You will find happiness one day soon."

Dona Mafalda's shoulders suddenly sagged. "I don't think so," she said softly.

"I know so," he said. "It is inevitable that a person like you will find happiness." Dom Carlos placed a kiss on her forehead. "You are a good woman, and sooner or later you will find your man."

Dona Mafalda tensed when Dom Carlos' lips touched her skin and then she relaxed. "I thought you didn't like me," she said.

"Whatever gave you that idea?" he asked surprised. "You and I have a secret, remember?"

"Oh," she sniffed daintily. That secret was also her daily tormentor. He was referring to the time she confessed her love for him and when he admitted that he was in love with someone else. "It feels that it happened ages ago," she said blushing.

"I remember," he said sheepishly. "And I'm quite flattered to have the attention of a woman like you—intelligent and damn pretty."

She smiled demurely, "Oh, Dom Carlos! You're just saying that."

"I never lie. You should know that by now."

Dolores, the nurse, was a pretty little thing—straight blond hair pulled back with a ribbon and falling softly on her shoulders, little white teeth in a small dainty mouth, big transparent blue eyes, and the frame of a waif. No wonder Dona Mafalda was upset.

Early in the day, Dolores had told Angela that Emanuel needed longer and more challenging walks. She thought that Dona Mafalda was shielding him too much, not allowing him to do anything, not even breathe deeply, and at that pace, he could get pneumonia.

"I'll take him for a walk," Angela offered and, with the assistance of the nurse, he was out of bed and getting ready for the walk.

"Where are we going?" Emanuel asked as soon as the gate closed behind them.

"To the windmill," Angela answered.

They walked slowly up the road like lovers on a stroll. She had her arm around his waist and could feel his struggle with each step. When they got to the windmill, he was covered with sweat. Angela opened the door and a cool breeze welcomed them. Doves cooed softly on the small stone cutout windows. The doves came in to check who inhabited their place and flew out again to perch themselves on the windows. Emanuel and Angela sat on the edge of a grinding stone, leaning against bales of hay stacked up against the wall. They sat there quietly with their heads against the hay, eyes closed as if asleep.

"How is your investigation going?" Angela broke the silence.

"Slowly, but surely," he said. "Getting information from people is like pulling teeth."

"Yeah, it hurts," she quipped. "It would help if every time you want to know something about someone, you share a story about yourself. Curiosity will loosen people's tongues." Angela proposed.

"My life is very boring," he said.

"I doubt it."

"What do you want to know?"

"I want to know about your first true love."

He thought for a while as if choosing from a long list of love stories. Then he repeated from memory:

Every time I love is true love,
It lasts for a year, it lives for a second
For a century or just a few days
But every time I love, is true love, always.

He gave Angela a self-deprecating smile. "Her name was Irene," he answered.

"Where is she now?" she asked.

"I don't know. I went into the military, lost myself in the city, and lost sight of her. Dolores, the nurse, looks like her."

"No wonder Dona Mafalda is jealous."

"Is she?" he asked incredulously.

"She is devastated," Angela said. "She can be a witch, but she cares…"

Emanuel softly recited:

She was such a witch,
You couldn't tell them apart
Between her and a snake,
But in matters of love,
Even witches have hearts
That break

Angela laughed, "A police detective who quotes poetry… that's quite a diverting strategy."

After a long silence, Emanuel asked, "Shouldn't you tell me why you brought me here?"

"I have nothing special to tell you. Dolores told me that you need exercise. Dona Mafalda spoils you like a little boy."

"She said that?" he asked, almost offended.

She laughed and they were quiet again. Emanuel broke the silence. "You seem to have a very special relationship with Dom Carlos."

"I love him," she stated simply.

Emanuel held his breath for a second. "You love him?" He was totally surprised.

"I do," she said.

"How?" he insisted

"How do you love people? You simply do. I love Dom Carlos with all my heart," she said.

"Does he know?" he asked.

"Of course, he does. I'm very open with my love."

Emanuel was confused with such candor.

"Are you… sleeping with him?" he asked evenly. He was thinking about Regina's verdict.

Angela felt her heart jump and blushed under his close scrutiny. Dom Carlos' rationale came to mind—about sleeping together. She said, "No, we aren't lovers. People talk, I know, but we aren't lovers."

"I've heard you are," he said.

"Then you're going to make up your mind, aren't you, Detective Santos? You also heard that I'm a witch, I'm crazy, a healer…"

He held her gaze. "And you are none of those things?" he asked evenly, knowing that she was toying with him.

"Depends who is looking at me and the heart they hold in my regard," she answered with some amusement. "What is your heart telling you about me?"

"I've told you that my heart is a foolish thing. My head does better," he said.

"That's the problem with men. Heart and head, like enemies—one must surrender to the other—and you are never whole."

He was uncomfortable with her assessment. According to her thinking, men were one rung below in the evolutionary process. He decided to move away from being prickly and get back to his investigation. He said, "I don't think you sleep with Dom Carlos. You couldn't pull off a love affair like that. You're not… duplicitous."

You have no idea how duplicitous I can be, she thought.

The doves cooed.

Dom Carlos was still sitting on the bench with Dona Mafalda when Regina Sales opened the gate and came in. "Well, well, Dom Carlos and Dona Mafalda. I feel overwhelmed in the presence of royalty," Regina said mockingly.

Dona Mafalda tensed. This woman was a prostitute. How do you behave in the presence of such a person?

Regina seemed to read Dona Mafalda's thoughts and smiled sweetly at the teacher. "I came to talk to you, Dom Carlos. There is something I need to tell you," Regina said, still looking at Dona Mafalda.

Before Dom Carlos could say anything, Dona Mafalda got up and walked briskly into the house. Regina laughed.

Dom Carlos turned to Regina, as she sat next to him. He caught the sweet, nutty fragrance of almond oil and felt slightly nauseated.

"I suppose you don't want to have dinner with me tonight?" she asked.

Dom Carlos looked at her for a second. This woman was once a girl, pretty and innocent. What had happened to her to be who she was now? When was the moment she saw herself broken or damaged?

"Steak?" he asked.

She laughed. "Keep an eye on Angela," she said quietly.

Dom Carlos tensed. "Why?"

"You should know why," she said. "And I'm not talking about the police detective falling for her right under your nose. I'm talking about Pedro Matias. He is planning to bring her hell, and part of that hell is to hurt you too. He told me about the abduction of the duck and about letting the bull catch Emanuel, even before it happened. But he also told me about a fantasy he has to hurt you, and I don't want it to happen. As for Angela... well... he never really desisted from his original plan... to physically hurt her—if he can find a way of not being blamed for it. Knowing Pedro, it's just a matter of time."

"Thank you, Regina. I will keep an eye out for all of us, including you."

She got up from the bench and said, "You know, most people don't like the police detective, but I do. He is a good man and what happened to him shouldn't have."

Before she closed the gate, she turned around and said, "Be careful. A storm is coming."

Dona Mafalda was elated with Dom Carlos' invitation to spend the rest of the day riding around the island. She put on a headscarf, sunglasses and a flower dress that complimented her skin. How lovely this afternoon would be.

On their way out, they went by Lucas' garage to fuel up the car.

"You said you were going to apologize to Lucas," Dom Carlos said. "Here's your chance."

"On my own time!" Dona Mafalda said, exasperated.

At the garage, Dom Carlos exited the car and disappeared, leaving Dona

Mafalda alone with Lucas—leaving her no way out other than to apologize for her disregard for his feelings.

Lucas and Dona Mafalda walked away from the car to the back of the garage, where there were a bench and potted geraniums under a shade.

Dona Mafalda cleared her throat a few times and apologized for the letter and for the unkindness of unrequited love. But Lucas was not listening to excuses why she couldn't love him. He could hear only possibilities.

She looked at him in complete silence, scrutinizing his face. Was that grease on his face? No, his skin was tanned and shaved. He had a broad mouth with well-shaped lips. His eyes were dark and kind. Why did she find him disagreeable? She forgot. Was it just because he was a mechanic? Yes, he was a mechanic. She was above his station. How dare he think that he could propose to her!

Dona Mafalda was lost in thought that Lucas read as doubt. He leaned in and touched her mouth with his. He pressed in and Dona Mafalda felt her lips part when Lucas' cool and soft tongue briefly brushed her lips and entered her mouth, searching for a response.

And then it was over. Dona Mafalda thought that she had melted all over the bench, and Lucas thought that maybe, just maybe, he had a chance.

Dona Mafalda abruptly pulled away. Offended and confused, she retreated to the car, running with small steps almost sideways with dizziness. She got in the car with Dom Carlos and they drove off in silence.

When Dom Carlos wanted to know why Dona Mafalda was so flushed, she was convinced that he had seen the whole wretched scene and was mocking her.

"You set me up," she said, after a while.

"I did not," he said. "I merely provided a chance for you to talk to him. You said you wanted to. What happened?"

Dona Mafalda stared at him to assess his sincerity. "He kissed me!" she said primly.

"What?" and he started to stifle a chuckle. But it was too late. His dimples showed.

"See? Everything is a joke to you!" Dona Mafalda accused.

"I'm sorry, but I didn't expect that he would have the courage." He stared at her mouth as if looking for the vestiges of a kiss. "How was it?"

"If you want to know, you kiss him yourself!" she said furiously.

Dom Carlos lapsed into full-out laughter. Dona Mafalda didn't resist and fell under the spell of his merriment.

The car was now flying like a demon, the wind and the sun were on their faces, and they were laughing about a kiss.

This was indeed a most wonderful day.

When Angela got home with Viriato, it was late. She tried to be as quiet as possible, but Hercules provoked Viriato and he barked.

"Angela!" Emanuel called out.

She made a grimace and peered into his room. The nurse wasn't there on her cot, where she should have been.

"I sent her home," he said guessing her question, "I don't need her to stay all night."

The nurse was always grateful when she didn't have to stay in Angela's house, and knowing that Emanuel had been quick to oblige.

The nurse thought that her fellow islanders were uncouth, cagy, and unprincipled. They often got caught up in ungoverned passions, creating disorder and strife and never recognizing the cause. If only her people could be like the Americans from the base—clean, polished, and civilized. Angela fit neatly into Dolores' profile—a brute that lived with animals as if they were people

When Angela turned around to leave, Emanuel caught her by the hand and she winced in pain. Emanuel held on to her.

"What happened to you?" he asked.

"Nothing, we were cooking and I burned myself."

"Were you cooking with moonshine... linguiça?" he asked.

"Emanuel," she said, "I'm tired and I want to go to bed. Of course, we cook with moonshine and linguiça! What a question!"

"You don't even cook with linguiça," he said impatiently. Then he added after a brief pause, "I have Lazarus' wristwatch for you."

Angela stopped in midstep. "You've done the test? When?"

"I gave it to Dom Carlos and he took it to the city to the station's lab. He returned it last night."

"Why didn't you tell me today at the windmill?" She felt that this was a pivotal moment. Whatever he said, it would surely change her life.

"I wanted to have a quiet time with you, so we could talk about it and process it in peace. I thought we would be interrupted at the windmill."

Angela was looking at him with wide eyes.

"Let's go to the terrace," he said getting up slowly.

When they went by the kitchen, Angela grabbed a jug of water and two glasses. *This is going to be a long night,* she thought.

They sat at the end of the terrace, close to the kitchen and away from the windows on the second floor.

"I'm tired, Emanuel. I want to go to bed and rest," she said in an edgy tone.

"The water in the wristwatch wasn't saltwater. Actually, there were traces of soap in it," he finally said.

"I'm going to kill that bastard!" she said as if talking to herself.

He said firmly, "I'll deal with Pedro Matias."

"You? You can't even deal with Hercules," she said.

"Angela," he said, reaching out and holding her hand. "Look at me. You have to promise that you will let me deal with this as I see fit. That man is dangerous because he is a coward." There was urgency in his voice.

"Tomorrow, will I remember the things I promise you now?" She brought her face closer to his. "Is that love that I see in your eyes?" she asked. "You said that it was self-evident. I can't tell."

"You're drunk," he said evenly.

"That's not what I asked. You are hard to read, so this self-evident crap doesn't work with you." She continued to observe him closely.

"Where were you?" he asked softly.

"I was with the Sacristy."

"Are you lying?" he asked.

"I never lie. Ask me anything."

"You're so drunk," he murmured, impatient and ill-humored.

"That's not a question—it's an unkind statement. Are you being unkind?" She sat back waiting for his response.

Emanuel was looking intensely at her.

"Okay," she said. "I'm going to bed. I'll kill Pedro tomorrow. With some luck, maybe he is dead already."

"What do you mean?" he asked.

"Nothing, Detective Santos. Go to sleep. Tomorrow things will look different."

"I'm sorry that everything is coming up like debris washed up by a storm. I'm sorry that I'm dredging up painful memories," Emanuel said.

"Are you asking for my forgiveness?" she asked.

Then she got up and left him alone on the terrace.

Emanuel looked up at the sky and sighed heavily. Then he started walking slowly to his room, thinking vaguely that Hercules was nearby to ambush him. He held an empty glass in his hand like a weapon. "Damn cat!" he muttered.

Angela climbed the stairs, her eyes full of tears. She wanted to scream until she couldn't scream anymore. She wanted to scream at God to make up His mind. Was Lazarus dead or not? "Take Lazarus from me for good or give him back! But don't make me doubt or hope…"

She opened the door—not to her room, but Dom Carlos'.

He was asleep, sprawled across the bed as if he had fallen from a high place. His hair was disheveled, with curls falling on his forehead. The open window let in the soothing night air, along with the moonlight. The moon was so high up, distant and small, accentuating the sky full of stars. Mozart was playing on the radio.

He looks like a fallen angel, she thought, *so beautiful, just like Lazarus.*

He snored softly. She took off her shoes and crawled into bed with him. She laid her head on his chest.

It will be just for a second, she thought.

He stirred a bit, instinctively embracing her. Then he woke up. "Angela?" he asked confused. He reached for the blanket.

She threw her head back and laughed, "You look like a Victorian maiden."

"Angela? What are you doing?"

"Who did you think it was? Dona Glorrria?" she said.

He was silent for a second. "Hawk, are you drunk?" he asked, getting up to light a lamp.

She was already lying face down on the bed. She tried to sit up and speak, measuring the words, trying not to slur them, "I don't know why I came to your room," she hiccupped.

"Boy, are you drunk," he said. "Come on. I'll help you to your room before you wake up the rest of the house."

"Can I stay with you just for a little while?" she asked.

Dom Carlos sat on the bed, his back against the headboard. "Okay, come here before you fall. But don't throw up!"

She swayed in her effort to kneel in front of him. Dom Carlos set his hands on her shoulders to steady her.

"Why didn't you tell me that you had Lazarus' wristwatch?" she asked.

"I wanted to spare you the anxiety of waiting for an answer," he said.

"Lazarus," she said softly.

"I'm not Lazarus."

She looked up, "I know, I was just thinking about him..." She started to weep. "Do you know that his wristwatch has soapy water in it?"

"Yes, I know," he answered, his heartbreaking.

"Sometimes I'm afraid," she said. "I'm afraid of losing people who I love and they are gone before I had a chance to tell them. Just like Lazarus. I don't think I told him enough times how much I loved him. Remember when I almost lost you on the cliffs? I had never told you that I loved you. If you had died, you wouldn't have known that I loved you. Zorro... It seems like a long, long time ago."

"Yes," he said gently. He thought about when he first arrived on the island.

She waited as if she had asked him an important question. He caressed her face. She asked again, "Have I told you that I love you? If you died today would you know that I love you?"

"Yes, I would," he answered in a soothing tone. "And I'm not going to die, today or in the near future."

"When Emanuel got hurt at the bull-fight, I was so sorry I hadn't told him that I cared for him. I was even sorry that I hadn't kissed him. I'm such a fraud. Why can't we show people what our hearts hold?"

He was curious.

She rested her head on his chest. "In the hospital, when I kissed him, I wanted him to know that I cared. He believes that love is self-evident. Doesn't it sound like bullshit? If you love someone, why don't you tell them? Why do we have to guess or try to decipher? Why are we so unkind, even in love?" She pulled back to look at his face, then asked, "Are you making fun of me?"

He put his head back, hiding a smile. Angela looked at his neck. She always thought he had a beautiful neck. Once she had kissed his neck when he got hurt playing Zorro. And she had kissed his mouth when he was sleeping full of painkillers.

"I kissed you once," she said softly.

Dom Carlos said, "Many times."

"I kissed your mouth once when you were asleep..."

"You little liar," he said trying to remember.

"You got hurt and were on drugs for the pain, remember? Remember when you were playing Zorro? I did kiss you. It was such a sweet feeling."

"And what did I do?"

"You moaned," she said.

"That's it, I moaned?" he asked surprised. Dom Carlos looked at her for a long moment.

"I love you," she said. "Just in case I die today, I want you to know."

"I know," he answered. "I love you too. You're not going to die today. You may die tomorrow with a hangover."

She said, like a confession, "I have a secret. I love more than one man."

She took his face in her hands and kissed him full in the mouth. First, it was a small, sweet kiss. Dom Carlos didn't respond. He closed his eyes. She kissed him again. And the sanity he was hoping to maintain was lost as he responded to her kisses. They kissed without saying a word.

"I love you," he murmured.

"Do you?" she asked full of hope. "Why didn't you tell me then? We must let people know that we love them before life comes around with its dirty tricks."

"I love you, Hawk, I've loved you for a very long time."

"You could become an addiction—like wine... *In vino veritas...*" she said half asleep.

Angela woke up as she always did, at five in the morning, with Hercules' fur tickling her face. She had a headache and an upset stomach. She had had a night full of silly dreams. She remembered having a midnight conversation with Emanuel. She knew for sure that he had talked to her about Lazarus' wristwatch, and maybe she had seen Dom Carlos. No, she had dreamt of him and Dona Gloria making love, while she watched with such a terrible ache in her heart.

Rosa was unaccountably late. Angela managed to quickly pull together breakfast, the smell of coffee, fresh bread and cheese inviting all to assemble around the kitchen table. The menagerie ate noisily, while the pretty nurse tried to hide her revulsion for sitting at a table with a noisome pig underfoot. Her American boyfriend would never allow such incivility.

Dom Carlos came around the table and sat next to Dona Mafalda. "I had a wonderful time yesterday," he said.

"I too had a wonderful time. Thank you, Dom Carlos. You're not half the nuisance you try to be," Dona Mafalda said in jest.

"I'm glad someone had fun yesterday," Angela said ill-humoredly.

Rosa came running in. Not only was she late, but she had big news. "Big,

big news," she said, outstretching her arms to emphasize the enormity of what she was about to say.

Everyone stopped eating and stared at her.

"Pedro Matias was caught by the Night Justice," she said breathlessly.

Emanuel was the first to react. "What happened?" he asked.

"They found him this morning tied to a harrow, spread eagle, naked, with lard all over his... his...you know..." and her hands went round and round her belly.

"Genitalia?" asked the nurse, grimacing.

"No," Rosa said frustrated, "all over his balls and dove."

Dona Mafalda gasped.

"There was lard everywhere! He had more grease on him than a frying pan," Rosa continued. "And the monsignor is coming to see you," she said pointing at Emanuel.

"Oh great!" he muttered.

And in a few minutes, the monsignor came charging through the door with his cassock flying about him, like a bird of prey claiming a victim for breakfast. Hercules ran out with a terrified meow. The monsignor was the only person who Hercules was afraid of. Viriato hid under the table with Nixon and Dalia.

"That cat has dealings with the devil," the monsignor said, pointing at the fleeing animal.

Everyone else wanted to flee too, but only Hercules was that shameless. The monsignor looked around as if assessing all whether they needed to exist. "You and you," he said pointing to Emanuel and the nurse. "I need both of you now."

And they left.

Dom Carlos looked at Angela. "What in the world has happened?" he asked.

She gave way to a weak smile, "Pedro, anything to do with Pedro is mayhem."

He slid around the table, put an arm around her shoulders, and kissed her brow. For a split second, she remembered something, and then it was gone. "I think I had a déjà vu," she said looking up at him. He smiled.

"Did I see you last night?" she asked, suddenly worried.

He hesitated, and answered evasively, "You don't remember what you did last night?"

"After I talked with Emanuel, I remember very little..." She stared at him.

With a tired sigh, she rested her face on his chest and listened to his heart quicken as she put her arms around his waist. "You are like an empty church," she murmured. "You are peaceful, quiet, soothing..." she said with her eyes closed, inhaling his smell of soap and a freshly ironed shirt. Then she dropped her arms and walked away.

Rosa came running into the kitchen to inform Dom Carlos that Emanuel, still mending from his fractured ribs, couldn't make the trip on foot. They needed Dom Carlos to drive him up to the barn.

8

A Storm is Coming

"Where are we going?" Dom Carlos asked the monsignor.

"To the seaplane, near the cliffs," the monsignor answered. He started to recount what had happened. "Pedro Matias stayed out all night. He does that often, but he always comes home in the morning for breakfast to start the day with his boys. When he didn't show up, his wife sent one of the boys to look for him. That's when they found him in his barn near the cliffs, tied to a harrow, naked, covered with lard. Hot lard had been poured over parts of his body, including his head. The man looks like a boiled potato!"

Dom Carlos drove along an age-old bull cart path up to the barn. The detective was growing paler with each bump. At the barn, a cluster of murmuring villagers failed to heed the monsignor's orders to go home. Pedro Matias was still tied to the harrow, barely conscious. No one had touched him—they had been waiting for the monsignor or the police.

Dolores knelt beside the man and examined the ties on his wrists and ankles—sword-grass. *Primitive beasts*, she thought. Then she requested a sheet to cover the man, opened her medicine bag, and extracted a pair of scissors. Gingerly she cut the tie over his mouth, careful not to pull it, fearful that his skin would come with it.

Pedro whimpered. "The Barcoses, little fuckers…"

His feet and hands were swollen from being tied. His genitalia glued to the side of his leg, looked like dead stems.

"This man needs to go to the hospital," the nurse said. "He needs immediate attention."

The nurse and the monsignor exchanged glances. They were afraid that an infection would set in, and he was feverish and suffering from dehydration. The nurse gave him pain medication and started the process of ungluing Pedro from the harrow, where the lard had solidified. The lard had been poured on hot. The top of his head was pink, bald, and with blisters. There was no screaming, no sounds other than weak moans. He was taken home on a makeshift gurney, and shortly an ambulance took him to the hospital.

Emanuel and Dom Carlos exchanged looks. This was the man who had made Angela's life hell for years. Not only her life, but the lives of all who came in touch with him—like a contagion.

Emanuel and Dom Carlos got in the car silently, full of questions and speculations.

Emanuel talked first. "He was accusing the Barcos family."

"I guess you have some sleuthing to do," Dom Carlos said.

They were quiet for a while.

Emanuel started again. "It should be easy to verify, but I don't think so. This looks like the work of the infamous Night Justice. Fernando Cardoso, according to my notes, was the last victim before Pedro. He tried to rape Luciana, a girl who was much maligned by a detective like me. Fernando also raped a girl from another village, a beggar, a prostitute, that came around with her aunt or mother and they begged for food and other things, sold sexual favors…Who would bring the rapist of a beggar girl to justice?"

"Very interesting question," Dom Carlos said. "No one cares about a beggar girl."

"I hope someone did," he muttered. "As for Pedro… a lot of people wanted to skin him alive," Emanuel said. "Especially Angela," he added.

Dom Carlos stopped the car in the middle of the road and looked at him. "And you!" Dom Carlos snapped. "Everybody knows that he set it up for the bull to catch you. If you look hard enough, almost everyone had a reason to fry the man, including you."

"I can't even slap Hercules, never mind tackle a man," Emanuel demurred.

They were silent for a while.

"I saw Angela last night," Emanuel said, never taking his eyes from Dom Carlos.

Dom Carlos started the car again. He asked, "You told her about the wristwatch, didn't you?"

"Oh yes, and that Pedro had been lying," Emanuel said.

"And how did she take it?"

"She said she was going to kill Pedro, or that he was already dead."

"She can't kill a fly, never mind a man," Dom Carlos muttered.

"Maybe it wasn't Angela I talked to last night then!" Emanuel said with annoyance. "Did you talk to her last night?"

Dom Carlos hesitated. Then he abruptly stopped the car again and told Emanuel to get out.

Emanuel was surprised. "Why?"

"Are you really interrogating me in my own fucking car?" Dom Carlos said angrily.

"I'm not getting out. I can't do all this walking alone." He looked at Dom Carlos with interest. "I'm going to tell you what I know: Angela came home last night smelling like a brewery, and smelling like... linguiça, the same smell that we found at the barn and on Pedro Matias. She had a blistering burn on her hand."

"Half of the village smells of moonshine and linguiça, and you don't have to be a detective to know that and women get blisters all the time," Dom Carlos said with annoyance.

"Angela doesn't cook with meat. Last night Angela smelled exactly like Pedro Matias did this morning," Emanuel insisted, "a mixture of moonshine, linguiça, lard and... hay?"

Dom Carlos warned, "Don't go accusing people."

Emanuel knew that he had hit a nerve. He smiled. "I'm right then, you're thinking the same thing."

Dom Carlos said, "Out! Out of my car!"

"I can't walk all this distance alone," Emanuel complained.

"Too bad!" Dom Carlos said, "Out!" And he reached across Emanuel and opened the door for him.

Emanuel stepped out with a moan of pain. He looked down the long and narrow dirt road ahead of him and sighed, as Dom Carlos' car disappeared, leaving him in a cloud of dust.

Emanuel was making slow progress up the road. He was sweating, out of breath and cursing Dom Carlos, when he heard a faraway voice call out his name. Then he saw a figure run down the path, waving her hands—Dona Mafalda.

That beautiful pain in the ass Dona Mafalda was coming to his rescue. *I think I love her,* he considered.

She reached him, out of breath and vociferating against Dom Carlos. She encircled Emanuel's waist, and became his human crutch again—by now she was quite the expert.

"God bless you, Dona Mafalda," Emanuel said to a smiling face. "I'm so grateful."

They arrived home, dusty and sweaty.

Dom Carlos was waiting for them in the garden. He said to Emanuel, "I need to talk to you." Both men sat distanced on a back garden bench, intently sizing up each other as if preparing for a duel.

"You're an overzealous police detective trying to build your career, and in the process, you'll sacrifice people. It won't be Angela." Dom Carlos said in a measured tone. "Stop that nonsense to connect her with the Night Justice. Pedro Matias has more enemies than water in the sea. Anyone of them could have done it. Why do you want to implicate her?"

There was a long silence. They both looked out into the garden as if the other wasn't there.

"I love her too," Emanuel said finally.

Dom Carlos felt his heart thump so loudly that he thought Emanuel had heard it too.

"I'm telling you this, to put your fears to rest about me hurting Angela." Emanuel got up and disappeared into the house, leaving Dom Carlos speechless as if he had been struck by a hypnotic incantation.

After a few moments, Dom Carlos got up and left, slamming the garden gate. He was going to find Angela. When he got to Ascendida's house, he didn't knock. There they were, the four, huddled together, embroidering a tablecloth. They stood straight up, their eyes fixed on him—whether out of fear or curiosity—as if he had two heads.

"I'm sorry to barge in like this, but I need to talk to Angela," he said.

The women exchanged meaningful looks before Angela trailed Dom Carlos up the pastures.

"It's going to rain today," Ascendida said. "We all need a good cleansing."

The menagerie followed Dom Carlos and Angela at safe distance. Viriato didn't like that kind of behavior. He had never seen Dom Carlos like that—disheveled and in a hurry like the world was going to end. This type of strife was more to Hercules' liking. He reveled in distress and now was laughing at the scene. Nixon was not passing judgment. He was going to wait and see the outcome of this little drama. And Dalia didn't care—she pecked the ground, disinterested.

"Keep walking," Dom Carlos said.

And they walked all the way to Ascendida's orchard, the small divisions of land, with quiet shade. The stone walls divided the small plots evenly as if a mathematician had taken the trouble.

When they sat under an orange tree, they were both sweating and out of breath. He threw a pebble at Hercules, took a few deep breaths and said, "Last night you came home smelling exactly like Pedro Matias' barn, and you were drunk. What in the world did you do?"

She said evenly. "And how do you know all of that?

"Because I saw you! You came into my room."

She stared at him and let loose her frustration. "So, it wasn't a dream! I thought maybe I went into your room, but I was unsure this morning and hoping it was all a dream."

"What do you remember from last night?" he asked.

"Well… I remember you taking me to my room…" She frowned and closed her eyes as if trying to remember. Then she looked at him with a certain alarm, "Did I do something stupid?"

"Your reputation is safe," he said.

"I'm serious!" she snapped.

He took her bandaged hand in his and said, "Me too. Dead serious. This is why I need to talk to you, about Pedro. He could've died. Those burns still could kill him."

"I hope he dies… He… was going to hurt you," she said.

"Did Regina tell you that?" he asked quietly.

She felt oddly exposed by his gaze. "I just had this terrible feeling that he was about to hurt you. He was hurting those I love. He hurt Dalia and Emanuel… and Regina revealed something to my mother…"

They were both quiet for a long while.

Then he asked, "You did it, didn't you?"

She was silent. He felt powerless, something that he didn't feel often. Then he tightened his arms around her as if he could protect her from the danger she was in.

"Damn it!" he said exasperated.

"He had it coming," she murmured.

"Hawk, you could've killed a man," Dom Carlos said, holding her head to his chest.

"He killed Lazarus!"

"You don't know that!"

"Yes, I do. Whatever happened to Lazarus, he is to blame!" she said agitatedly.

He released a slow breath and she pulled away from his embrace. She sat crossed-legged facing him and told him what he already knew and didn't want to hear.

"We knew that Pedro Matias was working on the seaplane, Dona Amelia told me. His sons came home earlier because she needed help with wood for the oven, but Pedro stayed finishing the chores. His dog, Ferocious, never leaves him alone. The dog noticed my presence and came up the road to meet me. I fed him—he's always hungry. I tied him to a post up the road. Then we waited for Pedro to step out of the barn. It was getting dark. As soon as he came out, I hit him on the back of the head with a tree branch. He went out like a light. We dragged him into the barn and you know the rest. We only did to him what he has been doing to other people."

He had noted the small alcohol cooker set on top of a boulder next to the barn where Pedro barbecued linguiça with moonshine for weekly gatherings with his friends. Pedro had provided everything the Night Justice needed to take care of Pedro. "When he came to, he was blindfolded and gagged," she continued. "We spilled moonshine on ourselves to cover any smells and drank a bit to give us strength, just in case," she continued. "He struggled like a pig ready for slaughter. I thought about Lazarus' back crisscrossed with scars from his beatings, and I thought of poor Dalia in his hands fighting to get off as he twisted her wing and broke it. At that moment, I saw Dona Amelia, always black and blue, Emanuel frightened running away from an enraged bull, and Pedro Matias responsible for all this malice. And I poured the hot lard." She lowered her head. "It was awful," she said. "It was awful because I didn't even blink. It came so easy to me."

Dom Carlos muttered to himself and wiped his face.

"Are you crying?" she asked surprised.

"I'm not crying! I'm sweating bullets!" he said, irritated. "You scare me half to death! Imagine all the things that could have gone wrong. You're incorrigible!" he said, full of frustration. "And you get on my case about Zorro?"

The orchard's hush would have been so peaceful had Dom Carlos contained his expletives. He rested his head against the tree and closed his eyes to hide the turmoil he was feeling. After a long silence, Dom Carlos asked, "Is the Sacristy responsible for the other Night Justice incidents?"

She answered sourly, "You mean the ones that have been happening since the beginning of time? The events from decades and decades ago? Those events?"

"Don't you be evasive with me! I am dead serious!" he snapped.

"So am I! Until now the police didn't give a shit about Night Justice, but if they think women have had a hand in it, you bet they will care! Leave us alone, because we are alone. We only have ourselves."

Dom Carlos was bewildered, sputtering as if he was choking on words. "I am terrified if anything happens to you," he finally said. "I promised Lazarus that I would protect you."

"Nothing will happen to me," she said irritably and stood up. Dom Carlos rose after her. She turned around and looked at that perfectly groomed man coming undone, and her heart melted.

She rose on her tiptoes and kissed him. She was aiming at his cheek but somehow it was his mouth that found hers. His lips tasted like tears and everything suddenly seemed gentler. Angela closed her eyes, moaning softly with the surprise response to her gesture. She vaguely thought about addiction as his kisses deepened. And she kissed him back, just as eager, having flashbacks, or remembering dreams.

Without a word, they pulled apart. He touched her full lips and started walking down to the house ahead of her. She was bewildered with that unexpected loving overstep and she hoped that the walk home would give her time to compose herself.

They reached the gate and walked placidly into the garden. The menagerie was waiting for her under the peach tree. Hercules stretched his arms to Angela. She picked up the cat and hid her face in his furry chest.

Emanuel and the nurse were observing the scene. Dolores had a twist of distaste on her little perky mouth. *Brutes*, she thought. She wasn't afraid of the cat. She had a protective bottle of water always in hand. The first time the cat stalked her she sprayed his face, and the cat howled in disbelief, running away and taking refuge under a bush. The cat never came near her again, unless he was with Angela, like now, looking her straight in the eyes, *bitch,* he was saying, *you and your little water bottle…*

Angela sat next to Emanuel on the garden bench. He smiled in that mysterious, hooded way that no one could read.

"Nascimento came by and asked me to give you a message," he said, still looking at her as if he wanted to discover her innermost self.

She looked surprised. "We just had lunch."

"The Sacristy will go to confession this afternoon, for you to meet them in church."

"Oh!" she said as if she expected something else.

"What collective sins do you have to confess?"

"Every Friday afternoon we go to confession. We tell the monsignor our sins." She gave him an impudent smile and continued, "It makes him feel in control to sort out the saints from the sinners."

"You told me once that at the end of the day we are all saints and sinners," he rejoined.

Angela could feel Emanuel's eyes on her—those probing, dark, mysterious eyes.

"Did you do that to Pedro Matias?" he asked.

"Would you believe me if I said I didn't?" she held his gaze.

He smiled. "Why don't you try me?"

"Whatever I say, almost everyone in the village can say the same."

"What would that be?" he asked quietly.

"That most of us can't stand the man. That he's done quite a few horrific deeds and has never been punished. Actually, people are surprised that the Night Justice took so long to get him," she said, trying to sound calm.

"I wonder why, why now, and who did it. I think I'll have to arrest the entire village if I want to know. I understand there is a long history of vigilante justice here. I need to talk with my boss about having to arrest the whole village... again. I don't think he'll like that."

He knows, she thought, closing her eyes.

"You do what you need to do, Detective Santos," she said and leaned her head back against the wall.

Emanuel looked at her profile—the long column of her throat, a slightly crooked nose, and parted lips as if she was praying.

"If I arrest you, would the whole village come to your rescue, as they have done in the past with other people?"

"I don't know, Detective Santos. Why don't you try it?"

And then they felt the rain. It came down first as a warning with thick and sparse drops and then strong and steady.

"Emanuel, the rain!" she said, jumping up and forgetting about threats. She was laughing—her arms opened wide, her face turned up to the sky. "Get up," she said. "Get up and take off your shirt."

"What?"

"Take off your shirt," she repeated. And then she proceeded to unbutton his shirt. "The healing rains, these are healing rains!" she said.

The rain, cool and abundant, fell on the thirsty island. Sounds of joy could be heard all around. People shouted, cows mooed, dogs barked, children were screaming with delight, and women ran in and out of their houses to set out jugs, pots, and pans to catch the rain. Rosa, Dona Mafalda, and Dom Carlos went out to the street to rejoice with the neighbors. The streets were thronged with laughing people, making singing circles, holding hands, like children playing in a schoolyard:

> *Rain, rain, perfect rain,*
> *Keep me wet and keep me sane*
> *Go down my roof,*
> *My water spout*
> *Drench my lover*
> *And kill my drought!*

Angela pulled Emanuel's shirt from the waist of his pants and looked at the mess on his back. His back was still badly bruised, with weeping abrasions, skin gaps, dark angry scabs, portending the development of lumpy scar tissue. She carefully removed the dressings, exposing his injuries to the healing rain.

Angela caressed his back, and her heart was full of sorrow—another beautiful person who would carry the scars of malice for the rest of their life. She encircled his waist and rested her face on his back, wet and battered, and then she kissed it softly, small kisses all over his injuries.

He tasted of iodine, salt, and rain.

Emanuel held his breath when her arms went around him, and he held them tightly against his waist. While the whole village rejoiced on the streets, he was in the garden being drenched with rain and kisses. He turned around in Angela's embrace and lowered his face to hers, kissing her full on the mouth. At first, she didn't respond but stayed there with her face turned up to the rain and to him, receiving both graces. Then she kissed him back. She answered his small and gentle caresses and then his deep and long kisses.

He thought about gratitude and love, and she thought about falling.

When he let her go, she laughed, her face streaming rain, her hair plastered on her neck and face. He kissed her again.

"Angela," he whispered. "Please promise me that you will stop it."

Then they heard Dona Mafalda's voice calling out, as if worried, "Detective! Detective Santos! Where are you?"

Angela pulled away. "I promise," she said, disappearing in the rain.

Dona Mafalda came running out into the garden, full of panic. Then she saw the detective without a shirt and the dressings drenched at his feet. He looked like he'd been ravished.

"My God, Detective Santos, what happened to you?" she asked pulling him by the hand inside of the house. "You don't believe all that nonsense that the first rain of the drought heals. Do you?" she accused.

"You bet they heal!" he said with a smile.

"Please, Detective Santos, don't turn into a peasant like them!" she snapped. "The only thing you may get is pneumonia," she said, gingerly padding him dry with a towel.

Emanuel held Dona Mafalda by the shoulders and said tenderly, "Thank you, my friend. Thank you for caring about me."

In the streets, the neighbors were still dancing and singing. Dom Carlos was caught in the singing circle, going around and around in the rain, thinking vaguely that the clothes he had on would be ruined. He looked at his Italian shoes soaked and dark with mud.

Regina broke the circle to hold Dom Carlos' hand. He felt a pang of tenderness for this woman, much abused and reviled. In the middle of the street, in front of all the neighbors, under the August rain, he kissed Regina Sales on the mouth—a long kiss that momentarily stopped the singing circle. The prince of every fairytale, the man of every woman's dream, kissed the village Jezebel on the mouth with all the tenderness he had in his heart.

In the church, the three women were looking at the door, waiting for Angela. She came in drenched and hurried. There was a line of sinners waiting to go to confession. One by one, the Sacristy knelt before the monsignor and one by one was sent to wait in the sacristy.

"Boy, I wonder what he is going to do to us," Nascimento said.

"If he hits me, I swear I'll hit him back," Ascendida said.

The monsignor had slapped her a few times over the years for being belligerent, for being aggressive, but Ascendida's patience with him was wearing thin. She felt burdened by his penances and demands.

"I think he is going to excommunicate us," Madalena said, thinking about Saul and how he had once offered himself to the monsignor for punishment in her place.

Angela was thinking about the kisses she'd received that day. She was bewildered with the sweetness of those two men and felt divided in her desires. The other three women looked at her with suspicion.

"Why are you so quiet?" Nascimento asked.

"I'm thinking about punishment. I deserve to be punished," Angela said.

"Don't be stupid," Ascendida said irately. "You don't think you've been punished enough? What's the matter with you, woman?"

Angela knew only too well what was the matter with her. How could she be with two men? Or more to the point, how could she not? She wasn't even thinking about what she did to Pedro Matias. With a shaking hand, she touched her lips.

"Confessing is the right thing to do," Ascendida said. "Otherwise, the monsignor won't stop until he unveils the truth. Confessing shuts him up, and that's the only reason we are confessing, not because we are contrite or need punishment." Her words sounded like gunshots.

"And this time, it's going to be the worst!" Nascimento exclaimed. "He's going to..." She was thinking about some terrible things the monsignor could make her do. "He's going to make me clean the church bell with my tongue."

The others looked at Nascimento, exasperated by her infantile projections.

Madalena said hopefully, "I think he's going to do the same old thing. Serve the old and infirm for a few months."

"I prefer to clean the church bell with my tongue," Nascimento concluded.

They laughed nervously.

The monsignor came in like a hurricane. "I'm glad that you all are so amused!" he said, full of indignation.

They stood up in front of him like little children.

"I can't believe your gall! Didn't you promise that your Night Justice days were over?"

They were silent.

"Answer me, damn it!"

"No, Monsignor, we didn't promise that," Angela said in a weak voice.

The monsignor zeroed in on her and slapped her across the face, once, twice, three times—knocking her head from side to side, the last blow hitting her right below the eye.

Ascendida stepped in front of him and said in a low voice, "Enough!"

Angela's ears were ringing and she was thinking about this afternoon's events—so tenderly kissed and now so thoroughly slapped.

Ascendida said, "We promised not to do anything to Pedro Matias, true, but Pedro Matias was continuing to do fiendish things. We promised to refrain, but we didn't promise not to do it at all—especially where justice is nonexistent in this place as it is."

"How dare you question and dissect my penances!" he said, raising his hand to Ascendida.

"Don't you dare!" she said grabbing his skinny wrist. "You won't hit us again. You will give us the penance that you decide upon, but you will not hit us. We had all the hitting we can take in this lifetime!" And Ascendida, that loyal but angry woman, was still gripping the monsignor's wrist when she started to cry.

Madalena was shaking and praying to Saul as if he was a deity. She did that often and things always seemed to get better. Nascimento was waiting for her turn. *Get it over with*, Nascimento thought, *just don't leave a mark that I can't explain to Jaime.*

The monsignor suddenly sat down, deflated. He held his head in his hands and said in a defeated tone, "You're going to be the death of me!"

I can only hope, Nascimento thought brightly.

And they waited. They waited for a long time. He seemed to be praying. Then he raised his head and started dispensing penances.

"Ascendida, your penance is to care for Mrs. Lourenço for one whole year. You care for her as if she is your own mother. Nascimento, you will work for the children in the Children's Home every day for a whole year. And you, Madalena, you will care for your father while he is sick. You, Angela, you're going to send that little nurse home and take care of the police detective yourself. You are going to be at his beck and call and assist him in his inquiries regarding the missing men. If you mess up with your Night Justice antics, I won't cover for you. Pray to Jesus that your deceitfulness won't end up in tragedy, with the four of you in jail. Do you understand?"

The women crossed the village in complete silence, each one thinking about their sins and penances. Ascendida was the first to talk. "Let's have tea. I have the house all to myself—no children and no husband."

"Where are your instruments of torture?" Nascimento asked, referring to Ascendida's family.

"With my parents, those wonderful human beings," Ascendida answered.

They felt comforted by the old familiar smells and warmth of Ascendida's kitchen. She made a fire, put water on to boil, and turned on the radio. The women sat motionless, still buoyant from the welcome rain, allowing the heat to dry their wet clothes, still clinging to their bodies. The soothing music in the quiet evening was like a tonic for their nerves. They were thinking about their road to redemption and the farce they maintained. They were not even penitent. They were manipulating a tired old priest by using religious dogmas against him as if his magic had perversely turned on the master. Poor monsignor! Poor old devil.

"I think the detective is suspicious of us," Ascendida said.

"Police investigators always are," Madalena murmured.

"He has been asking questions. He talked to my husband and to yours," Ascendida said, nodding at Nascimento. "Today he asked them where we were on the night of Pedro Matias' attack."

"I think the detective will leave it alone," Angela murmured. "Maybe he sees the justice in it… maybe he doesn't care…"

"And why would he do that?" Ascendida asked, her nostrils flaring in disbelief.

"We are just an excuse, if not a distraction. Many have come and gone. They really don't care if we kill each other here," Angela said quietly.

Ascendida erupted in anger, "They will care if they suspect that women are at the root of things. Mayhem created by men is one thing. Mayhem created by women is punishable with the fires of hell! You should know that by now!"

Angela answered as if she was talking to herself, "Well… here we are, in the middle of the ocean between two continents… like stepping stones across a brook. Motherland sends people here because of our location, not because we kill each other. Besides, people will never think that women would be so audacious… Remember, we have no balls and consequently no right to be incorrigible or lawless... We are obedient and virtuous. People will default to what they presume we are: weak women." She looked at Ascendida, who in turn snorted with disapproval.

"Just think," Madalena said dreamily. "If women were more courageous and men were kinder... like Saul."

They were quietly contemplating Two Brooks with courageous women who, without subterfuge, would stand up for themselves, and kind men who would support them. They knew kind men, but even they told their women to behave, to stop it, to be quiet, to not provoke, to be sensible. They wanted to fix things for their women, to fight their battles, to rescue them. Angela was thinking how she would have preferred to see Pedro Matias in jail for his deeds than to have burned him with hot lard, but the kind men she knew had never succeeded in bringing Pedro to justice.

9

So Tenderly Kissed

When Angela got home, everything was in place. Rosa had completed her duties and left. Dona Mafalda was in the living room with Dom Carlos, looking at the wet world outside. The menagerie was in the kitchen waiting for her, and Emanuel was in the woodshop working on his cases.

Angela lingered in the garden before entering the house: Everything looked cleansed by the rain. The brooks were running noisily, the crickets were singing joyfully, the moon was full and the sky was clear. She felt brand new.

Dom Carlos stepped out of the house to meet her in the garden.

"It's a beautiful night," she said.

"What happened?" Dom Carlos asked.

She knew what he was asking. "He slapped me and then gave me a penance," she answered quietly.

Dom Carlos let out a grunt. "I'm going to kill him."

"No, you're not. I got off easy," she said dismissively.

Maybe the kisses she has received that afternoon had caused more damage than the monsignor's slap. Maybe she needed to be slapped for her devious and shameless ways. Maybe she needed to be reminded of measure and restraint.

Dom Carlos gently touched her face. Then he asked, "What was your penance?"

"To be at the detective's beck and call," she answered.

Dom Carlos stared at her for a moment. Then he leaned in and kissed her. It was a lingering, tender kiss, one that makes a woman close her eyes and softly moan. She looked around, worried if someone had seen it. "Dom Carlos," she murmured, "What does this mean?"

"Shhh," he said. "We will talk later." He walked toward the house and Angela walked down to the woodshop, wondering if Regina was at her attic window peering into her garden.

Emanuel was happily surprised to see her.

"I just wanted to check with you," she said, "According to the monsignor,

I've been an obstructionist to your endeavors. My penance is to help you. Of course, I didn't confess about you kissing me this afternoon." *Or about Dom Carlos*, she thought with a vague smile.

"Penance? I'm your penance?" He didn't know if he should be grateful or offended. He said, "Well, I'll let that sink in... I don't know what to say... other than kissing is not a sin."

"Depends on who you kiss," she said, turned around and left.

As soon as she left, he returned to his task. He looked at the coffins. He had been looking at those coffins for a while, especially Isaac Lima's coffin. He had heard something about that coffin, but he couldn't remember what it was.

There was another knock on the door. It was Dona Mafalda.

Dona Mafalda closed the door behind her and in a conspiratorial tone said, "So... I hear that you're Angela's penance. How does it feel to be someone's penance?"

"How do you know?" Emanuel asked.

"I'm an informed person, Detective Santos," she said in a self-important manner.

"Does the monsignor impose penances like indentured servitude?"

"He does it all the time. You must admit that his plan and sense of practicality are flawless. You have things that need to be done and he gets them done through penances. The old, the sick, the poor are all cared for through penances."

"How about those who don't go to confession?" he asked.

"Most do."

Then he asked, "Give me an example of a big penance that someone got."

"Well..." she was thinking. "Ascendida cared for an old paraplegic until he died because she shoved the monsignor down the church steps. It's a long story about a miracle she wanted from a saint who came to visit. I wasn't here at the time."

Emanuel was amused. He asked, "And what was the miracle she wanted?"

"No one knows. She never said. She said she didn't believe in miracles, but apparently, she did."

Emanuel thought about life and its schemes. Maybe Ascendida didn't get her miracle, but the old man certainly got his. And Ascendida, the dragon with a heart, was still waiting for her miracle.

Dona Mafalda said, "Angela's penance was syncopated with a hail of slaps."

Emanuel tensed. "The monsignor hit her?"

"He slapped her," she said, "quite a few times. And if Ascendida didn't step in and restrain him…" She wanted to spark Emanuel's imagination.

She had been the recipient of such punitive attentions from the old priest… most women had been. She told Emanuel about her own altercation with the monsignor, "He blamed me because the procession of the Jesus crucified was a fiasco. Someone put sugar on the flower carpets and the ants almost ate everyone alive. They crawled up the bishop's vestments, and the priests and seminarians… they almost undressed in the street trying to get the ants out of their clothes… there were surplices, stoles, cassocks… flying all over the place. Even the bishop dropped his miter."

Emanuel smirked imagining the scene. Then he asked, "And why would that be your fault?"

"I was responsible for coordinating the flower carpets… someone played a trick on me by adding sugared water to the flowers," Dona Mafalda said.

Emanuel looked at Dona Mafalda recounting a strange story as if it was the most mundane thing in the world. She wasn't even embarrassed disclosing that a priest slapped her across the face. "Let's go home," Emanuel said. "I need to release someone from indentured servitude."

When they entered the house, Angela was reading alone in the kitchen. Dona Mafalda said good night and gave Emanuel a meaningful look.

He said in a low voice, "You are released from your penance."

She let out a sigh of resignation. "No, don't release me," she said. "If you do, he will give me something else, something terrible. To be at your beck and call isn't so bad. Actually, it's the nicest penance I've gotten all my life." She smiled.

He looked at her. There was a black-and-blue mark on her cheek, that face that only a few hours ago he had kissed so tenderly.

"Do you want me to be your penance, really?" he asked, feeling grateful.

"Yes, I do," she answered sleepily. "I really do."

"Okay then, I own you," and then with curiosity, "For how long?"

She thought for a second. "Ad infinitum, like hell," and she laughed.

He thought about balance. Someone's penance could be someone else's miracle, like Ascendida and the old man. And now Angela's hell was his grace.

Dona Mafalda, looking very pretty, was just arriving at the woodshop to talk with Emanuel when Hercules jumped out hissing. She screamed and fell on the brier roses. Her dress was caught on the thorns, she lost a shoe, and her perfectly coiffed hair was a mess. Emanuel came to her aid.

"Are you all right?" he asked full of concern.

"That cat, really!" she cried. "What a menace!"

Dona Mafalda tried to regain her composure. She said to a flustered detective, "Please stop trying to fix my hair! I'm fine!" Then in a softer tone, she said, "Maybe this is an omen. I think I'm making a terrible mistake going to the city."

He was perplexed by her statement. Going to the city shouldn't be a hazardous undertaking.

"Detective Santos, I hope we are friends," she murmured.

"I hope so," he answered, full of curiosity.

"I have a question that only a friend can ask another friend."

He waited intrigued. "Sit down," he invited.

They sat on Isaac Lima's coffin. He looked at her encouragingly.

She wrung her hands and said demurely, "I'm meeting a man in the city."

He opened his mouth to say something, but he didn't know what to say. So this was the mistake. He waited for her to explain.

"I… I have never done this before." She blushed.

He was still lost for words.

"I always thought that my first boyfriend would be an older, experienced man who could guide me… who I could… learn from…" She shook her head in frustration.

"And he isn't?" Emanuel asked.

"I made a decision to be courageous, to give myself to love, to experience life. This is one of the reasons I came to this remote place… because I lacked the courage to be different in a place where everyone knew me." She was quiet for a moment. She added, "I'm embarrassed to come across as the old cow I really am, an old cow that had never been kissed." She was trembling.

Emanuel put his arm around her shoulders. "You've never been kissed?" He couldn't hide his surprise. "How old are you?"

"See?" she uttered offended. Then she said more calmly, "People pass judgment on these things… a woman my age. Something must be wrong with me… and so on…"

"Is it Lucas?"

She was going to meet Lucas in the city because she was too ashamed to meet him in the village. But she couldn't say that to Emanuel. She just shook her head in affirmation.

"Why Lucas?" Emanuel asked, his interest piqued.

"Because he has been the only suitor consistent in his devotion. Or more aptly, I have no one else. This is my chance." She had never been as candid as she was now.

"Lucas is a fine man." After a long pause, he added, "I didn't know that you and Lucas were seeing each other."

"I felt terrible about that uncharitable letter I sent him. We talked a few times. He is a sweet man. I agreed to see him in the city, away from curious eyes."

"Why are you so nervous?"

"He thinks that I'm his superior, a knowledgeable being, and I don't even know how to kiss. I made a terrible mistake!"

He grinned.

"See? I don't want him to laugh at me either!" she said all flustered.

"Men are a really perverted bunch. We love women without experience. Lucas will love to teach you." He looked at her concerned face. She was staring at him doubtfully.

"Dona Mafalda, do you want me to kiss you?" he asked.

Dona Mafalda blushed so violently that Emanuel thought she was going to explode.

"I'm sorry, Detective Santos. I didn't mean to give you the impression that... I came here for you to kiss me!"

Emanuel held her face in his hands for a moment. She didn't move. She was very tense, hardly breathing, and vaguely thinking about an insect that paralyzed its prey—Emanuel's hands cupping her face had the same effect. He kissed her and caressed her mouth with his tongue as she parted her lips, instinctively, just like she did when Lucas kissed her behind the garage.

"See? You are a natural," Emanuel murmured. "Kiss me back," he said and kept on kissing her repeatedly on the lips until she kissed back. First, it was just a little peck and then she gained more confidence. She was inclined to his lower lip. It was a wonderful feeling to kiss a man. The world had a softness and a sweetness that could only be found in a kiss.

Emanuel moved away from her and smiled.

Dona Mafalda took a deep breath. She was trembling, felt weak, ridiculous, and good, all at once.

"Oh my... what a wonderful thing," she murmured.

Finally, she got off her perch on the coffin, feeling somewhat dizzy, and thinking that she hadn't done anything as wonderful as that, ever.

"Thank you, Emanuel," she said with a shaky voice. She paused and added hesitantly, "This will be our secret, true?"

"This is just between us," Emanuel said. He gave her a wide grin and kissed her again. "Enjoy your trip."

Emanuel got up after her and pushed the coffin against the wall. As he was doing so, Dona Mafalda helped him with the cover. She stopped midstream, with an expression of confusion.

"I thought this was—the now-famous—Isaac Lima's coffin," she said.

Emanuel looked at it and said, "It is. The last coffin Lazarus built."

"No," she said, looking into the box. "Isaac Lima's lining was dark brown, due to his promise to Our Lady of Carmo. Everybody knows that. This one is navy blue."

Dom Carlos stormed into the monsignor's house.

The monsignor got up and asked no less outraged, "What's this all about?"

"Shut up and sit down," Dom Carlos said.

The monsignor sat down as if he had been pushed by an invisible hand.

Dom Carlos sat across the table from him and the two men measured each other like mortal enemies.

"What do you want?" the monsignor said.

Dom Carlos said with an even voice. "If you so much touch Angela again, I will break you in two."

"My dealings with Angela are not your concern," snapped the monsignor. "It's between her confessor and God."

"Well, think again," Dom Carlos said. "Now I'm in the mix. Angela may not have a husband or family who will stand up to you, but she has me."

The monsignor made a grimace, "The hero," he mocked.

"No, I'm just a man who doesn't use and abuse women."

"How dare you to—" started the monsignor.

Dom Carlos interrupted him, "Be careful, Monsignor, I don't need much of an excuse to destroy you. You're a bully! You terrorize these poor people like a monster terrorizes children and all in the name of God. One of these days they will figure out that there is no power in your gods and demons—you use them as a tool to oppress and control. You disgust me!"

The monsignor's green fiery eyes were dark with rage. "I love these people!" he shouted.

"No, you don't! You use them for your own redemption, to cleanse yourself from your wickedness. You touch her again and I will destroy you."

"My God! You're in love with the girl!" the monsignor said between disgust and amazement. "I knew it!" he exclaimed with no little satisfaction.

"What the hell do you know about love?" Dom Carlos asked evenly and walked out, leaving the door wide open and the monsignor shaking with ire.

Dom Carlos needed a few moments to calm down from his shouting match with the monsignor. Before going into the house, he walked down into the garden and saw Emanuel and Angela in the woodshop. They were absorbed looking at a coffin.

"What are the two of you looking at?" Dom Carlos asked, entering the shop.

"Isaac Lima's coffin," Emanuel said.

"What is so fascinating about it?" Dom Carlos was now curious.

"This coffin should have a brown lining. Everyone seems to know that, and this one has a navy-blue lining," Emanuel explained.

"Don't look at me. I don't know how to make coffins, but I know for sure that Isaac's coffin had a brown lining. I saw it many times when I used to visit Lazarus," Dom Carlos said, getting very intrigued.

"Since Lazarus died, there were no more coffins made here. They are all made in the Carpentry Shop," Angela said. "I agree with Dom Carlos. Isaac's coffin had a brown lining."

Emanuel said pensively, "Someone died and Isaac's coffin was used?"

"I do the books for the business," Angela said. "I would have known if Isaac's coffin had been sold to someone else or a new coffin had been ordered. And if a new coffin had been ordered, what is it doing here still?" She looked to the two men, who were also looking baffled.

"May I look at the books around that time?" Emanuel asked.

Turning to Angela, Dom Carlos said, "You were sick with grief those first few months after Lazarus died. Your parents were helping you with the business… maybe your father sold it and forgot to tell you."

"Even if he did… Lazarus built this coffin with navy-blue lining. I know his work. He built this. He only had one coffin completely finished in the shop: Isaac Lima's," she argued with growing alarm.

"The only explanation I can come up with is that someone is buried in a coffin with brown lining..." Emanuel said.

Dona Mafalda had done something terrible. She had gone to the city to meet a man. What was she doing? She was meeting a mechanic! All her life she saved her virtue and now she was about to debase herself with a mechanic with greasy loins and a lusty heart. What was she thinking?

Lucas, removed from his garage and scrubbed to an inflamed pink, looked even younger. He had new shoes on that seemed like instruments of torture.

They had agreed to meet in Dom Carlos' apartment, for privacy and, in Dona Mafalda's case, because she was embarrassed to be seen with Lucas.

As soon as they entered Dom Carlos' apartment, Dona Mafalda looked around and was reminded of Dom Carlos' sophistication and lineage. She looked at Lucas and thought, *the poor man is terrified of me.*

They were in the middle of the living room.

Dear God, help me out. What do I do with her? I should have been better prepared. I should have asked Dom Carlos to be more specific. What does it mean to go with my heart?

Lucas, with tremulous hands, touched her shoulder and then started to unbutton her dress. She was speechless. This wasn't right. Didn't he skip a few steps? But what did she know about such matters? She should have asked the detective. She'd read Jane Austin and fantasized about that ill-humored Mr. Darcy, and she was almost positive that Mr. Darcy wouldn't do what Lucas was doing. She felt the floor disappearing from under her feet. She gasped and Lucas momentarily stopped and looked at her anxiously. Slowly he resumed the task of undressing her until her dress was on the floor around her feet. Then he took off every piece of clothing she had on until Dona Mafalda, pink and round, stood there, with no idea what to do next. The afternoon sun shone in and made her look like a fuzzy ripe peach. Again, for the second time on the same day, she thought of that poisonous spider that rendered its victims immobile. She felt like that, she couldn't move.

"You're so beautiful," he said with a strangled voice and kept on looking.

You incompetent peasant! Dona Mafalda said to herself.

Lucas was still staring at her when he felt the urge to cry. Finally, he had that elusive teacher naked in front of him and he wanted to cry. This couldn't be happening. He wanted to cry big loud howls, hide his face in her bosom, and let out all the pent-up love he had for her. And with a terrible sob, he started his shameful, inopportune crying.

Dona Mafalda was stupefied. Emanuel didn't say anything about crying. She saw her shadow tall and thin reflected on the wall by the afternoon sun. But the reality was that she was short and fat and was naked in front of a crying mechanic. She, Dona Mafalda, who abhorred anything that wasn't proper, could not be living this terrible moment. No man had ever seen her naked and now this *mechanic*, who had pursued her for months, was crying.

She hurriedly started putting her clothes on, with urgency, as if she wanted to turn back time.

Lucas was crying into his hands. He sat down on the rocking chair and rocked himself while sobbing.

What a fiasco, she thought. *What a gruesome fiasco. Now I know for sure that God doesn't love me.* Quietly she got up and left the apartment.

Emanuel was sitting quietly on the terrace when Dona Mafalda came home through the garden. She barely acknowledged him and went into the house in haste, almost bumping into Dom Carlos and Angela, who were coming out to join Emanuel.

"What's wrong with her?" Angela asked.

The two men exchanged a brief look. They both knew that she had met Lucas in the city and, according to her demeanor, things hadn't gone well.

There was an awkward silence.

"I talked to Madalena this afternoon," Emanuel said, steering the conversation away from Dona Mafalda. "She said that her father is getting better. So, I'll talk to him soon. She also said something intriguing... the mailman only delivers the letters to Pedro. When he was in the hospital, there were no letters. When he came home, the mailman came in the house and gave the letters personally to Pedro. Dona Amelia doesn't mind because Pedro gives her the letters, unopened, afterward. Madalena asked the mailman about this unusual service and the mailman said Pedro made the request around the same time Lazarus died."

They were thinking about this odd request.

Emanuel continued, "According to Dona Amelia, there is absolutely nothing out of the ordinary when she receives correspondence—a few letters from family in Canada, a few letters from the city regarding business."

"You think that he's waiting for something big to come in the mail?" Dom Carlos asked.

"That fucker buys everyone! He poisons everything! He should have died!" Angela said savagely. She got up and stomped off.

"Madalena says that he keeps on repeating the story that you and Angela are lovers," Emanuel said as soon as Angela was out of earshot.

Emanuel took a long look at Dom Carlos—so confident, so in charge... and so in love with Angela that even an utter stranger could tell.

"Married men have no business falling in love with other women," Emanuel said.

Dom Carlos stiffened and leaned forward in his seat to better gauge Emanuel's expression. He answered, "I'm not married."

"You are married. I looked into it."

Dom Carlos went cold. "What did you say?" he finally asked.

"Your divorce isn't final. Your wife, Vivienne, didn't sign the papers."

Dom Carlos felt as if the garden was spinning around. So that was why Vivienne was insisting on meeting?

"You didn't know?" Emanuel asked surprised.

Dom Carlos took a while to answer. "No, she was the one who wanted the divorce, not me. She hounded me for it and I signed. I assumed she was going to do the rest," he added with a cynical laugh. "I also signed over half of what we owned to her."

"Well, if the divorce really happens this time, she can ask you for the other half," Emanuel said dryly.

Angela returned with a jug of wine and sat next to Dom Carlos. She looked at him and asked, "Are you all right?"

"I'm fine," he mumbled.

Angela poured three glasses of wine and said to Emanuel, "Continue what you were saying, before my outburst about Pedro."

"This is what we know," Emanuel said, "Lazarus didn't fall into the sea with the wristwatch. Pedro Matias is lying. He found the wristwatch somewhere, but not on the cliffs... or Lazarus gave it to him. Again, it's not only that the water inside the watch face isn't seawater, but the watch has no scratches, no indication that it had been washed up by the sea. Pedro Matias goes to catch limpets, but Lazarus was afraid of the sea and didn't care for limpets anyway. Why would he have gone that night? It took Pedro Matias three hours to tell Angela that Lazarus had fallen into the sea. It's too long. You can imagine him hoping for his son to somehow surface alive or waiting for at the very least his body to wash up on shore. But three hours is way too long to delay.

"And one month before Lazarus' death, Saul and Manuel disappeared. Around that time, Angela's mother saw Lazarus making a coffin. She thought it was odd because no one had died. Everybody knows that Isaac Lima a long time ago had commissioned a coffin with brown lining. It sat in the woodshop waiting for Isaac. The coffin we have now in the woodshop has the wrong color lining. Where is Mr. Lima's coffin? There were no deaths in the village for twenty-five months while Lazarus was alive, according to the monsignor. This is what we know," he concluded.

Dom Carlos said, "It's possible that Pedro cooked up the story of Lazarus' death in the ocean and convinced Lazarus to go along with it. Lazarus may have taken a ship somewhere. The question is why? Why would Lazarus do that?"

"Maybe he was running away from… something… some crime?" Emanuel speculated, looking at Angela turning pale.

The three of them sat motionless in a heavy silence. Where to go from here?

"Oh, my God," Angela whispered. "Nascimento's dead man."

Dom Carlos and Emanuel were speechless. Nascimento killed a man?

Angela let out a muffled cry. She wiped her face with a tremulous hand, took a long breath, and said, "Isaac Lima's coffin was used for this dead man. And Lazarus built another one but made a mistake with the lining. It means that Lazarus buried this man, and he left because of it."

"What man?" Dom Carlos and Emanuel asked in unison.

Picking up the tension, Viriato started howling and Hercules was hissing like a fool, Dalia was flailing about trying to fly with her one good wing and Nixon squealed nonstop. Hercules finally fled, hissing.

For what seemed a long time, Angela sat with her face in her hands. Then she told them about Nascimento's night trips, stressing her condition as somnambulism, and the man—who might have been drunk—being dragged through the village eighteen months ago.

There was an uncomfortable silence.

"And you never told anybody about this?" Emanuel asked.

"We decided to wait. It could have been a falling-down drunk man. After all, no one died, nobody appeared…"

"Angela!" Emanuel said, exasperated. "This investigation is about men who disappeared! How in the world didn't you think it was relevant?"

"At the time, Manuel and Saul were accounted for—they had left. And Lazarus was still with us when that happened. This was Nascimento telling us something that didn't make sense… and no one showed up dead…"

"What in the world is happening?" Dona Mafalda's voice rang like a bell in the night. She was at the living room door peering into the dark, trying to figure out where the voices were coming from.

"Let's go inside," Emanuel said.

When they entered the house, they encountered Dona Mafalda fully alert and ready for an explanation. No one knew what to say.

"There was a break in the case," Emanuel finally said.

Dona Mafalda's curiosity was minuscule compared to the heartbreak she felt in seeing Dom Carlos so tenderly consoling Angela.

"Maybe we should all go to bed," Dom Carlos said. "We're all tired and tomorrow our thinking will hopefully be less muddled."

Both Dom Carlos and Angela stood up and disappeared up the stairs.

"Dom Carlos is in love with Angela. She is the one. How did I not see it before?" Dona Mafalda said. Her voice was quiet as if she was giving up on something cherished, as if she had been fighting a current and finally let herself go under.

"Do you think she feels the same way about him?" Emanuel asked, equally morose.

"I don't know. She loves everybody… it's hard to tell with Angela…" Dona Mafalda was so downcast that Emanuel felt like crying.

Emanuel didn't want to think about Angela and much less about Dom Carlos. He had a mountain of work to get through and he needed to focus. He was irritated with himself for allowing Angela to be a bright light shining in his eyes and blinding him from everything else. "You helped break the case," he said to Dona Mafalda.

"Me?" she asked, momentarily forgetting about broken hearts.

Emanuel went over the facts and events, while she listened with interest. The church clock sounded two mournful strikes. "What do you think, Dona Mafalda?" he asked.

She didn't know if she had the strength to shift gears from her heart to her head and talk about murder and mayhem. She let out a long sigh. Maybe murder was a good distraction from her disappointment. "Then let me give you a few scenarios," she started, clearing her throat to sound more enthusiastic. "Scenario one: Saul and Lazarus hurt and kill Manuel Barcos. They bring him up to the house and bury him in Isaac Lima's coffin. Question: What is the motive? Motive:

Manuel is pursuing Madalena even after she is married to Saul. Saul gets into a fight with him and kills him. He goes to Lazarus for help and Lazarus, wanting to help his sister out, helps Saul. The problem with this scenario is that Manuel Barcos had already left for Brazil. His family confirmed it, and his luggage hasn't been found. The monsignor says that Manuel should have gone to his house to get some money, but he didn't. Given his distress, it's more than likely that he just left when he found out the money for his journey came from Saul."

"Good deduction..." Emanuel said.

She continued, "Scenario two: Lazarus kills someone. Let's say he kills Saul. Manuel Barcos is already on his way to Brazil. Lazarus is assisted by his father in disposing of the body. They use Isaac Lima's coffin. Angela says that Lazarus was very strange after Saul and Manuel disappeared. A month later his father says he fell into the sea. But he didn't—he gets onto a ship and goes to some distant country because he can't live with the knowledge that he killed someone."

"What would be the motive for Lazarus to kill Saul?" Emanuel asked.

"This theory doesn't hold... it's weak," Dona Mafalda said with a wince. "It would be a stronger case if Pedro killed Saul and Lazarus was covering for the father, as he had done a million times in the past." She turned to Emanuel and added, "Also, it can't be Saul in Isaac Lima's coffin. He was too big."

"According to what people say about Lazarus he would never kill anyone, much less his sister's husband..." Emanuel said. "Now, I could see Pedro Matias killing Saul... they were always fighting... and then forcing Lazarus to cover for him."

"Yes, that would make more sense," Dona Mafalda said, spooning sugar into her tea. "Then Pedro Matias makes Lazarus leave because he doesn't trust him to keep the secret. This would explain why Pedro Matias has been waiting for the mailman all these months, to find out where Lazarus is and control receiving the letters. He must be afraid that Lazarus would write to his mother or Angela about it."

"He's waiting for Lazarus to write back to let him know where he is. But he doesn't know how to read and write... or he's lying about that," Emanuel finished.

"I'm imagining that Lazarus wouldn't put his name on the envelope, but a letter from Canada or America, Brazil or even Australia is unmissable. He would recognize the type of letter," Dona Mafalda said. And then with a gasp, "He must have the letters hidden somewhere if this scenario is true."

"Dona Mafalda, you have a fine brain," Emanuel said and reached across the table to softly pat her hand.

10

Rise Up, Lazarus!

Emanuel was still sitting at the kitchen table when Dom Carlos came down. "How is Angela?" Emanuel asked.

"I'm taking her to the city for a few days. She can rest there. And we have to divide our efforts and clarify these... speculations. I will check on Manuel Barcos' voyage and if he bought a passage to Brazil and used it. There will be a paper trail, I'm sure. Angela will check on Saul's bank transactions."

"I did that already and all I got was that someone used the passage. It could have been anyone, but go ahead, you may find something else... I'll pursue a few lines of inquiry here with Dona Mafalda," Emanuel said.

Dom Carlos raked his hair with his fingers. "What a mess," he said. He looked at Emanuel and asked, "Do you think Lazarus killed someone?"

Emanuel arched his eyebrows. "I don't know," he said. "I've never met the man. But what I know about people is that we are all capable of murder—given the right set of circumstances."

Dom Carlos said, "It's inconceivable that Saul and Manuel left on the same ship. They hated each other. And why would Saul leave if his major problem—Manuel—was going to disappear far away in Brazil?"

Emanuel said, "I agree. I'm going to interview the Matiases again, now that I have a better grasp of things. I'm also going to let loose Dona Mafalda on the Matiases. If there are letters from Lazarus, she'll find them." Emanuel smiled with the idea of Dona Mafalda taunting Pedro and snooping all over his house. "Dona Amelia will help if it has to do with Lazarus being alive."

The silence in Dom Carlos' apartment was perfect for rest and reflection. So much had happened in a few hours. Like when a dam bursts, they were rapidly being inundated by a flood of information that they couldn't process fast enough.

He made coffee and took a shower. Then he went to the bedroom to wake up Angela. He sat on the edge of the bed and tenderly shook her. She sat up, abruptly remembering all that had happened. She held her head in her hands and sighed deeply. *I'm going to be fine. No matter what, I'm going to be fine,* she thought.

She was afraid of that conversation, about love in metamorphosis, about the kisses she exchanged with Dom Carlos. She was also afraid that if they talked and clarified things, it would change their relationship for the worse. He believed that she didn't know her own heart. Here alone with him, she didn't want to talk about anything other than Lazarus and the missing coffin.

"I know that Lazarus would never kill anyone," she said.

"Maybe not. But it might have been a fight or accident and he panicked," he pressed.

She thought about it for a while. "Yes, I can see him panicking, trying to hide mistakes, like a little boy, afraid of being punished."

"Everything will be fine... eventually," Dom Carlos said quietly. "Let's go to the Café by the Sea. It will do us both good to go get something to eat and take in the beauty of the bay."

But seated in the café, they were too preoccupied to admire the scenic backdrop. They were absorbed by all that they needed to do and the perilous directions in which this search could take them.

Angela was thinking about her eroded dreams. Her life had dramatically changed and everything she knew was out of kilter. She had Lazarus' death certificate in hand, though Lazarus was probably alive somewhere in some country. He hadn't drowned, after all—he had left her. Why hadn't this occurred to her before, where now everything seemed so clear? What happened, that she, Lazarus' savior and protector, couldn't intervene and make right? Angela felt betrayed. Yes, he left her. Down deep she had always known that he was alive. But why had he left? He hadn't even tried to confide in her, to include her in making irrevocable life-changing decisions. Instead, he had sought out that monster of a father for support or guidance.

"Are you all right?" Dom Carlos asked.

"Yes, I'm better than yesterday," she said evenly. Something profound in her soul had shifted and she knew that she would never ever again cry over betrayal. "Everything is changed," she said finally. "Everything that I had was like a castle made of sand. One big wave washes over it and it's gone."

"Tomorrow we will know more," Dom Carlos said evenly.

Tomorrow Emanuel was coming to meet with them. He would have already spoken with Pedro Matias and Madalena. And Angela and Dom Carlos would report on what they had learned in the city.

"How did we not think of this before?" she asked, incredulous about her failure to anticipate the emerging chain of events. "Here we are with this scenario developing in front of our eyes and we never noticed it before."

"Before, we didn't know about Nascimento's dead man," he reasoned.

"Only Nascimento thought he was dead, nobody else—not Madalena, much less Ascendida or me. And where was the dead man? His body didn't show up anywhere."

"Nascimento's perspective is a bit shady... most of her facts are collected in the dark," he said playfully.

"That's not funny!" she snapped.

"It is funny in a sad kind of way. She sees things that no one fathoms, even a dead man," he said.

Bernardo, the waiter with mournful eyes and a droopy mustache, refilled their glasses and thought, *Son, don't laugh. An angry woman and a laughing man never end up well.*

The afternoon was waning and the city dwellers were hurrying home.

"Let's go, Hawk. Nothing here is going to change your bad mood. When we get home, you can beat me up."

She couldn't exactly explain why Dom Carlos was the target of her frustration. She couldn't help but think that it was his fault! He had made her love him. She'd been arrogant in her certainties and now she felt fraudulent as if she'd known that her doubts were always there and she never let them speak. But Dom Carlos knew. He knew that she was a headstrong child who had hardly lived and made rash statements about knowing her heart.

"I was born knowing love," Angela said. "Doubt was never part of my being because everything else issued from that gift of knowing love. Now I find myself leaping across chasm after chasm, no longer oblivious of the void in between. I don't remember when I started being so inflexible in my thinking about love and hate, life and death, compassion and unforgiveness, kindness and indifference. My hubris blinded me and I never learned how to measure up. I don't understand how I was betrayed by my own heart and how unprepared I've been because I thought love was enough. How can this feeling that I thought was a gift be so riddled with guilt? I've been so unworldly and arrogant for thinking that loving intensely was all I needed to understand everything."

She was quiet for a while and Dom Carlos, stunned by her admission, held his breath.

"You think that I'm confused," she continued. "I'm not confused. I know what I want and who I am. I want you and I'm ashamed because I should be thinking of Lazarus and how to bring him back. I feel guilty because I lust over Emanuel. But you, Dom Carlos, you are so familiar and dear to me that I feel that I've loved you for forever." She sighed as if a tremendous burden had been lifted from her shoulders. She looked at him pointedly and said, "Please don't say anything—at least not yet."

And the old waiter saw the glass of wine slip out of the man's hand and soak his beautiful suit. He knew it—the combination of a laughing man and an angry woman never, ever ended well, no matter what.

"Then there's the possible third scenario," Dona Mafalda said. "Lazarus," she said in a low voice, "could have drowned, after all."

Emanuel was surprised. They had agreed to discard that theory.

"Well... I was thinking of suicide." She let the words sink in.

Emanuel stared at her. "Go on," he said.

"We know that Lazarus was the last of the three to disappear. So, he's not buried in Isaac Lima's coffin... unless Pedro put him in there... but I don't think so... because Pedro is waiting for a letter to arrive and Manuel or Saul wouldn't be writing to Pedro. Either Manuel or Saul is in that coffin. Dom Carlos will find out this week if Manuel set off for Brazil or Australia. Suppose that Manuel left on his voyage. Then who's buried in Isaac's coffin? It has to be Saul, even as big as he was. And who was responsible? Pedro and Lazarus." She stopped, expecting a reaction.

"Go on," he repeated.

"Lazarus, by all accounts, was a kind, loving, beautiful boy. Yes, a boy. Angela grew into a woman, but Lazarus continued to be a boy. People say that Angela wore the pants in the family and that Lazarus looked at her as if she was everything. He was a broken spirit. He was the oldest and his father beat him mercilessly. Many of the beatings were for Madalena. Lazarus was always protecting his sister and getting the beatings that he could deflect from her. He also protected his mother when Pedro Matias was going to beat her. You see, he was the whipping boy... but he never stood up to that horrible man. I can see Pedro Matias involved with this whole thing and telling his son that he would go to jail or that something terrible was going to happen to him, or worse, something was going to happen to Angela. Lazarus may have taken the easy way out—jumping into the sea. You know that suicide is all too prevalent on the islands, don't you?"

Emanuel pondered. "Angela was the one who proposed marriage to Lazarus... he really didn't make any decisions, did he?"

"But, in his defense, Lazarus didn't want to get married because he was afraid of being drafted to fight in the war and leaving Angela a widow."

"But he wasn't drafted," Emanuel said thoughtfully. Emanuel was recalling Regina Sales' stories about the village, as she had tied him to the bed. "I've heard that it was the monsignor who paid a substitute to take Lazarus' place," he ventured. But what Emanuel heard from Regina Sales was that Dom Carlos paid a fortune to someone to go in Lazarus' place to the military. When he asked Regina how she knew, she smiled and held the information for later sexual extortions. "Do you believe it was the monsignor?" Emanuel asked Dona Mafalda.

"No, I don't. His sense of righteousness wouldn't allow him to do that for Lazarus and not for the other young men in the village."

"Who then?"

"Amelia Matias thinks it was because she prayed a novena. Angela thinks it was the miracle she asked of Father Cross."

"And you?" Emanuel was intently looking a Dona Mafalda.

"I think it was Dom Carlos. I can't think of anyone else who would be able to pull it off, or be interested and generous enough to do that for Lazarus and Angela."

"Dom Carlos?" Emanuel said, paying close attention to Dona Mafalda.

Dona Mafalda offered, "Yes, I can see Dom Carlos doing that. I also can see Angela finding a way. She protected Lazarus like a lioness. I wouldn't be surprised if she found him a way out of military service and the war."

Emanuel was pensive.

"I don't know if you noticed Pedro Matias' chipped teeth?" she asked.

Yes, Emanuel had noticed and had been informed how Pedro had his teeth broken. He smiled.

"Well," said Dona Mafalda, "the first Christmas after Angela and Lazarus got married, Angela punched Pedro in the mouth, breaking his teeth."

Emanuel shook his head in mild disapproval and laughed softly.

Dona Mafalda pressed on, "What I want to say is that Lazarus was weak, a broken spirit. Angela came into his life as a wife, protector, mother. But a lifetime of abuse can't be undone by a savior, and the abused don't grow courage from that. He could very well have killed himself. His father manipulated him like a puppet when Angela wasn't around, and even when she was around, he tried. She was always on guard, always alert. Remember the pig? Nixon? That pig was taken right from under Lazarus' nose and Lazarus lacked the courage to stop his father. Angela was the one who freed the pig. Lazarus left all the battling to Angela."

This was certainly a sobering thought. Dona Mafalda said with a shudder, "Assuming that Lazarus killed himself by jumping into the ocean, he would have taken off his wristwatch and maybe left it for Angela with a note that Pedro Matias later destroyed. But Pedro couldn't bring himself to throw away or destroy the watch and invented that story. This indeed could be the third scenario... unless Pedro pushed his own son into the ocean... which is too perverse to contemplate... even for Pedro."

"You're right about a third scenario, Dona Mafalda. Maybe a conversation with Dona Amelia would be helpful today regarding the letters, and anything else you think will provide clarity."

Dona Mafalda took out her notebook and started making a to-do list—she loved making checklists:

1. *Visit Amelia Matias.*
2. *Talk to Madalena about the letters.*
3. *Have a conversation with the mailman.*
4. *Check the passenger list for Manuel.*
5. *Check bank withdrawals/deposits for Saul.*
6. *Check the passenger lists of other ships in port eighteen months ago*
7. *What about Saul's mother, Carlota Amora?*

"Do we have everything?" she asked, showing Emanuel her list.

Angela and Dom Carlos arrived home without exchanging a word. Dom Carlos did what Angela asked him to do—remain silent. Sometimes love is.

He showered and reappeared in the living room in his pajamas, barefooted, and feeling refreshed.

"We have to talk," he said.

Angela looked at him steadily. She took a step toward him and crossed her arms. "Who are you?" she asked.

He frowned. "You know who I am."

"Do I? I also thought I knew my husband. I'm so gullible that even Lazarus was able to deceive me. What do I know about you?" she insisted. "You don't trust me either," she said quietly, and then she thought about Dom Carlos-turned-Zorro. That should have been a red flag that forewarned her that Dom Carlos was more than a kind man—he was a mysterious one.

He closed his eyes and said softly, "Please, Baby, don't judge me so harshly. Don't project Lazarus' actions onto me. Be patient."

It was such a strange thing to say. He had never called her *Baby*. What happened to *Hawk*, the strong bird that personified her island? A baby was such a vulnerable creature. Angela looked at him, trying to figure out who was this man pleading with her. Was he the ever-present, supportive, loving, caring Dom Carlos or an untrustworthy stranger with devious ways and a shady background?

He said, holding her gaze, "There are many things about me that you don't know. Give me time. But there is much that you do know... such as my love for you, and you know that, don't you?"

"Yes," she said softly. "I'm tired, I'm going to bed. I need distance from you and from everything else. I am full to the brim and if anything more happens to me today, I think I will drown." She turned and went into the bathroom.

Dom Carlos was already in bed when she emerged from the bathroom and settled down on the sofa. She looked at the ceiling, feeling small and stupid, insignificant, and defeated. All her life she'd been so sure about everything. She had seen only primary colors—no color blends. What was she going to do with the wave of doubt washing over her? She was too overwhelmed to consider how to deal with it.

She didn't sleep at all through the night, kept awake by the same doubts running around her brain, unresolved. Morning, announced by loud knocks on the door, came as a relief. Dom Carlos, still sleepy, opened the door to let in Emanuel and a jubilant Dona Mafalda. Angela squinted into their amused faces.

"What time is it?" Angela asked.

"Very early, my dear. We got a ride with a farmer," Dona Mafalda said, sounding very upbeat. She was ecstatic. To find Angela sleeping on the sofa made her feel like she had won something.

Emanuel was elated too. He looked at Angela and sat next to her.

"I'll make coffee," Dom Carlos said, barefooted, rumpled, and ill-humored, "You are way, way too early."

Dona Mafalda followed him into the kitchen, leaving Emanuel and Angela on the couch.

Angela looked up at Emanuel, freshly shaved and with his hair nicely combed. He looked so happy this morning. She got up from the sofa and picked up the sheets and the pillow. "I had a terrible night," she muttered. Her mood had not improved from the previous day. She felt that she would never be centered again. Finding out about the real possibility that Lazarus was alive, that he had left her, had done something so profound in her soul that she knew she would be forever changed. It was more than a loss; it was devastating.

Emanuel was worried. He had never seen Angela without her inner light. Even when she cried, you could see the light, beauty, and goodness within her. Now she was dim, closed, and distant.

Dona Mafalda's nonstop talking in the kitchen was animating the apartment.

"Hey," Emanuel said, holding Angela at arm's length and trying to look into her eyes. "Talk to me."

She looked up at him, "Lazarus left me, didn't he?"

Emanuel was silent.

Angela said, trying to sound light-hearted, theatrical, "Rise up, Lazarus!"

Emanuel squeezed her arms. Angela could smell her home on him. She leaned against his chest, taking in the freshly laundered smell of his shirt. She let out a deep sigh. He cradled her in his arms.

"Did you survive with Dona Mafalda in charge?" she asked.

"Barely. She was a total nightmare. She doesn't let me take food to my room and no moonshine. But at least she is tormenting Hercules. She sprays his face with the nurse's water bottle and doesn't allow him in the house. The most terrible thing is that she picked a fight with Regina."

Angela looked up, "Who won?"

"Regina." He smiled ruefully, bent his head, and kissed her on the mouth.

It was such a gentle, sweet kiss. Angela felt warm and loved by this police investigator looking for incriminating secrets that could put her in jail. She smiled with the thought and he kissed her again.

"You shouldn't be kissing me," she said.

"Why not? I can't think of anything more appealing than your mouth."

"Stop that nonsense," she said, pushing him away.

Meanwhile, Dom Carlos tried to have an innocuous conversation with Dona Mafalda, while making coffee. She gave him a sideways glance, assessing if she should be enjoying his discomfort regarding Angela and Emanuel when what she felt was a pang of sympathy. Unrequited love… it was so painful. Dona Mafalda thought of Angela and her sadness. Angela was her only true friend… other than Emanuel. So to see half of Angela gone—her joy and laughter—and in its place, something or someone that she didn't know, scared her.

When Angela came into the kitchen, Dona Mafalda said, "Oh, my dear, don't let these tragic events change you. You are one of the finest people I know." She placed a hand on Angela's arm. How true she spoke and how sorry she was that she hadn't said it before. Instead, she had criticized Angela for laughing at everything, for defending everyone, for loving too many people, for taking care of too many pets, for taking on too many causes.

"He left. He left me with this terrible sorrow," Angela said quietly.

Trying to soften the blow, Dona Mafalda said, "Darling, we don't know what really happened yet, but we will find out."

There was a knock at the door. They all looked at Dom Carlos, who with a grimace went to the door and hesitatingly opened it, letting Dona Gloria in.

"Good morning," she said, looking around the room and resting her appraising eyes on Emanuel. "Hearing the commotion so early in the morning, I was worried something bad had happened."

Dona Mafalda stepped in front of Emanuel and introduced herself, with steeliness in her voice. She moved as if she was going to lift her leg and mark territory around the room.

Dom Carlos said, "My friends came to visit—too early in the day, certainly, but just a visit."

Dona Mafalda knew about this woman. At one time, she thought that Dom Carlos was in love with her. She gave Dona Gloria a cold stare.

Emanuel was speechless looking at the morning visitor. So this was the woman, beautiful and perfectly put together, that he'd heard so much about.

Dona Mafalda stepped in front of Emanuel and said to Dona Gloria, "You don't mind if you visit some other time? You see, we're working on a very important project."

Dona Gloria was full of apologies and left. Emanuel started to laugh.

"I see no reason for your merriment," Dona Mafalda said, with her nose in the air, as if she had smelled something unpleasant.

Dom Carlos said irritably. "Our detective is full of mirth today."

Angela said, "She thinks that I'm Dom Carlos'… paramour… from France," and she pointed with head tilted toward Dom Carlos.

"And why would she think that?" Dona Mafalda asked, almost offended.

"It's a long story," Angela said.

Emanuel gave Dom Carlos a pointed look. So Angela didn't know about Dom Carlos' wife.

"What did you find out?" Dona Mafalda asked, trying to get back to the business at hand.

Angela answered, "We found out that Manuel Barcos bought a passage to Brazil. We had no way of knowing if he really went. We located the person responsible for the boarding on that day and he looked at Manuel's photo and said, yes, it looked vaguely familiar, but it was too long ago to clearly remember. There were two ships around that time—one on route to Africa and one to Brazil. We are assuming that Manuel boarded the ship to Brazil and it's possible that Saul took the one to Africa. The man on duty around that time, when the African ship was in port, had since died. So we have no way of confirming if Saul took the ship to Africa. If he was seen, he would have been remembered— he was a hard man to confuse with anyone else... We also found out that Saul didn't deposit the money for the month. As you know, every month he went to the city to make deposits. There was no deposit or visit from Saul Amora to the bank that month. Actually, the month prior he withdrew a substantial sum. We could assume that he'd been planning to do something with it or leave." She sat quietly as if spent from sharing this information.

"We can then deduce that he gave Manuel the money for him to leave, and or he left himself." Emanuel reasoned.

"I also talked to Madalena," Emanuel continued. "She said that prior to Saul's disappearance, Manuel had written her letters requesting a meeting. She later found out that Saul intercepted the letters—with her father's help. He waited to see if she would betray him. And she did when she went to say goodbye. She could only explain Saul's sadness by assuming that he knew he was going to leave because of her betrayal."

Emanuel was thinking. Everybody waited and he continued, "But I'm not convinced of this. It's more likely that he left because his father hadn't died in Africa—at least this is the rumor. Saul doesn't strike me as a man who quits so easily after he fought so hard. And why now when Manuel was leaving? Saul isn't the romantic type to surrender to big romantic gestures. That was more Manuel's style. Madalena said that she fell in love with Saul. He was kind, loving, and patient. He was consistent and caring. He understood her doubts and waited for his love to take root in her heart. And it did."

There was a long pause. Emanuel looked at his audience one by one. "Now, does this sound like a man who would take off leaving his mother and his wife behind because of one love encounter? I don't think so. I also spoke with

Carlota Amora, the devoted mother. An interesting thing about Mrs. Amora is that she doesn't sound paralyzed or desperate, or in mourning as one would have imagined. She was always sad, but never desperate with grief. As for Pedro Matias, he says that the letters he was waiting for had to do with business. That, we know, is a lie. He can't read and Angela takes care of the business. Dona Amelia said that there is nothing different with the letters. She has family in Canada and they write once in a while. And we also know that the mailman gave him the letters first. Was he waiting for Lazarus' letter? And how would he know if he doesn't know how to read? But every time I speak with Pedro I know that he's lying about something. I am almost positive that he is the key... that he knows everything."

Dona Mafalda broke in, "Dona Amelia will be looking for the letters. The poor woman has renewed joy thinking that Lazarus is alive." She looked at Angela, almost afraid to continue.

"Please," Angela said, "I won't break. Just get on with it!" There were no tears. She was distant and collected as if she was a spectator.

"I'll break Pedro Matias down, eventually," Emanuel said. "It's just a question of time. But because he is sick, the nurse doesn't allow me to talk to him more than a few minutes at a time."

Dona Mafalda said, "We also spoke with the Barcoses. They received one letter from Manuel—a strange note, more like it. They showed it to us. It was from Brazil and very brief as if he had been in a hurry: '*I'm well, don't worry about me. I will write later.*' They received the letter only a few weeks ago. It's his handwriting, they say. Strange, don't you think, after so long? But, according to what people know of Manuel, it's like him to get distracted and forget everything else. His family says that the business of life always took a back seat with Manuel. The horse that was left at the port was Manuel's. He took it to the city and left it there to be picked up the following day. Saul didn't take anything—not the car, tractor, or horse and if he boarded that ship to Africa to be with his father, he must have walked or caught a ride to the city," Dona Mafalda concluded.

"But since we are coming clean, clarifying things..." Emanuel said slowly as if measuring every word, "Angela should know that you paid a substitute to take Lazarus' place in the military." Emanuel looked at Dom Carlos.

Angela was startled. She put a hand to her chest and looked fixedly at Dom Carlos. "Did you?" she asked astounded.

Dom Carlos held her gaze but said nothing.

"I thought that my prayers were answered," Angela said looking at him, not understanding how miracles happened.

"They were answered, after all... but that has nothing to do with the case, Detective," Dom Carlos said coolly.

"It tells me that you deeply cared for Angela and Lazarus, putting to rest the rumors that you wanted Lazarus gone because you were in love with Angela."

"I'm glad your Shakespearean conjectures were put to rest," Dom Carlos quipped.

Dona Mafalda put her hand over Dom Carlos' hand and squeezed it. She had tears in her eyes. Bending slightly toward him, she said in a whisper, "You're a good man, Dom Carlos."

Angela was very still looking at Dom Carlos, never loving anyone as much as she loved him at that moment.

"Well," Emanuel said, breaking the spell, "We're done for today." He rose and looked at Angela. "Are you coming home?" he asked.

"Not yet," she answered. "I have a few more details to iron out."

Dom Carlos rested a hand on Angela's shoulder.

Emanuel hesitated a second as if he was going to say something, but Dona Mafalda grasped his arm, opened the door, and escorted him out.

"We need to talk," Dom Carlos said as soon as the door closed. They sat next to each other. She was feeling like a shameless hypocrite. Lazarus was alive somewhere and she was feeling more guilty than happy. Her sense of loss was greater than when Lazarus disappeared because then she had believed that Lazarus had loved her without limits, and now she knew that something stronger than his love for her had moved him. She was disoriented. Instead of focusing on Lazarus being alive, she was thinking of her loss. She had thought that his love was infinite, constant, and never-ending.

Dom Carlos held her hand, and Angela looked up. She said, "Lazarus is alive and that changes things with us... doesn't it?"

He answered, "What does it change, Angela? We've never been anywhere, you and I. A few kisses... a promise to talk about love, about the phases of love... but nothing else."

"Make love to me then," she said quietly, looking into his eyes.

He blinked a few times, completely taken by surprise, "What?"

She shook her head and smiled sadly. "See Dom Carlos, how cagey you are?"

"That's the wrong answer," he said.

"I didn't realize that I was being tested," she said, pulling her hand away from his.

Dom Carlos bit his lip and Angela could tell that he wanted to say something but was holding back. She waited without moving her eyes from his face.

"Am I being tested?" she asked quietly.

Dom Carlos let out a frustrated expletive. "I won't make love to you to satisfy the reasons you have," he said. "You want to stick it to Lazarus because he left. You want to resist Emanuel because you're falling for him. You want to make love because you think I have a lover!" Now he was upset. "You also tend to go off on a tangent when you don't want to deal with unpleasant issues. You don't want to think about Lazarus, so you talk about making love. You feel that we're getting close, so you run to Emanuel. Grow up, damn it!" He crossed the room away from her. They were quiet for a long time. Angela was looking at his back and thinking that he didn't look like Lazarus at all. When had they become different?

He said, "You can be incredibly insightful, courageous, and good. But you can also be immature and irresponsible. Don't fool around with people's feelings."

"Look who's talking—the universally renowned heartbreaker!" she said with tears brimming in her eyes.

"Be careful, Angela," he warned.

Angela had never seen him like this—sensual and dangerous all at once—not the safe Dom Carlos that she knew. This was Zorro.

"People do different things when they're overwhelmed," she said, now less confident about the outcome of her outburst. "Ascendida goes into the garden and weeds, Madalena cries, Nascimento engages in voyeurism, Luciana sings love songs, and Regina cooks. What do you do when you're overwhelmed?"

"I deal with it. There's no point in avoiding your burden. It's yours and you deal with it!" he said, trying to contain the tone of his voice.

"How mature of you," she said evenly. "Am I a burden?"

"You are!" His voice was low but clear.

She flinched as if she'd been struck.

"Suppose that I said yes. What then? You would run away. You've been running away from me for a very long time."

11

Talking About Love

They were in the middle of the room, provoking each other.

Dom Carlos said, "When you think about Emanuel, you run away from me. When you kiss and hug him, you run away from me!"

Quietly she responded, "You do the same with Dona Gloria."

"Dona Gloria?" he asked in disbelief.

"You take advantage of that poor woman because she is in love with you. You hide behind her adoration. You put her up as your shield when you want to create illusions. You are such a pair! She is poised and perfect, like you. And it occurred to me that I could lose you to this woman with perfectly fitted silk dresses, fashionable shoes, and coifed hair. She may be the feminine version of you, with your tailored clothes and Italian shoes. You two are beautiful and elegant. Look at me, I'm an oaf."

Dom Carlos walked up to her and rested his hands on her shoulders. "You have no idea how far off you are," he said. "I'm not interested in Dona Gloria, and you are not an oaf. You're the most beautiful person I know."

You are not an oaf—this cannot be the beginning of a love confession, Angela thought.

"Now you're making fun of me," she said discouraged. "One thing I know is that I'm not beautiful. I'm many things, good things, but not beautiful."

"You are to me," he said, caressing her face. "And I'm so sorry I kissed you, I really am. This is precisely the thing I wanted to avoid—to confuse things. But when I kissed you, I didn't know that Lazarus was alive."

She looked up at him, dismayed. "You're sorry that you kissed me?"

"I am very sorry," he said and repressed a grin.

"Oh! That's a terrible thing to say," she said meekly. She couldn't stomach his jesting, not now when so many things had left her raw. She took a long breath. "I know that Lazarus is alive and I love you, I know that you're an insufferable man and I love you. You're a jester and a heretic and I love you... no matter what... I love you," she said in a whisper, his gaze on her face.

"Say it again," he murmured.

"You're an insufferable heretic," she repeated.

He laughed. "At last," he said, "What took you so long?"

He had loved her for so long. Now that everything had unfolded, he wondered how he had been able to endure it. No one would ever take her away from him. The detective could try, Lazarus could come back on a horse of fog like the lost king Dom Sebastião, but Angela had been his since the first moment he knew of her—like a curse that he couldn't break.

She opened her eyes, startled by the blaring, dissonant sounds of the city. She was disoriented for a few seconds.

He laughed.

"Have I been snoring again?" she asked, reaching up to touch his face.

"Yes, it's one of your many charms," he said and kissed her. There was no haste, no urgency. They would love each other with deliberate slowness, knowing that when they returned to Two Brooks, they wouldn't be able to act like lovers. They would be acting like their old selves—no love affair.

At least this was what Angela wanted. She needed to have everything cleared up with Lazarus. She had no patience for gossip—all that talk around one kernel of truth that in the end bore no resemblance to anything real.

"I have to tell you something about me," Dom Carlos said. He sounded nervous and when he raked his hair like that, it was a sign of distress.

Angela was curious—a revelation about Zorro? And he told her about Vivienne and the aborted divorce.

They looked at each other. The sounds of the city came in through the open veranda doors, so indifferent to their plight: Laughter, cars beeping, snippets of conversations, and the smell of coffee from the corner café.

"Was that the big secret?" she asked, coming out of her stupor.

"One of them," he answered.

"What are the others?" she asked.

"They have nothing to do with us."

She was looking at him so intently that he felt uncomfortable.

"Why should I believe you?" she asked.

"Because I never lied to you," he said, slightly offended.

"No, you just didn't say anything. Silence can be a lie."

The evening was tinted orange by the setting sun disappearing behind the cathedral. Angela touched his face and he held her hand to his lips. She was thinking about life and its little cruelties. She and Dom Carlos were both married to someone else.

"I love you," he said, caressing her face. "I love you so much that sometimes I think I can't breathe."

She rested her face on his chest. The sound of his heart was the most soothing sound she knew.

"Emanuel knew that you were married, didn't he?" she said.

"Hmm," he harrumphed. "I saw him kissing you yesterday," he said, pulling a strand of her hair. "You looked up at him and *bam*! He kissed you."

She laughed. "Did it make that noise, *bam*?"

"I'm serious, Hawk," he said, taking a handful of her hair and tugging, pulling her face to his.

"I will tell him, in my own time," she said. "Let's just enjoy it, just the two of us, without people looking in and making assumptions. It will be our secret for now, until all is cleared up," she closed her eyes and concentrated on his kisses. "It will be fun to sneak into your room and ravish you, soundlessly, in the middle of the night, while my lodgers sleep so innocently…"

He grinned. "Do you promise?"

Suddenly Dona Mafalda came to her mind. She held her breath.

"What is it?" he asked.

"Dona Mafalda," she said. "She is going to be devastated."

Dom Carlos groaned. "I'll tell her… when the time is right. We've talked about love before."

"Why were you talking about love with Dona Mafalda?" she asked, full of curiosity.

"I'll tell you, when you tell me the conversations you had with the detective… tit for tat?"

"There's nothing to tell," she said.

"In that case, same here," he murmured in her ear.

"How about Regina?" she insisted.

"Regina doesn't talk about love. Her thing is sex," he said.

"That day when I rescued you from her –"

"You didn't rescue me," he interrupted. "When you heard me scream, I had been stuffed with beads already. You were too late, Superwoman."

Dom Carlos locked the door of the apartment with a sigh. He wished they could stay there forever, away from all the calamities waiting to fall on their heads. They drove home after supper, quietly enjoying the silence and the breeze. Dom Carlos had his hand resting on Angela's thigh, rubbing it ever so softly, the radio was playing love songs, and the night was perfectly dark.

When they arrived at Two Brooks, the village seemed to be asleep—the streets, the houses, the gardens, except for the Music Club House and the Carpentry, where men were playing music and cards, their peals of laughter gradually fading away as Dom Carlos drove through the night.

They stopped outside the garden gate.

"Are you ready for this, Baby?" he asked.

Angela grimaced. No, she wasn't ready, but she had to face it. And she thought about the changes in her life lately, including the unsettling change from *Hawk* to *Baby*. Somehow it felt like she had lost status, that she had gone from a position of independence and strength to one of dependency and weakness. She much preferred *Hawk*.

As soon as they entered the garden gate, they sensed a thousand eyes upon them. A match was struck and a candle was lit, illuminating the welcoming party.

Emanuel. Dona Mafalda. The menagerie.

Viriato and Nixon came to them, sniffing and making friendly sounds. Dalia untucked her head from under a wing and stared at Angela. Hercules, coming out of the shadows, walked slowly up to Dom Carlos and looked him up. *Where have you been?* Hercules hissed.

But who was that shadow right next to Emanuel? The monsignor!

What was the monsignor doing at ten o'clock at night in a dark garden? This could only be bad news. She looked at him in open dismay.

"Monsignor, what happened?" She remembered the many times she'd seen him announce sorrow, humiliation, and disgrace. What was it now?

Dona Mafalda, sitting away from the monsignor, was unusually quiet. She smiled at Angela. Her smile was compassionate—this alone meant trouble—Dona Mafalda was rarely compassionate.

Dom Carlos placed a hand on Angela's shoulder.

"I bring great news, my girl," said the jubilant monsignor. "Lazarus is alive!"

Angela felt her head get very big and very light and then she fainted. Everybody screamed, including the monsignor. The menagerie made terrible sounds and Dona Mafalda and Emanuel tried to quell all that squealing and howling. The monsignor was shouting, trying to gain control of the situation.

"Dom Carlos," said the monsignor, "I need to talk to you. Let Detective Santos and Dona Mafalda attend to Angela. We need to talk."

But Dom Carlos was already carrying Angela's limp body in his arms, cursing the menagerie and the monsignor.

Emanuel went up after them. He said, "We'll take over. Please go and talk to the monsignor. It's important."

When Angela opened her eyes, Emanuel was kneeling by the side of her bed. He smiled and kissed her. She mentally counted—*bam, bam, bam*. "Everything is unraveling, isn't it?" she asked softly.

"Yes, that's what we wanted, isn't it?" he answered.

Dona Mafalda came into the room and sat next to Angela. She held her hand between hers, tapping it gently as she did to the children in school when they were upset. She said, "When we told Dona Amelia about our suspicions, that maybe Pedro had letters hidden in the house, she didn't rest. She turned the house upside-down and finally found a few letters in the barn by the seaplane. They were hidden behind the boulder in the corner of the barn, wrapped in an old shirt."

Angela closed her eyes with relief. "Where is he?"

"We don't know," Emanuel said. "He wrote from different ports. There aren't many letters—about three, but they all say basically the same thing—he doesn't know where he will end up. The last letter was from six months ago. Except for the letter he sent to Dom Carlos through the monsignor. That one is from a month ago."

"Such a long time," Angela murmured. "And why didn't he write to me?"

Dona Mafalda and Emanuel exchanged glances.

Dona Mafalda looked to Emanuel before saying, "Pedro Matias knows how to read. He has been faking illiteracy to serve his own perverted purposes. But, yes, he knows how to read and write. He answered Lazarus' letters."

"That devious bastard!" Angela whispered. "I had a suspicion...Tell me about the letters."

"Don't you want to read them for yourself?" Emanuel asked.

"Just... give me an idea. I don't want to be surprised again."

Emanuel started with a summary of events. "The first letter was sent three months after his disappearance. It was sent from Cape Verde. He told his father that he was going to follow his advice and go away for good. He never mentioned the reason. He spoke to his father as if his father was controlling the situation. He spoke about you and how he wanted his father to leave you alone, as part of the deal for him to stay away. The second letter came five months later. He asked his father to write to an address in North Africa. It was a brief letter, saying that he would be in Africa for a few months. The third and last letter was sent six months ago from Angola. Pedro Matias wrote to him about the monsignor stirring up trouble and asking for an investigation. Lazarus alluded to that in his response, and he expressed his doubts if he had done the right thing, that *they* should have faced the consequences. Who was he referring to when he wrote, *they*? Was he talking about his father and himself or about Saul and Manuel, or all four of them? It isn't clear. But he never talks about the events that made him leave, only the terrible consequence of leaving you."

There was a heavy pause. Emanuel and Dona Mafalda glanced at each other. Angela sensed there was more. She waited, looking expectantly at both of them.

Emanuel held her hand and said, "Lazarus alluded in his last letter to your love affair with Dom Carlos. Pedro Matias said something, either to be vicious or to serve some sick purpose. Either way, it backfired. I don't think that Pedro Matias wanted the monsignor to know. I suppose it is about this that the monsignor wants to talk with Dom Carlos. The letter to Dom Carlos was about that."

Angela colored deeply. She felt as if she had been fried, she was so red and hot. She closed her eyes, not wanting to look at either Emanuel or Dona Mafalda.

"We know it's not true, my dear," Dona Mafalda said. "We know you're not lovers."

"As for Pedro, the man lost his tongue," Emanuel said. "The monsignor berated him to no end, but he didn't open his mouth, He was as quiet as a sepulcher." He continued, "Lazarus' ship did go to South Africa and on to Australia. However, Lazarus might have stayed in Angola and later boarded a ship to South America. We don't know. In a work for passage arrangement, he probably would have gone undocumented."

"Can't you make that bastard talk?" Angela asked, feeling that old familiar anger well up from her belly to her throat.

"Even if he does… He can always say that he helped his son leave an unfaithful wife," Emanuel said, not revealing to Angela that Pedro was already using that line.

When the monsignor left, the four of them—Emanuel, Dom Carlos, Angela, and Dona Mafalda—remained at the kitchen table. The familiar smells of soup and bread were so reassuring. The menagerie was in the chimney room, exhausted by the events, except for Hercules who was nowhere to be found. Dona Mafalda lit two lamps and placed them both next to Dom Carlos, who was going to read the letter to Angela.

"First, let me read you the letter that Lazarus sent me. I'm assuming that you've been told the rest?" Dom Carlos said, looking at Angela and unfolding the letter.

> *Dear friend,*
>   *So many things happened for me to be here writing this. I don't even know if I should write this letter, but my father told me that an investigation is going on about my disappearance and that you and Angela are being implicated because you are lovers. True or not, it doesn't really matter. Angela always deserved a better man than I was. She is strong and good. She was my angel, but you are far better suited for her than I am. I am sending this letter to the monsignor because he will know what to do. I don't want people to think that Angela is responsible for my disappearance because she was in love with you. Everything that happened to me was of my own doing. Saul and Manuel are also gone. My father has nothing to do with this other than to try to help me. Some things are irreversible and there is no point talking about them. I am gone for good, and the others are as well. I really died, as sure as if I had drowned. Please look after Angela.*
>   *Thank you for being so good to us. I will always remember and love you.*
>
> *Lazarus.*

Dom Carlos placed the letter on the table. Angela wept silently, her tears falling on her linen blouse and spreading a wet stain of sorrow. Emanuel and Dona Mafalda felt intrusive and useless.

"I'm so sorry," Dom Carlos murmured.

"I will talk to Saul's mother again," Emanuel said quietly, "I'm curious about the letter Lazarus sent to the monsignor as a *confession,* and as such the monsignor couldn't reveal its contents… but again, according to the monsignor, there was nothing in that letter that could clarify anything."

"We should go to bed," Dona Mafalda said, completely drained.

"Are you okay, Angela?" Emanuel asked.

"Yes, I am." She gave him a brief smile and thought, *bam*!

Lucas had been thinking about Dona Mafalda since that humiliating day in the city. But what could he tell her? What kind of excuse could he make? Not only didn't be have an excuse, but he was dying of shame. He should at least apologize.

That morning, bright and glorious in its clear sun and light air, Lucas set out to Angela's home to apologize to Dona Mafalda. He would wait for her all day if need be, but today would be the day.

He knocked and Rosa answered. He asked for Dona Mafalda, who was having breakfast, and Rosa went to get her.

When Rosa gave Dona Mafalda the message, she turned red and then pale and said nothing. What did he want now? Peel her like a banana in the middle of the garden and run home? No, she wasn't going out to see him.

Lucas waited in the garden for a long while. At last, Rosa emerged from the house and sadly shook her head. "No, she doesn't wish to see you."

He left, thinking that he didn't deserve any better treatment. She should've come out and beat the hell out of him. That's what she should've done.

If they were not so worried about the recent events, they would have known that something was afoot with young Lucas and Dona Mafalda, but everyone was quiet and withdrawn and there was sadness all around. They had no attention for romance or foolishness.

Rosa was serving breakfast, surveying the mournful table. "Dear Jesus," Rosa said with some frustration, "at least we know that Lazarus and Manuel are alive. Why the long faces?"

Emanuel looked up at her and thought that they could be diverted and enlivened by a good piece of gossip. "Anything new, Rosa?" he asked and listened to Rosa's enthusiastic narration—something to do with the bishop getting an electric shock. The bishop wasn't used to microphones and confused the microphone with the holy water sprinkler.

"As soon as he plunged the microphone in the holy water, the sacristan, who was holding the holy water silver bowl, flew across the cathedral like a giant bat, and the bishop was thrown against the altar. There were terrible screams. The bishop had his dress over his head and people didn't know if he was dead or alive. It was terrible!" Rosa scanned her audience. No one had shown much interest in the bishop's near electrocution or the sacristan's flight across the church. If this didn't make them laugh, then they might as well die because nothing else would ever move them. Rosa harrumphed and left the room.

Emanuel got up and walked out to the garden. He looked up at the sky. It was blue and beautiful, but he couldn't find any joy. He ached.

"Are you all right, Emanuel?" Dona Mafalda asked softly.

"Yes," he lied. He sat on a bench and she sat next to him.

"You are in love with her, aren't you?"

His silence was more eloquent than any answer he could give.

"I'm sorry that you're hurting," she said, lightly touching his arm.

"You also have been in love with Dom Carlos for a very long time, haven't you?" he offered, looking at her with kindness.

Her first thought was to deny it. But she was tired of self-denial and denial to others. "Yes, I fell for him the first moment I saw him. And I told him—a long time ago. I don't think he took me seriously, or he is too much of a gentleman and made me forget that I was once brazen enough to confess my love to a man." She was quiet for a long moment. Then she added, "It's amazing the things we do when we are in a foreign land... this place is foreign, isn't it?" She laughed a sad, short laugh.

"But you have Lucas. I have no one," Emanuel reasoned.

Dona Mafalda blushed. She put her hand to her chest. "Oh, dear," she said.

Emanuel frowned confused and waited for an explanation.

"It was a disaster!" she mumbled.

How could she say, *he peeled me like a banana and left me there with no idea what to do, and... cried.* She sighed and resigned herself to be courageous to the end. What did she have to lose? She was so far away from home with the self-imposed responsibility to be a paragon of virtue, and why? Who had demanded such sacrifices of her? As sad as it sounded, this police investigator was maybe the only friend she had in this place... maybe Angela was also her friend, but the girl was so young and volatile...

Emanuel waited and finally she told him in a monotone voice, trying to keep out any inflection that could highlight her embarrassment. She expected Emanuel to laugh, but he didn't. He placed his arm around her shoulders and said, "I'm so sorry."

She looked up with a grateful smile. She was in so much need of friendship, of another person to look at her and listen without judgement. She never thought it would be a man, a policeman, and worse yet, a man purported to be a gypsy, but there he was—her gypsy friend, kind and empathetic. She said in a quiet voice, "If a man needs experience, he can get it with another woman, at a brothel. It's acceptable and even recommended. But a woman... Is she supposed to save all that lack of experience as a gift to a man? It makes no sense. I think this is the only part of one's life where lack of experience is valued."

"These societal rules were created by men," he said.

"And women, like idiots, follow," she answered with more sadness than resentment. "And after a certain age, to be a virgin is a defect, not a virtue and people perceive you either with suspicion or pity."

Emanuel didn't need to comment. If she had never been kissed, she certainly never had had sex. He felt sorry for this pompous, self-righteous woman.

"I must sound too ridiculous, if not outright pathetic," she added.

"Not at all," he hurried to say, "Women wait for a man to come along and be their... everything. There's quite a lot to ask of a man, you know. I have a friend who was terrified of having sex with a virgin. He heard about the pain and the blood, and some stories about the screaming and having to go to the doctor to have the hymen surgically removed... He wanted nothing to do with a virgin."

This struck Dona Mafalda as kind of funny. Women were keeping their virginity as a gift and some men were afraid of it. She laughed—a short, utterly amused laugh. She laughed again and Emanuel joined her.

When they stopped laughing, Emanuel said, "I... could teach you."

She took in a sharp breath. "That wouldn't be proper," she said.

"No, that wouldn't," he answered. "But men also made that rule. They go and learn from a prostitute, and that is proper, but a woman can't learn with a friend."

"Indeed, that doesn't sound fair," she said pensively.

"Sex also complicates relationships," he said.

"I don't want to lose you as a friend," Dona Mafalda hurried to add.

"I don't want to lose you as a friend either. But if I... teach you, there will be no romantic expectations. We are both in love with someone else," he reasoned.

"I lack the courage," she said quietly. "I wish I was this bold woman who didn't care about these social norms... but I'm not. I'm terribly conservative, I'm afraid." It sounded like an apology.

Emanuel said, "You have to live by your principles. Sex is for one to rejoice in, not for one to feel guilty about... although I'm sure the monsignor would say otherwise." He chuckled.

She looked at him appreciatively, and they fell into a reassuring silence.

"He's married, you know," he said softly. "I'm telling you this as a friend. Please don't share it." Emanuel feared he was becoming a gossip just like the villagers.

Dona Mafalda jumped. "Who's married?" she shrieked.

"Dom Carlos, in France. He thought he was divorced."

"Does Angela know?" Her voice had a faint ring of joy.

"She didn't. I don't know if she does now."

"Now I understand that whole farce at his apartment the other day, with Dona Gloria." Dona Mafalda was feeling betrayed, but she was not sure by whom. "He lied to those poor women: Dona Gloria, Angela, and God knows who else!" she said.

"Something like that... lied or didn't clarify the truth, which ends up being the same thing."

Dona Mafalda's face fell into a mask of gloom. "How did Angela get under your skin?"

Emanuel pondered. Then he said, "I don't even know when. I think it was in the very first hours of meeting her. She left something open in me, like a wound, and I think that's how she got in."

"You make her sound like a virus or infection. She did the same to Dom Carlos," Dona Mafalda said softly. "He met her once and he came looking for her the next day, although some say that he visited the monsignor's house even before he met Angela—so the story is a bit shaky."

Emanuel thought about that cloudy connection between Dom Carlos and the monsignor. It surfaced every so often.

Lucas had made a decision. He was going to learn all there was to learn about lovemaking. He would never again feel so out of sorts that he would start crying in front of a woman he wanted to have sex with. He always cried when he felt overwhelmed, but he never thought this would happen when he was with a woman. He was going to talk to Regina Sales and she would help him. It didn't take long before Lucas knocked at Regina's door. When Regina undressed, Lucas was mesmerized to notice the huge difference between Regina and Dona Mafalda. Dona Mafalda was small, round, perky, and rosy. Regina was big, saggy, and dark. Her breasts bounced low around her waist. Dona Mafalda was light-skinned with very fine and fuzzy hair, like a peach. Regina had dark hair all over—on her legs, under her arms, between her legs. He was fascinated by Regina's rawness.

And then he felt it again—the need to cry. And he did.

Regina was taken aback and sat quietly on a chair waiting for something to happen. But Lucas continued to weep. Regina had seen many unexperienced men react in many different ways to the prospect of sex for the first time, but she couldn't remember anyone crying.

He explained to Regina his predicament. She fastened her eyes on his swollen lips and strong erection.

For an entire month, Lucas went to Regina every day. He was a dedicated student and, consequently, she produced the most attentive and creative lover on the whole island. The problem was the crying. She couldn't wean him from that. He cried the hardest when she instructed him to hold his orgasm. With this request, Lucas disintegrated in tears but obeyed. He surrendered to Regina. Anything she wanted to do, he let her do it. Anything she had to teach, he wanted to learn.

Feeling completely prepared, he would request another meeting with Dona Mafalda. He was convinced that he wouldn't be the only one crying. Dona Mafalda was in for a big surprise.

Dona Mafalda, in turn, had accepted Emanuel's offer to teach her the techniques of lovemaking. When Dona Mafalda made this decision, she waited for him to go into his office, at night, as he always did. Everyone was in bed, Rosa had gone home, and Emanuel was doing work in the woodshop.

She knocked at the door and without waiting for the answer came in. He was surprised to see her.

"I accept," she said breathlessly.

"What?" he asked confused.

"Your offer to teach me how to make love."

He was speechless. He had said that quite a while back. He thought she decided to decline his offer owing to her principles, and he had been relieved because he had volunteered his services in a capricious moment of complete and foolish generosity. He shouldn't have offered, and she had been wise enough to pass it up.

He sat down on Isaac Lima's coffin and motioned for her to sit too. Dona Mafalda was not Regina Sales. He should have been more careful with his sexual liberties.

"You can't do it, can you?" she said smiling sadly. "Me neither, it would be too strange."

"I was caught by surprise," he explained. "We can try…" He took a deep breath.

"Okay," she murmured and waited for instructions.

The first day of school was truly special for Dona Mafalda, but this morning she looked particularly luminous. She winked at Emanuel who was thinking about last night.

He thoroughly enjoyed having sex with Dona Mafalda. He still could hear her gasp of surprise and then delight. He grinned remembering their dialogue about repeating lessons.

"You never repeated a lesson, Dona Mafalda?" he had asked.

"Many times," she answered demurely, not sure if he was serious.

"Good," he said. "Let's do it again."

"Okay," she said.

Emanuel came out of his reverie when Angela touched his shoulder and said, "You're looking very chipper this morning. Whatever thoughts you're having, they must be exceedingly pleasant."

He smiled at Angela and winked at Dona Mafalda.

Dona Mafalda blushed and concentrated on that sweet ache at the bottom of her belly. She had never felt anything so special. How special it would have been if it was Dom Carlos making love to her, or if she was in love with Emanuel? Sex was such a wondrous, marvelous thing.

Dom Carlos came in and Rosa winked at him.

"Why are you winking at me?" Dom Carlos asked.

"I don't know," Rosa answered, "everybody seems to be doing it this morning."

12

The Lessons

September came with brisk mornings and sunny afternoons.

Emanuel had spoken often with the monsignor about the missing men, but there had been no new developments or breaks. Carlota Amora hadn't given any signs that her son had written from anywhere and Madalena was slowly accepting Saul's absence. The Barcos family was hoping for Manuel to write again. Assured that their son was alive and well, all they needed was just another letter. And Angela was coming back to her own self, accepting that Lazarus was gone and plunging into her work, managing her businesses, helping with village affairs, and working with the monsignor on the church's festivities. Pedro Matias was up and about. He no longer had that spring in his step and the hair on the top of his head didn't grow back, but he was doing his work, going to the Carpentry and to the Music Club House and occasionally to Regina Sales. He continued to claim that Angela and Madalena were the reason why Saul and Lazarus had left. Dona Amelia was now living for the arrival of the mailman. She waited for him, going from window to window as if looking at the street from a different angle would miraculously produce a letter. She prepared the mailman's favorite foods as if special care would make him bring news from Lazarus.

The village fell back on the most simplistic, moral-laden explanations of the events: Madalena betrayed Saul and he left, or he was looking for his father who, after all, didn't die as they thought, and was somewhere in Africa looking for gold.

Lazarus left because Angela fell in love with Dom Carlos, and Lazarus being weak and childish couldn't compete. But Dom Carlos didn't seem in love with Angela. He made himself scarce for days at a time. The rumor was that he had a lover in the city and the villagers had seen him, many times entertaining Dona Gloria—having lunch or dinner or going to the cinema with that beautiful woman.

At home, Dom Carlos became bold and went often to Angela's room.

Quietly smiling at her horrified face, he was deliberately slow and teasing in his lovemaking. He enjoyed the duplicity of playing the innocuous businessman and Zorro, the outlaw, stealing around in the darkest hours of the night.

"Not a sound," he would whisper in Angela's ear, while they listened to Dona Mafalda's chatter outside the door. He was possessed by Zorro and pushed his game to the brink of disaster by announcing an absence of two or three days, but coming back in the middle of the night, sneaking into Angela's bed.

Angela had lost. She lost Lazarus and Dom Carlos. "It served her right for betraying her husband!" was the opinion of the day. "And now the detective is in love with her," the whispers ran. The village muckrakers had a field day: "That girl is a witch, and then she ruins every man she touches."

After dinner, Angela went to meet with the Sacristy.

As a result of Nascimento's penance working in the orphanage, she and Jaime were going to adopt a little girl from the orphanage. Her name was Manuela.

Manuela had the heart of a warrior who took life as a ground that had to be fought for and won each day. Life was a proposition that couldn't be trusted and consequently, Manuela never smiled. She had become hypervigilant to threats—always prepared to be betrayed. So when Nascimento took a special interest in her, Manuela was suspicious. Something good seemed to be happening and good didn't happen often. She knew sorrow, loss, and mayhem, but not joy, peace, and security.

Now Nascimento promised herself to abandon her nocturnal outings spying on her neighbors. She needed to be a good example for her new daughter. The promise made, Nascimento decided to take one last eavesdropping expedition before Manuela came home.

And tonight she had a marvelous story to tell the Sacristy about Dona Mafalda and Detective Santos having sex on a coffin.

"No!" the other women said in unison.

"They didn't…," Angela started and trailed off. She thought Emanuel was in love with her and here he was riding Dona Mafalda. Angela recalled the time when she surprised her parents in the act and her father had told her that his mother was teaching him how to ride a bicycle.

Nascimento said, "Yes, they did. I didn't have high expectations looking in on the detective, but who do I see coming to the woodshop? Dona Mafalda. I couldn't resist. What would she have to say to him at midnight that she couldn't say in the light of day? I stepped onto the bench right under the window. The detective had an oil lamp lit in the back of the woodshop so they couldn't see me. They talked for a little while and then he started to kiss Dona Mafalda... and giving her instructions."

They gasped and Angela said, "No, not Dona Mafalda."

"Oh yes, it was Dona Mafalda. She had her back to the window, the detective was facing it, and he closed his eyes and opened his mouth holding his breath. He caressed her head and said something. He had his hand up her dress for a long time while the poor thing moaned like an owl. He pulled her dress up, almost over her face, and pulled her underwear down... pink lace. And he... he pulled his pants down and rammed into her, right there on top of Isaac Lima's coffin. She let out a scream, and he caressed her face, kissed her softly, like a lover, but didn't ease up on her, thrusting his hips, ramming that marvelous thing into her. She looked like a ripe fig, round, and melting. She was very proper, biting her hand to not scream. Suddenly, she gives this terrible shriek and bends her back as if she was possessed. Her legs go up in the air and around the detective's hips. I didn't expect that, and I fell off the bench on top of your rose bushes. But they didn't hear me. The detective was so engrossed in giving it to Dona Mafalda... that when I looked in again, he was saying something... I couldn't hear it because he was saying it with clenched teeth and climaxing." Nascimento clenched her teeth and tried to demonstrate—only succeeding in looking epileptic.

Everyone was quiet.

Angela felt utterly despicable. She was jealous. She was jealous, after she stole Dom Carlos' heart, became his lover, knowing that Dona Mafalda was deeply in love with him, and now she didn't want Emanuel to make love to anyone.

"Hey," Nascimento said, poking Angela. "This is funny and you're not laughing. You're jealous!"

Angela snapped, "I'm not jealous! I'm just concerned. I like Dona Mafalda."

"So does the detective," Nascimento said. "He was really sweet to her, explaining something... She shook her head and he started all over again. I've seen people have orgasms, but never a polite orgasm like Dona Mafalda's."

"That's a stupid thing to say!" Angela said savagely, "Orgasms cannot be polite!"

"Well, Dona Mafalda can have them." Nascimento insisted. "It must be her royal blood. She bit her hand, arched her back, curled her legs around his hips, and pinned him to her, but no screaming this time. Very polite."

The women were laughing about polite orgasms, except Angela.

Oh, she was a deceitful one! For shame! Madalena thought.

"Angela," Nascimento said, giving her a stone-cold stare, "Explain yourself!"

Angela told them about Dom Carlos.

"I'm going to sneak up on you as I did with Dona Mafalda and compare politeness…," Nascimento said.

"Well, everybody is saying that Lazarus left because you were having an affair with Dom Carlos," Madalena said.

"People believe what they want," Angela snapped.

"Rosa told me that Emanuel kissed you. I didn't believe her. What is going on with you, girl, if you are sleeping with Dom Carlos?" Ascendida asked accusingly.

"It started in the hospital when he got hurt. First, it was almost a joke. I kissed him because the nurse thought I was his wife… And every so often he kisses me and tells me that he is waiting for my *fall*."

Ascendida was full of sarcasm. "Your fall? You're married still, you're sleeping with Dom Carlos, who is also married, you lust over a police investigator from the motherland, and you think you didn't fall yet?" Angela's friends were looking incredulously at her as if seeing her for the first time.

She said, "Dom Carlos is going to France. He announced it during dinner. I was surprised, even Nixon was surprised. Everyone thinks that he is going to France to get a divorce so he can marry the pretty woman in the city, Dona Gloria. Little do they know that he wants a divorce to marry me."

"What about the church? Lazarus is alive and Dom Carlos is married. You will be excommunicated and will burn in hell when you die!" Madalena accused with alarm.

Nascimento was imagining the monsignor grabbing Angela by the neck and kicking her out of the church door as if she was a soccer ball booted out by a goalkeeper.

Every day for two weeks the villagers harvested the grapes. They helped each other and, at the end of the day, celebrated with singing circles, a good meal, and sweet wine. The wine was now in the big wooden vats, and the women and children who stomped the grapes to extract the precious juices walked with stained feet and legs, like branded creatures, until November.

Angela was walking home under a beautiful September night, after helping Ascendida and after having too much wine. She was thinking about broken hearts.

Poor Olivia and Samuel, she thought. Joaquim Linos, Olivia's boyfriend, came back from Canada, full of rings, hats, and new clothes and had asked someone else to marry him—he had asked Lucia. Lucia, who had been in love with Samuel all her life, didn't resist and said yes because she wanted to go away to a clean, shining, faraway place. Samuel knew that Canada was stronger than love and he sat on the wall of the threshing circle, dignified and sad, eating figs to appease his sorrow, while Joaquim Linos and Lucia went round and round in the singing circles, singing "The Thief in the Middle":

> *It was midnight*
> *When the middle thief came*
> *He knocked three times*
> *On the middle door pane…*

Emanuel sat next to Olivia and said softly, "I broke your eyeglasses when I fell on you at the bullfight, didn't I?" And he took her in his arms and danced like a lover, inside of the singing circle. She smelled of fresh pine needles, grapes, and tears; there was a sadness about her, like a fog that lingered, like the island when assaulted by the white salty veil.

Now walking home, Angela thought of broken hearts and balance. She felt wholly out of balance with herself as if she was pitching wildly in a storm-tossed sea. Olivia had made her think of greed—the greed of the heart. She loved Dom Carlos but thought of Lazarus with his seductive beauty and innocence. She thought of Emanuel's soft mouth on hers, his unpredictable and stolen kisses. She felt indecent and greedy.

Indecent and greedy, she repeated to herself before she entered the woodshop. The light of the Petromax lamp blinded her for a second, and Emanuel stood up, pleasantly surprised with her visit.

"I was hoping that you were up. I wanted to talk to you," she said.

"Me too. I needed to ask you something," Emanuel said.

While Emanuel got something out of a drawer, Angela started to think about him and Dona Mafalda. She wanted to laugh and, yet, there was nothing funny about anything. What would he say if she said, "Let me see if you have a marvelous thing?"

"This," he said showing her a balance book with the expenses for the house: wood, grain, nails, cement, etc.

"What about it? she asked.

"Look at the date. This is the date around when Manuel and Saul disappeared."

She looked to where he was pointing. It was for cement—nothing strange about cement.

"What were the improvements around the house that needed cement?" he asked.

She thought about it. She couldn't think of any. She frowned.

"Think about it. This was around Christmas. Not really a time when people make improvements with cement. You would have noticed if Lazarus had."

"I… can't think of anything, but if I do, I'll let you know," she said.

Emanuel put the book away, crossed his arms, and asked, "And you? Why do you want to see me?" He noticed her fidgeting with her necklace—a sure sign of nervousness. He waited.

"I'm going to marry Dom Carlos," she blurted out.

"What?" he asked in disbelief.

"We're engaged," she said.

"Since when?" he asked in the same confused tone.

"No one knows yet, because of the latest events. Everything happened at once," she said, evading his eyes.

Emanuel paled, then said, "I thought you were falling for me…"

Angela lowered her eyes, took a deep breath, and said, "I did fall for you. I, who didn't believe in *falling*." Her voice had a ring of panic. She thought she knew everything about herself, and here she was confused and ashamed about her divided love. How could she be confused about love? "I love Dom Carlos in a way I can't explain," she concluded.

"Because he looks like Lazarus," Emanuel said.

"No!" she denied defensively. "He's nothing like Lazarus. If you had met Lazarus, you wouldn't say that."

Emanuel didn't insist. He knew what people said, that Dom Carlos and Lazarus looked like brothers, even in temperament, only their fates were different.

"I only told you and the Sacristy," she said after a long pause.

"Why the courtesy?" he asked dryly.

"Because you can't kiss me anymore. It's not fair to either of us and much less to Dom Carlos," she reasoned.

"Oh! God forbid if we are unfair to Dom Carlos!" He said, throwing his hands up in the air in a theatrical gesture. He stormed to the back of the woodshop and stared at her waiting for a better answer.

"I'm sorry. I know I am hurting you..." she murmured.

"He's married already," he said.

"I know, he told me."

"I love you," he said. "I should have told you sooner, but there were so many things going on."

"I know you do. You've told me every time we kissed. But I also love Dom Carlos and I have to make a choice."

She lowered her eyes, not able to absorb Emanuel's disappointment.

"You also love Dom Carlos..." Emanuel repeated slowly. "*Also* implies that you love me too."

"Yes, I love you too," she snapped. It sounded more like a scolding than a profession of love. She turned around to leave, stopped, and said with her back to him, "I don't know if I love him more, but I've loved him the longest." She imagined Dom Carlos, in bed fast asleep with a book opened on his lap, while she was in the woodshop exchanging love confessions with Emanuel. "I want us to be all right, Emanuel. Everything became so tangled. I don't know how to deal with complicated... I've been always so focused on one thing, so sure about my decisions and feelings, and here I am... divided. Forgive me."

"I don't know. I don't know if I can," he answered quietly.

As soon as Angela left, he too went home, quickly climbed the stairs, closed his door, and got into bed. He couldn't remember being as frustrated as he was now.

His cases had died with a whimper instead of a brilliant finale. The case of the three disappeared men had been more or less explained, where his superior urged him to close it. The Night Justice case had stalled out because the monsignor suddenly became silent and unhelpful and asked the chief to stop his pursuit into a matter that could never be resolved. His other inquiries had been negligible—a few Night Justice incidents, but nothing really serious. He couldn't sleep. He got up and went out onto the landing and knocked softly on Dona Mafalda's door. There was silence. He knocked again and her door opened a crack. She peered out with a sleepy face.

"Emanuel?" she said. She turned around to light a lamp.

"May I come in?" he asked. Now that she stepped aside to let him in, he didn't know what to do with her questioning gaze. She had hair rollers on the top of her head, the side of her face had the imprint of the pillow, and her nightgown was slightly askew, allowing the view of a creamy clavicle.

"I can't sleep," he said. "I'm too charged, too frustrated."

"Can I help?" she asked. She was thinking along the lines of having tea, some good conversation, a stroll in the garden, looking for clues in his cases, playing a little music on her Victrola. She put on a robe and started to take off the rollers.

"Can we have sex?" he asked.

She blushed deeply and let her arms down, leaving the curlers in place. She felt awkward. "Now?" she asked.

"Please," he said.

"But..." she started to meekly object.

"Please," he said again.

"Okay," she murmured but didn't move.

He turned her around swiftly and said out of breath, "On your hands and knees."

She climbed on the bed with Emanuel behind her, lifting her nightgown and exposing her buttocks, spreading her legs apart, and holding her thighs against him, as if afraid she was going to flee.

He fumbled with his pajamas.

She felt ridiculous, not sure if she should look back or help him with the pajamas... He swiftly entered her, as if it was an emergency. His thrusts were so sharp that her rollers hit the headboard, making a funny scratching sound. She felt exposed, silly, swaying back and forth with the impact of his thrusts. Not in a million years would she had ever thought she would be in this strange village having intercourse on her hand and knees with a gypsy. She heard him utter the same thing as before, as he climaxed. And this time, there was no mistake—he was saying Angela's name.

She felt unsettled, unloved, and sad.

After he was done, he kissed her brow tenderly and said, "Thank you."

The following morning during breakfast Angela announced that Dom Carlos was going to France at the end of the week.

"Business, Dom Carlos?" Dona Mafalda asked.

"No, Dona Mafalda, personal." He looked at her for a second and said, "Can I talk to you this morning?"

Dona Mafalda was curious about his request and right after breakfast they went into her room, like old times, she turned on the radio and he sat across from her.

"Remember our secret?" he asked.

"Yes, that you were in love with someone…"

"Do you know now who she is?" he asked quietly.

"Well… it's Angela. However lately, you've been comingling with that pompous woman, Dona Gloria, so I don't know what to think."

"It is Angela, it has always been Angela. Dona Gloria knows that. And no, I have no romantic involvement with Dona Gloria, although we spend time together when I'm in the city. She enjoys my company and I need the distraction and the illusion. I wanted to let you know before my engagement with Angela became public," he said.

"Dom Carlos, you don't owe me anything!" Dona Mafalda said quite flustered.

"Of course I do! You were the first person I confessed to that I was in love. And you've been my friend. Sometimes I haven't deserved it, but you have been there for me and Angela."

"Do you also know that Emanuel is in love with her?" she asked, searching his face.

"Boy! How can I not?" he said throwing his hands up in exasperation. "And she loves him too," he said in a much quieter tone. "The difference is that we've loved each other for a very long time, in different ways—love in metamorphosis, but love nonetheless."

"How silly to believe that familiarity breeds contempt," Dona Mafalda murmured. She felt her heart break because this was the day she had feared for so long. She became teary. That mourning fado made it worse—she turned off the music. "Be happy, Dom Carlos, I'm glad that it is Angela. She is the closest friend I have."

He got up and kissed her brow. "Now I have to let the others know— Angela's parents, Rosa, Regina, the monsignor…" His voice trailed off with the unpleasant prospect of having to explain and defend his love for Angela.

When Angela told her parents, they shook their heads in bewilderment.

"What about the church?" her father asked.

"I can't receive the Eucharist… but I can go to church," she said dispiritedly.

The following morning, during breakfast, Dom Carlos told Rosa and Emanuel. Someone dropped something.

"Is this a joke?" Emanuel asked.

"No, no joke," Dom Carlos stated simply. "I'll stay in France for as long as it takes to get that divorce, but when I come back I'll be a free man, and we'll marry."

He got up, went around the table, and lifted Angela's face to him. "You will marry me, Angela, won't you?"

She smiled and felt her throat tighten with the emotion, "Yes, I will."

"We are going to talk to the monsignor," Dom Carlos said.

"You should sell tickets for that," Emanuel said bitterly. It seemed that he had been holding his breath since Dom Carlos announced his engagement with Angela.

"Oh, dear!" Dona Mafalda said anxiously. "He's going to slap you again, Angela."

"I don't think so," Dom Carlos said, sounding quite calm. "And if he does, I'll shove this miserable village down his throat. This is a dreadful place, judgmental and vindictive. Maybe he will choke or die poisoned." He left the room and Angela followed him, resigned to announcing their intentions to a foiled, irate monsignor.

The end of the morning was such a special time of day—calm and promising many more hours of light, unlike the quiet, fading light of evening.

Dom Carlos and Angela walked slowly up the village, enjoying the calm before the storm. When they reached the monsignor's house, Dom Carlos stopped at the door before knocking. He looked at Angela. She was pale and her heart was racing.

"Don't be afraid," he said and knocked.

When the monsignor opened the door, he already knew. They came in and sat staring at each other.

"I suppose you came here to deny the rumors," the monsignor said coldly.

"What rumors?" Dom Carlos asked.

"That the two of you are together," he said impatiently

"No," Dom Carlos said. "That's not why we are here."

The monsignor and Angela looked at him. He was enjoying himself. He had that promise of a grin on his face. "We came here to let you know that we are getting married," he said evenly.

The monsignor jumped back in his seat, knocking into the chair behind him. Then he turned on Dom Carlos and Angela. "You can't do that. You can't marry because you are married, *already*!" he yelled.

"No, Angela is a widow, and I will be a divorced man in a few months."

"You can't marry in the church, man. You can't marry in the church even if Angela is considered a widow! And I say *considered* because we know that Lazarus is alive."

"He is? Who says? After all, he wrote a letter to me, though I can't put my hands on it. And a letter to you, which was a confession. And you can't share confessions, can you?"

"No, but I can be a witness to your letter!" the monsignor said with a great deal of satisfaction. "So, you see, you can't get married. The church will not allow it!" The monsignor glared at him.

"And who needs the church to get married?" Dom Carlos asked. "We'll go to France or England and leave this black hole."

The monsignor turned purple and advanced on Dom Carlos, who said, "This would be the time that, if I was a woman, you would slap me. Right? Or hit me with a missal?"

"You bastard!" the monsignor said, raked with ire.

"That has been established already, Monsignor," Dom Carlos said with such loathing that Angela recoiled. "Like father, like son!"

She was pale. She was looking at these two men locked in combat that seemed way out of proportion with their difference of opinion about where they could get married. She guessed this was an inconclusive battle in a costly, long-drawn-out war.

"Oh, dear God!" Emanuel said in a whisper. He had entered the monsignor's house while no one was tending the door. He had a scheduled meeting with the monsignor, who was obviously occupied berating Dom Carlos and Angela.

Angela got up and looked down the hallway. Emanuel was leaning against the wall as if waiting for her. She walked quickly to him. "Come, I think they're going to have a fistfight!" she said with urgency.

He shook his head. "I don't think so. They hurt each other in different ways."

Their furious voices carried down the hallway.

"You, Monsignor. You are a hypocrite! You have no moral authority to tell people how to love or deal with the ones they love."

"I paid for my sins! I am exiled on this godforsaken island and have been a servant of God ever since!"

"Your sins!" Dom Carlos laughed. "I guess you can't get rid of them, can you? Because if you could, I wouldn't be here making your phony sainthood a living hell!"

The monsignor sat with a thump and lowered his head. He was like a deflated nightmare, reduced to nothing. "I have been good for these people. And I love them. My past mistakes are mine to expiate, but I have been a servant of God."

"You aren't even remorseful," Dom Carlos uttered sadly. "You are just concerned about balancing your ledger just in case your promised chair in heaven was in question. You disgust me."

"And you want to punish me by ruining Angela. Yes, you will ruin her! Because she is deeply religious and you'll force her to live outside of the church. And you'll ruin her because she won't be happy! If you love her, you wouldn't ask her to make that sacrifice!"

Angela was about to enter the fray and plead her case when Emanuel grabbed her by the arm and held her next to him. He shook his head and said, "Let them sort this out. This isn't about you. You're just a tool." *A knife, a gun, a rock,* he thought.

They heard Dom Carlos threaten, "I'm leaving for France tomorrow. But I will be back for Christmas. And you, you leave Angela alone. If you so much as hit her, yell at her, do anything…I'll finish you off."

He slowly walked out of the room as if he had just had an everyday chat. Angela and Emanuel were waiting at the end of the hallway.

"Come on, Baby," he said touching her face. "Let's go home." He didn't acknowledge Emanuel.

Emanuel walked into the study where the monsignor was holding his head between his hands.

"So, that's it. He's your son."

The monsignor looked up and asked, "Does Angela know?" He looked smaller.

"I think that she was too scared to understand the exchange." Emanuel paused, waited for the monsignor to say something, and then proceeded, "I've heard that Dom Carlos came to Two Brooks in pursuit of a woman and a pig. I guess they were right, without even knowing half of it." Emanuel's voice was cold.

"I offered to be his friend. But he wanted me to acknowledge him as my son. I couldn't do that," the monsignor said quietly.

"So instead you became enemies," Emanuel stated flatly. "Very Christian of you."

"Don't judge me, because you don't know!" the monsignor answered. His color had returned and he was sitting up straighter in his chair.

"Let me tell you what I know," Emanuel said, taking a seat across from the monsignor. He started in a measured tone, "I was raised in an orphanage. Most of us there, like Dom Carlos, were bastards. However, the nuns, saintly creatures, had come up with a story for each one of us. Every child came from loving parents who had died. No child had been abandoned. Of course, I checked and there wasn't a shred of truth in my story—those nuns were pretty good little liars. My parents were gypsies, young and unmarried. My mother died and my father thought that the world didn't need another gypsy baby, and he took me to the nuns. Those nuns loved us and we loved them back. However, the priests who came to monitor, administer, check performance in the orphanage, were a different story. They were pedophiles and rapists. The nuns protected us from them. But, those monsignors and bishops got in the habit—pardon the pun—to have sex with the nuns. Rumors had it that most of the nuns were raped. One of them was Sister Rosario. I found out later that she died of a really mysterious illness—childbirth. So, you see, as much as I can't stand Dom Carlos, I am with him on this."

The monsignor blinked as if he had emerged from a trance.

"I loved Sister Rosario," Emanuel said as if remembering something sweet. "She was the closest thing to a mother. I remember her turning around, looking at me, and saying good-bye."

A heavy silence fell between the two men. The monsignor finally said, "I became a monsignor very early on. And then I met her—Carolina. She was very beautiful. Dom Carlos looks like her. She was very young, very lively, full of merriment—in some ways much like her son. And I fell for her. When she became pregnant, her parents emigrated to France. I knew she was with child, but the problem had been taken off my hands, and I never asked further. But I knew. My superiors also knew and I suggested this exile. A priest was needed in this remote place. There was a need for leadership. I had much work to do, and much to atone for. I always thought that Carolina had a girl and not a boy. And that girl would be like Angela."

"Where is Carolina?"

"She died five years ago. That's when she told her son about me. He thought he was the son of Carolina's husband. She married an older man and immigrant also, but a very wealthy one. He adopted Dom Carlos even before Dom Carlos was born. Dom Carlos was not born a bastard, and he was raised with love, privilege, and money." The monsignor paused and Emanuel waited. "So, what does he want with someone like Angela?" the monsignor asked. "I think that he is using her to punish me because I love that girl. Of all the children I baptized, that one grabbed my heart the first time she looked at me with those knowing eyes. Dom Carlos has known this. He says that he loves her, but he is driven by a compulsion to take her away from us here, to deter her from a path of goodness and good form, to let me know that he too can do damage to the people I love."

13

Love in Metamorphosis

Emanuel pondered. He didn't like Dom Carlos, mostly over Angela. Had the circumstances been different, they would have been friends. But what he knew of people, he couldn't see that type of guile in him. "I don't think he is that malicious," Emanuel said.

"I don't think he is either, but he is blinded by rage. He thinks that I took advantage of his mother, the woman he loved above all things."

"Did you?"

The monsignor was quiet, reflective. After a while, he said, "I did. She was a kid of fifteen and I a man of thirty. I was a priest and the spiritual director of a group of young people. She was a member of that group and I seduced her. I was weak and succumbed to my feelings for her. As much as Dom Carlos wants to think that he is different from me, he is doing the same thing—falling for a child and taking advantage of her. He said it: Like father, like son."

"What now?" Emanuel asked.

"I don't think he ever wanted me to be his father. He just wanted to humiliate me and show me as a fraud to my parishioners. He had a father, one who loved him totally. Why take public what happened thirty some odd years ago? It would destroy this village. My credibility would be gone."

"And so would your penances," Emanuel said.

"Don't dismiss my penances as arbitrary or as random. This village has not had poor people since I started here. Through the penances, people support each other as communities should. If a person sinned against someone, what good would it do to say ten Hail Marys? But if someone needed wheat or corn, or a debt pardoned, wouldn't it make more sense to address that need? This village has not seen one person without food or shelter since I've been their priest—mostly through penances."

How much did the monsignor know about the Night Justice? He probably knew all of it through confession. If the village confessed all other sins, why not the punishments meted out by Night Justice? But if they revealed their acts of retribution during confession, the monsignor couldn't report those responsible to the police. How perfectly cunning these people were. There was nothing simple about these islanders.

"You think this is the reason that Dom Carlos didn't expose you? That he sees the value of what you are doing?"

"I know so. He is, after all, a good man. He is a good man," the monsignor sighed. "And Angela became the punishing element. He won't expose me, because it would hurt a lot of people, but he will exploit someone who I love dearly—Angela."

"I can't believe he's that calculating. He loves Angela." Emanuel said.

"Yes, he loves her, no doubt," the monsignor mumbled.

"And so do I," Emanuel said. "And she broke my heart."

The monsignor looked at him without surprise. "I suspected that," he said. After a pause, he added, "She loves with a stubborn streak. She still loves Lazarus, I'm sure. If she loves you, it will be forever."

Emanuel was quiet for a long while. "I would have married her in the church, in a synagogue, at the end of the world, I wouldn't have cared. I have never been in love like this... and I know that she loves me." There was a heavy pause. "That hurts more than anything else because she loves me, but she chose another man," he added.

"Love is a trickster," the monsignor said. "So much can change in a short while."

Emanuel left the monsignor's house with renewed hope. She loved him, she had said as much. And, yes, he could feel it in the way they kissed. Dom Carlos had plenty of trials and tribulations to overcome before he could marry Angela. And life was a peculiar proposition—things changed all the time. He would be there in the house while Dom Carlos was in France.

When Emanuel got home, Rosa was preparing lunch for one. Everyone else had gone somewhere and Emanuel ate alone.

Sometimes the island got the best of him. It was like a contained, round, green prison that in little more than one hour he could drive around, and all that was left was imagining what lay beyond the horizon. There was no place to hide, no place to go. Living on an island was like living under a spotlight, continuously on, without reprieve. The islanders were sly and cagey, and at the same time, they were childlike and innocent. They could be cruel and violent and then loyal and easygoing. There were times when Emanuel wished for something straightforward like a murder, a clear-cut crime. But, on Hawk Island, nothing was clear—even the way they loved. He sighed and hoped that Dona Mafalda would come home and keep him company. He felt a surge of happiness when the gate opened and she came in. He felt sexually excited. How could he ask her again?

She walked with resolve, each step sounding like the beat of a drum accompanying her silent *no, no, no.* She could see the lust in his eyes. She sat next to him and gave him a side glance.

"Dona Mafalda," Emanuel said softly, "Let's have sex." He looked at her stupefied face. "I know we don't have romantic feelings for each other, but, I do enjoy having sex with you."

Dona Mafalda's face was showing her line of thought. *What was this man thinking? Let's have sex? Like, let's have a cup of tea?* "Because you can't have it with Angela!" she stated flatly.

"And you can't have it with Dom Carlos!" he retorted defensively.

Dom Mafalda felt a dull pain in her heart. Dom Carlos, her achingly dead dream. "It's the middle of the afternoon," she protested.

"I know how to tell time!" He answered, almost annoyed. "I know the perfect place," he added. "The windmill."

The windmill? That lonely place, full of hay and fleas, perched on top of a gigantic outcrop ... Was this the place he was proposing? Since Dom Carlos had announced his engagement, she had felt so sad... so alone... so critical of everything and everybody. Maybe sex would help. Maybe sex would push her into a different mindset; anything better than what she had been feeling of late. "Okay," she murmured.

Okay? Was she saying okay again? She couldn't believe it! What was it about sex that the first thing she thought to say was *okay?*

"Come then." And he grabbed her by the hand almost dragging her up through the pastures to the windmill.

Dona Mafalda was panting and heaving to keep pace with Emanuel, and thinking about some farmer lurking behind a stone wall, witnessing her disgrace, being dragged by a gypsy up the pastures to have sex in a windmill full of bugs and bats. She looked around, but the afternoon was quiet and serene. As soon as she entered, he locked the door with a wooden contraption. Immediately, he started to undress as if his clothes were on fire. And in no time, he was completely naked in front of a perplexed Dona Mafalda. He was aroused and breathing heavily from the brisk walk.

She crossed her arms and scowled at him.

"Don't make me beg," he said, looking at her forbidding face.

"And if I said no?" she asked petulantly.

"I would throw myself out that window," and he pointed to the tallest window where a pair of doves were looking down at him. *Coo, coo,* the doves called.

Dona Mafalda had never seen a man totally naked like that. His penis was standing up against his belly, shining like a talisman. She was startled by his beauty and frowned again, mustering her courage to be tough. Emanuel thought that she was his emotional, itinerant latrine—right there for his use anytime he got the urge. He needed a good lesson.

"It will be on my terms," she said, still with her arms crossed over her chest.

"Okay," he said.

"That's the right answer," she said. "Sit over there." She pointed to the grinding stone. He passively obeyed. He felt the bale of hay on his back, prickling his skin, and the rough stone grating his buttocks. He would sit on hot coals at that moment if she asked.

"You have to keep your eyes open, so you can see who you're having sex with," she said. "And every time I ask you a question, you have to give me the right answer."

He looked at her with feverish frustration. "What's the right answer?" he asked, vaguely thinking about the Spanish Inquisition.

"You have to say okay," she whispered in his ear. "No matter what I ask, you have to say okay."

"Okay," Emanuel said.

"See how fast you learn?" she said looking at him. "You can only climax when I tell you. And keep looking at me," Dona Mafalda instructed.

"Okay," he said breathlessly.

With deliberate slowness, Dona Mafalda stepped out of her pants, walked up to him, and slowly sat on his erection. He moaned feeling himself slide into her and closed his eyes.

"Open your eyes, Emanuel," she warned.

He opened his eyes and stared at her in his attempt at obedience.

"When you climax, you have to say my name," she said, swaying her hips. "When I say so," she added and continued her leisurely swaying.

"I didn't teach you this…," he said panting.

She smiled. "What's my name, Emanuel?"

"Mafalda," he whispered, sweat beading his skin.

She swayed slowly from side to side while he bit his lip and stared at her, his eyes glazing over with the effort to hold on.

"Now," she said sweetly.

"Mafangela!" he moaned, convulsing under her gaze.

There was dead silence. They were both still for a few seconds and then Dona Mafalda got off his lap, stepped away from him, and pulled up her pants. Before she opened the door to leave, she looked back at him and said calmly, "My name is not Mafangela. But that was an improvement."

When he got up, his buttocks were raw, oozing spots of blood from sitting on the grinding stone. The doves called again, *coo, coo.*

Dom Carlos said, "I wanted to destroy him. I established my business in Hawk Island and then I came to Two Brooks to become the bane of his existence. When I found out that the monsignor was my father... this sanctimonious, unrepentant self-styled demigod... I just wanted to expose him for the hypocrite he is."

Angela felt something disconcerting taking place in her heart.

Dom Carlos continued, "I didn't expect to love this place and much less to find value in the monsignor's work. I was divided between my goal to expose him and the damage it would do to people who I ended up caring about... My vengeance turned on me and I didn't know what to do with the monsignor. So, we fought all the time and insulted each other."

And that disconcerting feeling taking place in Angela's heart exploded. "Then... after you quench that thirst, what are we to you? Do you really love me or am I just a tool to punish that poor old devil, because you know he cares?"

"Please, Angela, of course, I love you!" he said somewhat irritated. "Right before Lazarus died, I was going to leave. I couldn't be with you in a platonic sense for the rest of my life. And then... I stayed because Lazarus was gone and I was in love with you... We make each other happy. We are right together."

He held her face in his hands to look at her up close. "I love you," he said.

"I know," she said quietly. "I always thought that your love was some sort of a miracle... impossible and yet mine."

Dom Carlos loved her that night with the desperation and sadness of one who wants to destroy doubt and Angela felt terrified as if a warning had gone off in her head. "Please don't go," she said. "Stay here with me. We don't have to get married."

He frowned slightly with her unexpected request. "Your parents would kill me," he said. "Besides, I want to marry you and you wouldn't be happy without proper civil status. It's bad enough that we can't marry in the church."

"I don't care about those things. I only care about you," she said with urgency as if her life depended on it.

"I will be back. Nothing will keep me from you, nothing, not even death."

"Don't talk about death!" she wailed.

When Angela fell asleep, Dom Carlos went down to the woodshop. He wanted to talk to Emanuel. He entered the woodshop and closed the door. "She knows," he said.

The two men were leaning on a bench, arms crossed over their chests and their hearts beating wildly. Emanuel was thinking about Angus Pomba and how right his instincts had been, if not his ethics, and Dom Carlos was looking down at their feet.

Much could be said about a person's shoes. Emanuel, for instance, one could tell that he wasn't a vain man. His shoes were scuffed and well-worn and had been resoled several times. On the other hand, Dom Carlo's were expensive, urban style, and perfectly matched with the rest of his attire.

"No matter what happens between you and Angela, I will be here, as her friend," Emanuel said. There was a long silence before he added, "The Night Justice incidents stopped and the pattern didn't make sense—mostly isolated incidents of people doing bad things to each other and blaming them on the Night Justice. The monsignor changed his mind and asked the superintendent to drop it. It was a fiasco through and through. I'm closing the case."

Dom Carlos looked at him with curiosity. "Don't sound so honorable, Emanuel. If you looked me up, I did the same with you. You're a highly-skilled, experienced police investigator, and, yet, you seemed to be, at best, half-hearted in your investigation of the Night Justice. You're here for something else, maybe political, maybe not. The African war isn't popular, especially here on Hawk Island. The Americans don't like that war either, and Hawk Island is… well… a whore to American needs…"

"You have no basis for that statement," Emanuel said. "I'm just a police detective trying to do my job and not let politics get in the way... my report will be... well, disappointing, but... these things happen." He grimaced.

"This place can break a man," Dom Carlos said.

"As you know, the Night Justice incidents happened all over the island, not just in Two Brooks," Emanuel answered. I was able to bring to justice other people in other villages. And I will solve the case of the disappearing men. I'm almost there."

Dom Carlos had a gleam of amusement in his eyes.

Emanuel returned a cold look. Dom Carlos was quiet and Emanuel continued, "What happened to Angus Pomba couldn't be lumped with the Night Justice events. It was a separate incident. He used violent means, he was certainly abusing his power, but his death was an accident. He was gored by a bull. It wasn't the work of Night Justice." He paused for a while, then let out a heavy sigh and said, "These people are sneaky. I've never seen anything like it."

Dom Carlos responded with a low chuckle. Emanuel joined in the levity.

"Night Justice hasn't always been just," Emanuel said. "Men have been killed and women have been beaten and raped by the Night Justice. Power is a dangerous inebriant. There's nothing noble about vigilante justice."

"Keep an eye on her, though," Dom Carlos said quietly. "I don't trust Pedro."

"Of course, I will. It goes without saying. When will you be returning?" Emanuel asked.

"I'll be back for Christmas," Dom Carlos said.

Emanuel nodded and Dom Carlos left.

Dona Mafalda was thinking that the house without Dom Carlos was like a church without a steeple—indistinguishable. That energy of laughter and fun was gone. Dona Mafalda tried to keep positive, but she was deflated. Every laugh or smile seemed unconvincing, put on like a mask. She was saying goodbye to a dream—to marry Dom Carlos. She had always known that he was her impossible dream, but now it was real. He had gone to France to get a divorce to marry Angela. He said it right there just a few days ago in front of everybody and privately in her room, "It's Angela, It has always been Angela."

She needed a lover. Not someone to have sex with, but someone to love her. She sorely wanted to have that feeling of being loved. She promised herself that she was going to give herself that chance by accepting Lucas. She didn't want a man making love to her while thinking about someone else, like Emanuel, even when she used sex to try to compel him, at least at that moment, to think only of her. That *Mafangela* episode in the windmill convinced her that she couldn't keep doing this to herself. She needed loving. She knew it was a sin to be weakened by the desires of the flesh. She had been virtuous, good, dedicated and God didn't care if she was alone and desolate. He didn't provide her with someone to love her. Maybe God didn't care. Maybe He had nothing to do with it and the rules were made by mean-hearted men. Who would she harm if she had a lover?

She needed to talk with someone unconstrained by religious beliefs. She needed to talk with Dom Carlos. He certainly didn't believe in anything the Catholic Church had to say. But he was gone. How much she missed that man! She should have appreciated him more while he had been around. But he would return. Wouldn't he?

And Dona Mafalda, aching for Dom Carlos, sought Lucas, who with love and hope in his heart taught her about veneration.

Angela woke up every day convinced that Dom Carlos' absence was just a bad dream. She would convince herself that he was downstairs reading and waiting for the others to have coffee, or that he was feeding Nixon under the table. But she wasn't dreaming. Dom Carlos was indeed gone and he had left a hole in her life as if a grenade had exploded.

Emanuel and Dona Mafalda stopped asking Angela if Dom Carlos had written. Angela was avoiding going out because she didn't want to tell people that he hadn't written or called. At the Sacristy meetings, no one asked anymore. Angela fell into a state of indelible sadness.

Dona Mafalda was very attentive, spending the evenings in the living room grading student papers while sitting next to Angela. A book in her hands, Angela would stare at the same page. Instead of working in the woodshop, Emanuel would sit with the two women. Most of the conversation was with Dona Mafalda, who would put down her red pencil and go into the kitchen to get tea — unless they talked about sex, and if they did, they drank moonshine. Emanuel talked about some of the cases he was pursuing and would invite Dona Mafalda to offer her opinion. But the conversation always went back to Angela, the village and its people—troubled and anxious.

The moonshine was on the table. Emanuel and Dona Mafalda were talking about sex. "Well… he cried." She looked at Emanuel for a few seconds and then added, "He will always cry. He gets so overwhelmed, he can't help himself."

"And…?"

"And… he makes love to me. And I can feel the difference…I mean, between having sex and making love, even with the crying." Like a sailor, Dona Mafalda downed a shot of moonshine in one gulp. Emanuel did the same. They glanced over at Angela with her head bowed over a book, still staring at the same page.

The conversation shifted from sex to the patron saint and the upcoming festivities in October. Dona Mafalda had been elected unanimously to be the committee chair. Only she could deal with the village in turmoil as it was. Intent on taking over the village's Holy Ghost festivities, the bishop charged the monsignor with organizing a vote of the village residents to win the approval of his plan. The villagers were, however, dead set against voting because it would air their dirty linen of how fractured they were. Most wanted to continue to do the same things that they had always done, but the bishop was sticking his nose into their business once again.

"If there is a vote, who will you vote for?" Emanuel asked Dona Mafalda.

"We can't vote," she said. "We're not members of the village society."

"And what does it take to become a member?"

"A lifetime of suffering," Angela answered, without lifting her face from her book. They hadn't thought she had been listening—still never turning the page. The night was chilly. Angela hugged herself and looked at her companions. "Should I light a fire?" she asked.

"I will," Emanuel said. "Just enjoy your tea, honey."

Honey. When did he start calling me honey? Angela thought. "The way you are performing your lodgers' responsibilities pretty soon I'll be the one paying you to stay here," Angela said.

"That sounds good to me," he answered and smiled.

"The monsignor called me today," Angela said after a while, her voice trembling.

Emanuel tensed. "What did he want?" he asked, giving a knowing look to Dona Mafalda.

"The monsignor received a letter from Dom Carlos' wife, Vivienne. She told the monsignor that she and her husband were working on a reconciliation. She asked the monsignor to steer me away from her husband," Angela said tonelessly.

"Oh, my dear!" Dona Mafalda said, running to her.

"I've been trying to work up my nerve to tell you," Angela said.

"That may not be true, darling," Dona Mafalda said.

"I know it may be a ruse from Vivienne, but she wants to keep the marriage."

"Takes two for a marriage," Emanuel said, and then felt like a fool for stating the obvious.

"He didn't want the divorce in the first place. It was Vivienne's decision, and now she decided to keep the marriage," Angela said in a steady tone. "Maybe away from all this turmoil, things look different to him. Maybe being away from us, all his reasons became… unimportant, irrelevant. Maybe he got it out of his system and he's done with us," Angela said, trying to be brave. She didn't want to think about Dom Carlos and his sophisticated wife— petite, refined, fashionable, lovely. In comparison, Angela felt like a brute. Her fingernails were broken, her feet were rough. What was she thinking? He would never come back for her. And why didn't he write? Why? She had written so many letters, with no response. She had called the only phone number she had and was always dismissed—he wasn't home. Angela closed her eyes and started to silently cry. Dona Mafalda hugged her and made soothing sounds. "I don't want to cry anymore, I don't!" she wept on Dona Mafalda's shoulder.

Emanuel got up and went into the garden. The roses were still blooming, stubborn little things. The wild daisies were coming up everywhere. The garden was dark and cold as he was. He could hear both women weeping inside and he felt helpless. He wished he could punch Dom Carlos right in his perfectly chiseled Roman nose.

After a while, Angela came out to the garden. She looked into the night, not saying a word, as if Emanuel was not there.

"Are you all right?" he asked.

"I'm like a cat, always landing on my feet," she said, her voice dangerously steady.

Emanuel stood behind her and wrapped his arms around her shoulders. His body heat was warming her back and she could feel his heartbeat softly drumming. She felt comforted at the same time she felt that she was being reclaimed. She was too exhausted to analyze her situation, and she gave in to the simple comfort being offered. They stayed there in the night, listening to the sounds of crickets and other little creatures.

"I thought you were angry with me," she said.

"I am, I'm furious with you," he answered.

She made a sound like laughter. "Did you curse me?"

"No, honey. I couldn't wish you hurt," he said. "Is that Hercules?" he asked, pointing to two green lights on the wall.

"Since Lazarus fixed that wall, it's his favorite spot."

"When was that?" he asked.

"Maybe a few days before he… left us," she said, choked with emotion.

"Don't cry, honey," he murmured.

"What happened to Joan of Arc? Was she totally consumed by that fire?" Angela sobbed.

When they went back inside, Dona Mafalda had already gone to bed. In the kitchen near the fire, looking at the flames spewing fascinating colors, they sat for a long time in companionable silence.

She looked at him—so handsome, so patient. "I'm sorry I hurt you. I'm sorry I have a greedy heart."

"What is a greedy heart?" he asked.

"One that wants everything," she answered.

"Do greedy hearts ask for forgiveness?" he asked.

"They should," she said, knowing full well that he was trying to make her laugh.

"Try me," he suggested.

"Forgive me," she said.

"No," he answered quickly.

She chuckled. "I know what you're doing. You're trying to rescue me from my sadness."

"How am I doing?"

"You're a master." She held his gaze for a while and then asked, "Why are you still here, Emanuel?"

"I like it here. Two Brooks is full of criminals. I'll have work for the rest of my life… I still don't know who fried Pedro… I secretly think that the only crime committed was the loss of all that good lard." He chuckled.

She said quietly. "It was inevitable that one day fate would get him."

"You're not going to tell me, are you?"

"I have nothing to tell you. You can't solve that case."

"Don't be so sure, Joan of Arc. I may surprise you yet."

As he was mounting the stairs to his room, he was thinking about Angela. His love for her was devouring him. How could he have let himself be caught so unaware? If he at least had been warned that a man could love in such a way, he would have protected himself. He had always thought that he was in control and suddenly, like a child playing with a dangerous toy, he was so wounded that he could hardly see beyond it.

The preparations for the festivities were going without a hitch. Under Dona Mafalda's direction, everybody had their specific job. The Music Club House was not only a place where the men gathered to drink and gossip, but Dona Mafalda set it up as the control center for the festivities. Even Regina Sales was invited to join in the preparations, where she had been given the brush-off in the past. Dona Mafalda wasn't going to snub anyone who wanted to help out. She had learned her lesson about exclusion.

After much foot-dragging, the monsignor finally announced that the vote about the Holy Ghost would take place on the last day of the festivities. The village was divided between those who wanted the Holy Ghost to continue as a pagan feast, who were unflatteringly dubbed the *Terrorists*, and those who wanted the Holy Ghost to be incorporated into the church under the control of the diocese—mocked as the *Petticoats*. The Terrorists were vilified for revolting against the authority of the church ("like the ungodly"), while the Petticoats were scoffed at for hiding behind the bishop's skirts ("like children tied to their mother's apron strings").

The village was hopelessly divided, and Dona Mafalda was furious with the monsignor. Not able to vote, she was quite able to influence, and influence she did. She decided to make a last bid to convince the monsignor to defy the bishop. The village council looked at her with foreboding. Shaking their heads, they warned, "Dona Mafalda, he's going to hurt you. Don't walk into the lion's den."

Dona Mafalda wouldn't listen. As she entered the sacristy, the monsignor turned around, already bristling with her presence. But Dona Mafalda was emboldened by her courage mustered over the last few months and was not about to back down now. "I came to ask you to postpone this vote. I think it's a disservice to the village and to the patron saint to get mixed up in this divisiveness." Dona Mafalda's voice was strong and firm, but inside she was terrified. *What if he hit her again?*

"How dare you come here and tell me what to do! I will do what's best for the village and you should stay out of it! You're not one of us!" the monsignor yelled.

Through the open door, Dona Mafalda saw Maria Gomes draw nearer.

"I'm as much one of you as you are, Monsignor," she answered calmly.

"How dare you! ..." he advanced toward Dona Mafalda.

Maria Gomes opened the door and saw Dona Mafalda's terrified eyes following the monsignor gaining on her, his hand already poised in the air to strike the teacher.

A person can think a million thoughts in a second. Dona Mafalda was thinking about her hands. She had never lifted her hands in an act of aggression to anyone. And now, a monsignor was making her choose between committing an act of violence or an act of cowardice. She couldn't hit a monsignor in his sacristy. But then she saw Maria Gomes standing there, just like her—a victim of the monsignor's wrath—ready to take her again in her embrace and console her after the slap, as she once had.

Before the monsignor's raised hand struck her face, Dona Mafalda punched him in the nose. He stepped back as much from surprise as from the impact. A pail of holy water, ready to replenish the holy water bowls, tipped over and splashed over the floor. The monsignor, still staggering to regain his balance, slipped and fell, sitting in the holy water with his cassock absorbing the water spread across the floor. The spectacle reminded Dona Mafalda of an old bat struck by a broom.

Maria Gomes screamed and the first arrivers for the mass came running to the sacristy. The monsignor saw a few faces looking down at him while Dona Mafalda and Maria Gomes held each other, trembling.

"I'm fine!" the monsignor yelled. "I just slipped and fell, but I'm fine!" He looked at Dona Mafalda and Maria Gomes. He got up and shook off his cassock. "I will take your recommendation under advisement, Dona Mafalda," he said for the benefit of the growing audience.

Both women looked at each other, walked out of the church and down the village side by side, fast and quiet as if on a mission. When they got to Maria Gomes' house, they entered the gate and hurried in.

Maria's husband was getting ready to go to mass and eyed them curiously. He asked, "What happened to the two of you? It seems as though you saw the devil."

"Almost," said his wife in a strangled voice. "Go to mass and we will go a little later. We have a few errands to do for the feast."

He left, glancing back at the trembling women.

When they found themselves alone, Dona Mafalda started to cry. She cried from deep within, making guttural sounds as if she had something stuck in her throat. Maria Gomes held the poor teacher, shaking with sobs and panic, in her arms and consoled her.

"He deserved it. He has deserved it for a very long time," Maria said, smoothing Dona Mafalda's curls. "Boy, right on the nose! Poom!" Maria added.

14

Blind, Bruised, and Broken Hearts

It was not even noon and Maria Gomes took out the moonshine. She filled two small glasses and immediately downed hers. Dona Mafalda looked at Maria, questioning the wisdom of drinking moonshine so early in the day.

"Come on, Dona Mafalda. You're nervous and this will relax you," she said, downing a second one.

Dona Mafalda took her glass and followed suit. The last time she had had moonshine, she was talking about love. She remembered its bitter taste and Emanuel's face when she told him about Lucas. Now here she was drinking moonshine because she punched a monsignor. Why was God provoking her that way? This village was going to transform her into a drunken, violent old harlot. "I've never hit anyone in my entire life," Dona Mafalda said, deflated.

"The monsignor was a very good start," Maria replied. They were silent. Then Maria added, "My dream, for a very long time, has been to slap him. I see my open hand flying and then land on his face with a satisfying *Thunk*!"

Dona Mafalda looked at her in surprise. Doable dreams, after all, seemed so impossible. "But why does he hit people?" Dona Mafalda asked in frustrated protest.

"He hits women and children. He doesn't hit men," Maria answered.

"He's going to run me out of this place," Dona Mafalda said. "He is going to petition for a new teacher."

Maria looked at her for a long while and then shook her head sadly because she knew he would.

"I like it here," Dona Mafalda said in a weak voice. "God knows why, but I do."

"We like you too," Maria said and broke into sobs.

Dona Mafalda thought about Dom Carlos. If he was here, he wouldn't let the monsignor run her out of town. But he was gone, and he wasn't writing and no one knew his whereabouts in France.

Oh, how she missed Dom Carlos!

Angela received a letter from France. She was trying to decipher if it was in Dom Carlos' handwriting. It looked like his handwriting, but her heart was racing and entertaining her doubt. She had written so many letters to the only address she knew and, without an answer to any of her letters, she thought that she had the wrong address. Not one letter until now. Not one response. She looked at the letter and weighed it in her hand. It was so light that it seemed the envelope was empty.

She opened it and read,

> *Angela,*
>   *After much reflection, I have decided that my marriage is worth saving. I am sorry if this causes you pain. Thank you for everything you've done for me.*
>   *I will send over the paperwork from my attorney to finalize our business together.*
>
>   *Be well,*
>   *António*

She fled to the windmill and closed the door. She wanted to cry alone. She would have one good deep and savage cry and then she would not cry ever again over men who left her. There, in the silence of a chilly afternoon, she cried while the menagerie sat outside crying too. Even Hercules was meowing like a lost kitten.

Emanuel entered the kitchen and looked for Angela. Rosa looked at him sideways, lifted her eyebrows and said, "Oh, yeah! The mailman came and brought a crying letter."

"A what?"

"A crying letter," she repeated.

Emanuel waited for her to explain. "A letter that makes you cry," Rosa said, as if it was too obvious to require explanation.

"Who was the letter from?" he asked.

"I don't know. I only know that it was a crying letter, like those that come from Angola or Mozambique, when a soldier dies."

"Was Angela crying?"

Rosa looked at him as if he was dim, "Why do you think I know it was a crying letter?" Rosa asked. "She went to the windmill."

Emanuel walked up to the windmill. The menagerie was outside all huddled together as if they were cold. Hercules was sitting with his chin resting on Dalia's back. They looked up at him as if saying, "*Do something!*"

He knocked on the door and entered. She was sitting with her back against the wall, with the letter in her hand. He sat next to her and she gave him the letter without saying a word. He read it and frowned.

"Quite a laconic letter," he said.

"It stands to reason that a letter like this would follow the monsignor's letter—first the monsignor to prepare me and now this," Angela said, now without tears.

Emanuel was still examining the letter. He was frowning slightly. Somehow that letter didn't fit Dom Carlos. Could distance change a man that much? How much hold had Vivienne over him? Could it be that Dom Carlos lost his fervor and focus on vengeance against the monsignor and Angela was intertwined in all of that?

"I'm sorry that you're hurting," he said kindly.

"I'm tired of hurting over men who leave me," she said.

"Let's go home. It's cold and it's going to rain soon," he said, helping her up.

"Not yet, let me stay here for a little while. Here I have no memories of him."

They sat silently, with the menagerie whimpering outside.

"Shouldn't you at least let those poor bastards in?" he asked, indicating the door and the animals rasping to get in.

"What do you do with a broken heart?" she asked, looking up at him as if waiting for a recipe.

"I'm still trying to figure that out," he said.

"Oh, Emanuel!" she said crestfallen. "Are you talking about me? Are you saying that I broke your heart?"

He gazed at her for a while. "Angela, when I say I love you and you take another man, what do you think it does to my heart?" he asked, more peeved than he wanted.

"I didn't think... that you loved me... I knew you loved me but not like—" she murmured.

"What?" he interrupted. "Do you think that only your love for Dom Carlos is noble, great, and worthy of pain?" Emanuel asked, feeling his annoyance grow.

"Forgive me, I was thoughtless."

"No!" he said sternly. "I will never forgive you. You are thoughtless and self-absorbed." And he briskly left the windmill, ahead of her, disappearing down the lane.

Why did he do that? This was not about him. He went there to console her and he ended up reverting to accusations and name-calling. He turned around and ran back into the windmill. Angela was sobbing into her hands, the letter lying on the floor. Emanuel took her in his arms and hugged her. He too was shaking with sobs.

"I couldn't help myself but love him more than anything else…" she cried, her face buried in his chest.

After the incident in the sacristy, Dona Mafalda had gone home and straight into her room without dinner, certain that she was going to be fired. The following morning the monsignor summoned her to his house. Dona Mafalda fully expected that he would inform her that a new teacher would be coming to replace her. But she also knew that he would never hit her again.

She knocked and he answered. His nose was slightly swollen. He motioned for her to enter. She remained calm.

"I want you out of here right after Christmas. I commissioned a new teacher and you are no longer needed."

"I'm not leaving," she said evenly.

He gave a laugh that sounded more like a shout. "You have no choice, woman!"

"Oh, yes, I do. You may bring in another teacher for the children but I will stay here." Looking straight into his eyes, she added, "You may think that you own everybody, but you don't own me. And you can't make me go."

"Oh, but I can! Don't you dare defy me!"

"Really? How can you make me go? You're a bully and a hypocrite, and you don't have a hold on me."

"You won't find a job on this island. I will make sure of it."

"And what would be your reasons? Would you lie? What would you say?"

"You're a bad influence on the children. You dared strike their priest! You sleep around with a mechanic, young enough to be your son!"

Dona Mafalda said evenly, "You're a pathetic man." And she left.

The monsignor was shaking. He was losing control over the village because these foreigners were influencing the residents and changing the way they looked at the world. First, it was Dom Carlos, then Dona Mafalda, and to a certain degree Emanuel.

The whole village already knew that Dona Mafalda would be leaving by Christmas. The children were sad and silent. That donkey of a monsignor was always sticking his nose where he shouldn't. They loved Dona Mafalda. They wanted her. The villagers were thinking about the good the monsignor had done for them, but also the harm he could cause.

Dona Mafalda sat at the dinner table. She was sure that the conversation was going to be about her leaving. Angela and Emanuel were looking at her, waiting for an explanation.

In less than two days, the monsignor had completely disrupted Dona Mafalda's life. Sunday morning she was coordinating the festivities, Tuesday morning she was being told to pack.

"You're not leaving," Angela stated. "You're not leaving."

Dona Mafalda smiled. "I could stay, but it would be too difficult for the children and quite bizarre for all of us. What would be my role?"

"You could stay and start that higher education school that you talk about. Instead of people going to the city to study, you could prepare them here and they would only go to the city for the exams. You know there's a tremendous need for that in this part of the island." Angela was speaking with such hope that Dona Mafalda felt touched by her enthusiasm. "And the children could always visit you and be inspired by your school," Angela continued.

"But the monsignor wants me out of your house. Where would I go?"

"This is my house," Angela said angrily. "I'll talk to him. And the new teacher will likely be staying here with us. There's room for everybody."

"Where will she stay?" Dona Mafalda asked.

"She'll stay in Dom Carlos' room. I'll put his things away," Angela said softly. "Or send them over to France, now that I know he is at that address."

"Oh, darling, I'm so sorry," Dona Mafalda said, forgetting her own troubles for the moment.

"He won't be coming back," she said.

Dona Mafalda stretched a hand and touched Angela's shoulder. "I'm so sorry, darling."

Emanuel got up and left. He and Angela had been avoiding each other since their meeting at the windmill. The more Angela thought about Emanuel, the more remorseful she felt. He was trying to support her in her grief and she dismissed his broken heart as something unimportant, as a crush or feelings easily overcome.

The festivities started with the procession of the patron Our Lady of Lourdes. The altar was so beautiful in white and blue that even the monsignor let out a grunt of admiration. The flower carpets on the street were all white, the philharmonic played with zest and perfection, the windows were adorned with beautiful throws and hangings, the children wore freshly polished shoes and their clothes were starched to a perfect stiff white. This was a village that wouldn't allow a bishop to divide them.

Dona Mafalda was working so hard that she failed to notice anything different about Lucas. But Lucas was different. Dona Mafalda heard it first from Rosa.

Rosa was setting the table for breakfast and said that Lucas was engaged to the American girl who had arrived two weeks ago for the feast. Dona Mafalda dismissed it. Impossible! Lucas was crazy about her. There would be no shining Canadian or American able to compete with her. Dona Mafalda never thought very highly of emigrants anyway. They left, covered with dirt and lice, and came back shining like a brand-new penny and thought they could steal other people's boyfriends. These islanders were self-indulgent and lazy at home. They lacked the motivation to strive for a better life. If they worked half as hard at home as they did in foreign lands, maybe they would be successful here. No, Dona Mafalda didn't like emigrants. She was thinking of poor Olivia. There she was, looking at Lucia and Joaquim getting married, while Olivia, as the main soloist in the choir, was singing her heart out while her heart was breaking. Poor Olivia.

These instant Americans, fraudulent and unreal, were the nightmare of those who were left behind. They came back to harvest the very best because they had a strange and promising world to offer. But Dona Mafalda was not a poor Olivia—she was Dona Mafalda and she had no use for Canada! No, these gossiping tongues didn't know that Lucas loved her. He adored her!

She kept their relationship a secret because of her position as a teacher and Lucas being a mechanic and all... She had refused marriage, true, but he was her man. Marriage had been out of the question, but then she had learned that he came from a lineage that could be traced back to the 1400s.

Emanuel and Angela were on the terrace because Dona Mafalda had summoned Lucas for tea. She wanted to get to the bottom of that bothersome rumor. But then they saw Lucas leave as if he was on fire, leaving Dona Mafalda stunned. They got up at the same time as if choreographed, went to Dona Mafalda, who said in a small voice, "Rosa was right. He's going to marry that American girl." There were no tears, no drama. Dona Mafalda sat down and said, "He thinks that I'm not committed to him because I don't want to get married. He said that I treat him like a second class citizen... that I'm embarrassed to have him in my life... and that he wants to end our relationship... that he isn't educated but nevertheless proud..." Dona Mafalda couldn't believe the gall of that mechanic. He, who had been so humble and so in love with her, just dropped her as if she was nothing.

"Is there an American girl?" Angela asked.

"Yes, and he can't even pronounce her name. They'll be married next year." Dona Mafalda sat down and pondered. He had asked to marry her almost every time they were together and she always said no. But he was always ready for sex, even after she said no. "That pig," she said in a low tone. "That pig!" she yelled. The menagerie left the room. They had never heard Dona Mafalda raise her voice. They ran out, all at once making sounds of alarm, except Hercules who sat at the door amused. *What happened to the queen?* The cat smirked. Nixon was completely terrorized with screams about a pig.

Dona Mafalda covered her face for composure. After a while, she said, "Time can fix everything," and went up the stairs with the dignity of the queen she considered herself to be.

Emanuel looked at Angela and asked, "Must everyone in this house have a fucking broken heart?"

Angela murmured, "Poor Dona Mafalda. I think she was too stuck on herself and didn't allow her love for Lucas to grow. I don't blame him. And if some prince or duke or count came along, Dona Mafalda would have dropped Lucas faster than he could say *mechanic.*"

It was a dark and crisp night. Angela sat holding her arms close to her body. She said, "People can be incredibly insensitive and dismissive of other people's feelings."

"Look who's talking!" Emanuel said.

"To my defense, I thought that I was for you more of a... conquest than anything else."

"What are you saying?" he asked offended.

"You… sleep around… easily. I thought if you loved me, you wouldn't sleep with other people… so I thought your love for me was a passing thing."

"Who did I sleep with?' he asked angrily.

"See? You don't even remember," she said. "You had sex with Dona Mafalda, with Regina, Dona Gloria, and God knows who else, while you confessed your love for me."

Emanuel made a sound of disbelief. "How in the world do you know that?'

"I know everything. I've told you before that I'm a witch."

"Then if you know everything, you should've known that I never loved a woman as I love you. I didn't make love, I had sex. And while I was having sex, I was thinking of you! There!"

"Oh, please! Don't give me that tired excuse. Shame on you, Emanuel! How can you have sex without love? It makes you an equal to Hercules or Viriato."

They were quiet. He didn't mind so much to be compared to Viriato but to be compared to that dirty nasty cat was more than an insult.

Angela was thinking of Dom Carlos, thoughtful, always present, always sure, loving, funny, and laughing about everything he could. He loved her just by being with her. He didn't have to have sex to love her. But when they did, it was as if the rest of the world didn't matter. She missed his attention to everything—to business, to her moods, to the village, to his friends. He was so much part of her that she hurt as if a limb had been cut off. She trusted his love—but he was gone.

Emanuel's thoughts rested on his hours of loneliness, thinking about Angela in the arms of another man and how he ached as if he was about to die. He thought about Dona Gloria's beautiful body, Dona Mafalda's inexperience, willing student, and Regina's devouring appetite. Sex was for him like a balm, an elixir. It eased his loneliness, if only for a minute. He was feeling that urge again, that need to be inside a woman to feel whole, cared for, kissed, and held. There was nothing in the world like the body of a woman.

"It is so unlike him to do something like this," Angela said to Emanuel.

"Lucas?" Emanuel asked.

Angela realized that her thoughts had run away from her, and Emanuel was staring. "Are you talking about Lucas?" he asked again.

"No," she said, "I was talking about Dom Carlos. It's unlike him to just disappear without a word, like a coward."

"He came to Two Brooks as if he was dropped by the heavens and took off as if he was swept away," Emanuel said evenly.

Angela looked at him, trying to decipher his meaning. "You think he left for good, don't you?"

"Yes. Just like the monsignor did to his mother—gone."

Emanuel looked at her for a long time and confessed. "Yes, I use sex to make me feel better. But I close my eyes and I see you. I have loved you for a very long time."

"Why didn't you tell me when you first realized it? When I kissed you in the hospital and when we kissed under the rain? You told me that you didn't want to love me. That's what you said," she reproached.

"I was fighting the undertow. I was remembering Angus Pomba, Sebastião Perdido, and all those poor bastards who came to this village before me. I didn't want to love you. God knows I didn't. All I wanted was to get rid of you... I wanted to kick you out of my heart because you hurt," he said quietly.

"I've been kicked enough lately," she said sadly. "But I know what you mean. If Dom Carlos or Lazarus came back, I wouldn't trust their love either. And I want to kick them out of my heart too, like a deadly virus."

"What if Dom Carlos comes back?" he asked.

"No, he won't come back. Why would he? He already knows all there is to know about the love I can give him. And he chose not to take it."

"Yes, I know all about getting the short end of the stick when people make choices, especially choices about love."

Angela got up from the chair. She was cold and angry. She looked at Emanuel for a long time. Then she said, "I always trusted Dom Carlos' love, that he was faithful and steady. How could I be so wrong? But you, my dear detective, you were always on the lookout for a woman to stick your prick in. You are generous with your body and with your loving. How could I know that I was not one of those fleeting fucks, to release your tension, like a pill for a headache?"

"You make me sound like I am a—"

"Whore!" she finished. "Right now you have an erection the size of Atlantis. As soon as I leave, you'll go to Regina, or to the city by foot, to give it to the ever-expectant Dona Gloria, or worse yet, to poor broken-hearted Dona Mafalda."

Angela turned around and went up to her room, leaving Emanuel like a leering statue on the terrace. No, he wasn't going to Regina or Dona Gloria. He was going to knock at Dona Mafalda's door and ask her to have sex. Angela and Lucas could go to hell. There was nothing better to ease a broken heart than a good fuck. There was nothing wrong with a good fuck! He walked quietly by Dona Mafalda's door without knocking. He got into bed, brooding, "Damn it!" he said.

He was lying awake when the door opened softly and he saw the profile of the woman standing, as if undecided.

Then she came in and said, "Would you? Would you love me tonight?"

He got up and brought her to his bed, without saying a word.

"Anything goes," she murmured as he tossed her nightgown on the floor.

"Anything?" he asked in disbelief.

"Yes, we both need revenge sex. I'll avenge you with Angela and you'll avenge me with Lucas."

Dona Mafalda added, "Light the lamp, Emanuel. I want to see everything and I want you to do the same." And she placed a little bottle of oil on the side table.

"I promised Lucas two things if he stopped crying—fellatio and anal sex," she said, lifting her face to his. "He never got it."

He moaned softly. He had a mental image of Dona Mafalda having a checklist of all the sexual acts she wanted to try—and perhaps even in her enthusiasm marking off some with an exclamation point.

They laid quietly side by side after their revenge session as if sleeping. Emanuel was thinking about Angela's accusation regarding his depraved ways, and Dona Mafalda was thinking about how low she had fallen.

November was cold and rainy, foretelling a hard winter. The new teacher was coming to replace Dona Mafalda. Also, the vote for the Holy Ghost sponsorship was going to happen that month. The monsignor hadn't held the referendum on the last day of the patron saint festivities because of the punch on the nose, but he was going to have that vote. The village was abuzz with the upcoming event.

At the Music Club House, men and women gathered to hear about the referendum. António Dores, the monsignor's right-hand man, was trying to win over those sitting on the fence. Some villagers weren't sure whether a vote against the monsignor was, in effect, a vote against God.

Dona Mafalda was running the meeting, much to the monsignor's dismay.

There were six hundred citizens in the village of Two Brooks. Six hundred votes were expected. In theory, a household could have some votes for the Petticoats and some for the Terrorists. But the men, having the opportunity to make a public show of their authority, voted on behalf of their families.

In households where the opinion was divided, the man of the house prevailed. Upon finding their parents on opposing sides, children didn't know what they should be—a Petticoat or a Terrorist? And so they fought as if they were enemies in a civil war—brother against brother, sister against sister, each one vowing loyalty to one parent, prepared to cast the other out.

Some women had never been slapped by their husbands, other than when they were determined to vote differently from their husbands. It may have been just one slap and just that one time, but their husbands paid for it for the rest of their days, because their food was never as delicious, their wives' arms were never as open wide and their lovemaking was never again offered, and many times it was denied. And if these husbands looked into their wives' eyes, they saw a dull, vacant look where light used to be.

The village administrator, Victor Costa, explained the referendum process. There were two parties—the Petticoats and the Terrorists. It was not one vote per household but one vote per household member, but still, winner take all. The household head would cast as many votes as members of their household.

António Dores had started his campaign against the Terrorists. If the Terrorists won, the Holy Ghost would become profaned, and the Petticoats would get a brand-new Holy Ghost, new crowns, new philharmonic, a new Music Club House, a new choir and a new theatre group.

If some villagers were illiterate, they weren't stupid. António was claiming that even if the bishop didn't win, the wishes of the majority would not be respected. The upshot was that even the undecided voted against the bishop because of his purported dirty politics.

And then Victor Costa said, "But this meeting isn't over... We don't want Dona Mafalda to leave. She has been the best thing that has happened to our children. As your administrator, I went to the Department of Education and submitted your petition. Today I received confirmation—Dona Mafalda will remain with us."

People got up screaming and applauding. Angela held Dona Mafalda's hand and smiled at her. Dona Mafalda paled and felt lightheaded.

"The new teacher will also be coming to the village, but to assist Dona Mafalda because we're a village with more than sixty children. Dona Mafalda will have someone working alongside her instead of replacing her," Victor announced, his voice quickly drowned by screams of joy and applause. "I will go and tell the monsignor… and as we all know, he will insult me and threaten us all, but these are our children and it is about time we take a stand."

Dona Mafalda let two big tears of gratitude run down her face. She knew so little about these people. She had made assumptions, but she didn't know their hearts. For the first time in her life, she felt completely humbled. She was beside herself with joy, not so much because she had her job back, but because the village stood against the monsignor on her behalf. This was the equivalent of facing up to a bloodthirsty, death-dealing monster.

"My mother and other people, including Regina," Angela said in Dona Mafalda's ear, " they went to every house in the village to sign a petition, stating that the village of Two Brooks wanted you to remain the teacher. Almost everyone signed, except, of course, the obvious ones…"

Dona Mafalda was sitting across from Emanuel during dinner. Once in a while, she looked at him with disapproval.

Angela said, "I know everything!"

"Know what?" they said in unison, wide-eyed and breathless.

"I don't care if you're having sex," Angela said in a low tone as soon as Rosa left the room. "Just don't think that you're fooling me."

"Angela!" Dona Mafalda said righteously. "Emanuel and I are not sexual partners or anything of the kind."

True. After that strange night of fellatio and anal sex, Dona Mafalda refused to have anything remotely sexual with Emanuel. She had lost it. When that dirty mechanic dropped her like a sack of potatoes, she was bound to lose control and she had lost it. How could she have gone to Emanuel and acted like a deviant? Two Brooks was rubbing off on her—she was becoming unhinged, out of balance. She could hardly recognize in herself the woman she had once been. She was now mending her ways and getting back to being the woman she should and could be.

As for Emanuel, he too wanted to turn a new leaf. He could go without sex no matter how often and how seriously provoked he was. And he was going to do it, if not for Angela, at least for himself. He didn't want to be a slave to his sexual appetites. When he went to the city, however, he was unable to resist Dona Gloria with her deliriously tempting ways. He played in his head strategies of self-control, while Dona Gloria undressed in front of him and said, "Anything you want, Detective Santos. Anything." And like a condemned man eating his last supper, he succumbed to Dona Gloria's invitation. But he resisted Regina and her juicy steaks. That should count for something. If he loved Angela, he was going to be hers, at least in his heart.

He lowered his head to the plate and said under his breath, "No one is getting it in this house, it seems…"

Dona Mafalda slapped her napkin on the table and left in a huff. Emanuel and Angela smiled in amusement.

Life without Dom Carlos had left Angela, for a long time, without the capacity to smile or feel joy. Her smiling at Dona Mafalda's indignant response was a good sign.

Slowly she started to feel like herself as if she was thawing from a deep freeze. She was again feeling her soul like one feels a foot or an arm that had gone numb.

Sitting quietly in the garden enjoying a glass of wine, Angela thought of the new teacher who soon would be coming to the village. *Another woman for Emanuel to have sex with,* and she couldn't hide a smile.

"What are you smiling about?" Emanuel asked, sitting next to her.

"If I tell you, you'll start another fight with me."

He took her wine glass and sipped. "No, I won't. I won't fight with you again."

"Why not?"

"Because we never fought before and suddenly Dom Carlos leaves and we're fighting. Why are we doing that?"

"To resist each other, I suppose," she said taking the glass from him.

"Why do you want to resist me?" he asked so simply and directly that it made her smile.

"Because you'll leave if I become romantically involved with you. It seems that for me 'to have' is easy, but 'to hold' is impossible. I don't want you to leave."

To have and to hold, what ruthless intent, Emanuel thought. Silently, they kept on sharing the glass of wine back and forth. "If you make love to me, it's to avenge your heart and stick it to Dom Carlos. It's not because you love me," Emanuel finally said broodingly. He was thinking about Dona Mafalda's revenge sex. As much as he had enjoyed it, he didn't want the same with Angela. With her, he wanted her love, not her vengeance on another man.

"No. If that was the case, I would've done it already. Gone into your room and fucked your brains out, like Dona Mafalda did the night Lucas dumped her," she said matter-of-factly.

"Do you spy on me?" he asked startled.

She laughed. "And you think that you're the detective." She lightly touched his face. "You are a gorgeous pain in the ass, but you're no match for me." She rested her head back against the wall and closed her eyes.

"All my life, I have looked for you," he said quietly as if talking to himself. "I found you on this small, inhospitable island and it became the sweetest home I have ever had. But you broke my heart, Angela, because you loved me and you let me go. It would have been easier if you had never loved me."

She was surprised by his confession. She had expected him to say something funny or flippant, but not this.

"We had this conversation before," she said, getting agitated. "I thought I was circumstantial. You fall for every woman you see, so I thought that you eventually would move on."

"Couldn't you see the difference? Don't you say you know everything? I've told you that love is self-evident and you chose not to see mine." Emanuel was tense.

"See? We're fighting again. You are incorrigible!" she snapped. Then she added more demurely, "I've asked you a million times for your forgiveness. There's no point in asking you again. You'll deny me."

"There is a way," he said.

"What is it?" she asked, gazing at him impatiently.

He smiled briefly. "You have to know on your own. If you don't know it, there's no point."

"See? You're being difficult," she said.

15

Life without Dom Carlos

Things around the house had normalized.

Angela was not even avoiding Emanuel. They often sat in easy silence—reading, listening to the radio or music on Dona Mafalda's victrola. Dona Mafalda was on her quest to find her most virtuous self. Becoming more rigid and judgmental than before gave her the backbone to keep on the right path to avoid temptation.

The lodgers were coming in and out in a steady, manageable stream, creating a diversion for Angela and the rest of the family. Rosa was so busy that she hardly found time to gossip.

"What's happening out there, Rosa?" Emanuel asked.

"If you only knew," she said.

"Please tell us," Emanuel coached, preparing himself for a good laugh.

Dona Mafalda and Angela studied Rosa. As much as they professed to hate gossip, they couldn't resist it.

"They're saying that Emanuel is sleeping with Dona Mafalda," she said.

Angela laughed and Dona Mafalda harrumphed. Emanuel grinned and added to Rosa's story, "You should tell them that I am sleeping with you both—Dona Mafalda on my right and Angela on my left."

Dona Mafalda looked up from her book and said peevishly, "Your irreverence is shocking. Such levity is impudence at best and a provocation at least. You enjoy being insolent."

"Since Lucas left her, she uses even bigger words than before," Rosa whispered to Emanuel.

He chuckled and Dona Mafalda got up in a huff and went up to her room.

Emanuel followed her example. Tonight he would go to bed early. He had things to think about and he needed rest. He had to seriously think about the conversation he had had with the monsignor and the strange request he had made.

The church bell struck two mournful rings that echoed through the dark village. Emanuel was so lost in his thoughts that he didn't hear the door open.

She stood next to the bed, like a ghost, looking down at him.

When he opened his eyes and looked at her shadow, he let out a howl of fear, as if he had been set upon by a murderer. And then he realized it was Angela and she was shaking with laughter. They waited a few seconds to see if his outburst had awoken the house, but not even the menagerie had stirred.

"Light the lamp, Emanuel," she said. "We are going to have a talk and I hope you are wearing pajamas under all those blankets."

Emanuel lit the lamp and looked at Angela. "What are you doing here?" he asked.

"I found the way," she said.

"You think so?" he asked, imagining how terribly embarrassed he would have been, had he been naked under the bedcovers. Presently he was so self-conscious that he felt his flaccid penis rest against his leg as if knocked unconscious by surprise.

She sat next to him as if this impromptu visit was no big deal. "Yes," she said. "I was in bed thinking about what you said and I knew the way to your forgiveness."

"What is it?" he asked, turning to her.

"I must confess my love for you and ask you to marry me."

"You think that's what I want from you?" he asked half surprised.

"I don't think. I know."

"Why don't you try me and see if it works," he said.

He was still sitting on the bed, but Angela got up, knelt at his feet, and said holding his hand in hers, taking slight notice that his pajamas were unbuttoned. "Please marry me, Emanuel." She looked up at him and waited. The weak light created shadows dancing on her face.

"No," he said quietly.

She wasn't surprised. She said in a tone she would have used to convince a fearful child, "Don't be stubborn. You know that's what you want."

"I don't trust you," he said in the same quiet tone.

"I've loved you since the first day I saw you. Know that I will always love Lazarus and Dom Carlos. It's the way I am. You have a scoundrel for a penis that needs to be always thrust into someone, but I know that you're an honorable man and you'll be faithful, as I will be to you."

He sighed deeply and held onto her hand.

She waited for an answer, looking up at him.

"You should have left out the *scoundrel penis* and the other two men to make it a true love confession," he said as if he was pondering on the validity of her statement.

She lowered her head until her cheek rested on his knees. He adjusted himself on the edge of the bed and held his breath, feeling slightly disoriented. He caressed her head.

"I love you," she said, getting off her knees and sitting next to him.

He shouldn't put himself in harm's way, but he couldn't deny what he felt for her and he couldn't deny himself the chance of living it. This was his time to love her completely. He knew that he was stepping in front of a loaded gun. Angela's love could kill him as much as the absence of it.

It was almost morning. The sun had not yet lifted the orange bar across the sky when Emanuel and Angela gave in to each other, without hurry, without words, and after a long while quietly fell asleep.

As if ordered by the same voice and in protest, the menagerie started making noises in the kitchen. Before they could wake up the other lodgers, Angela went to the kitchen to appease them, and Emanuel followed her a few minutes later. Angela built a fire and sat in front of it. Hercules, Viriato, and Dalia fell asleep, but Nixon sat in front of Emanuel looking at him fixedly. The pig was not only sad—he was a sad, staring pig.

"That pig is trying to intimidate me," he said.

"Who?" Angela asked.

"Nixon, the only pig in this kitchen," Emanuel answered.

Angela laughed and called Nixon to her. She scratched his head and talked soothingly to the animal. It was raining hard and the sound of it made the comfort of the kitchen even warmer. Nixon oinked softly and rested his snout on Angela's knee. *Where is Dom Carlos?* the pig asked.

"I don't know, darling..." she answered.

Emanuel looked at her and frowned. She laughed. It was never a good idea to talk to a pig and to a lover at the same time.

After a long silence, she said, "My heart is no longer made of glass. It won't break. Like metal springs, after being stretched, they remember and spring back to their original shape—so my heart can be bent out of shape, but will return to its original form with time." She smiled at his intensely serious face.

"What a strange thing to say," he said, struck by that alarming statement. He was not sure that he would like Angela with a bendable heart. "Can this new heart of yours love me?" he asked.

She looked at him for a long time before answering, "I will love you, always, even without a heart."

He let his fingers run through her hair, disentangling the strands and wrapping them around his hand.

"I feel so much happier since you forgave me," she said.

"I didn't forgive you!" he objected. "You still have years of expiation."

"Yes, you did. I know that about you."

"What else do you know about me that I don't want you to know?" he asked and pulled her hair until her face touched his.

"You never close your eyes when you make love," she murmured.

He looked surprised. "Why should I?"

"I don't know. I think most people do."

"And some people don't. I don't," he answered defensively, knowing that he was lying and calling up Dona Mafalda's lesson. He thought about his ass skinned by the grinding stone, and his strangled cry *Mafangela*.

"Is it because you want to make sure you're making love to the right woman?" she asked.

He was quiet for a moment and then said, "I dreamt so often about you... that I closed my eyes and let myself be with you. Now I want to take every moment in—not take a second for granted. Now that I have you..."

Angela felt her heart expand for this sweet beautiful gypsy who loved her with his eyes open. They fell into a long, peaceful silence.

"Tomorrow I have to travel." He finally said. He was thinking about the conversation he had had with the monsignor and the promise that followed.

"Work?" she asked.

"Yes," he lied.

"Should I worry?" Something vague and melancholic had lodged itself in the back of her mind.

"No, I'll be back, I promise you."

The new teacher arrived on a wet, cold Saturday morning.

"I am Prudência Piedade de Jesus." The woman at the door was someone not to be taken lightly. She was tall and strong with the musculature of a stevedore, very high brow, protruding teeth and eyes, and short, limp, straight hair, tucked behind her ears. She looked like the caricature of a giant rabbit. It was hard to tell if she was late or even mid-thirties. Prudência was not a pretty woman. She smiled at Angela, waiting for her to say something.

"Come in," Angela said, and in a swift movement took her heavy, unwieldy suitcase. But the new teacher laughed heartily and snatched the suitcase from Angela as if it was a piece of paper. "I'll take it, my dear," she said. "You're a slip of a girl and this is heavy. It's full of books."

After the new teacher put away her belongings, she announced that she was going to talk with the monsignor, per the village council's request.

The monsignor waited for the new teacher all day long. He was too keyed up to do anything else. Every now and then, he patted the pocket of his cassock, where Vivienne's letter rested like a contagion, but he didn't want to be distracted by it. He needed all his presence of mind to deal with the new teacher. Yet, his thoughts kept on diverting to Vivienne and Dom Carlos.

Although he was happy that Dom Carlos was out of the way and falling back into his wife's arms, there was something skewed about the whole thing. As much as he didn't want Dom Carlos to come back, as much as Dom Carlos irritated him and even provoked him, he had grown to respect his strength and integrity. The man stood behind the things he believed in. There was something off about the whole thing. Dom Carlos would never just disappear. He would write or return to tell Angela himself of such a weighty decision as to return to his wife. He would never turn his back on Angela. He would never act like his own father.

Startled by the knock on the door, the monsignor flung it wide open with a force that seemed like it would break the door off its hinges. "Come in!" shouted the monsignor.

Miss Prudência stepped back in agitation. She didn't expect a small man with lunatic eyes to open the door and yell at her. She stayed rooted at the door.

"Didn't I tell you to come in?" he shouted again.

She entered warily.

"Sit down!" he ordered. "I've been told that instead of a man, as I requested, they sent me again another diabolical woman!" the monsignor said, looking at her with frank disapproval.

She sat down and said, "Well, I am a woman and very proud of it—diabolical remains to be seen." She knew that instant that she had walked into a trap.

"I am the monsignor of this village," he said. "This village is my business. Whatever happens here is my business. So if you understand that, you will have nothing to fear by being a teacher with Dona Mafalda. A man would have been better in order to teach that arrogant woman a lesson, but you'll have to do. As long as you report to me and follow my orders, everything will be fine."

He looked at her perplexed face for a moment. "What are you gawking at?" he asked impatiently.

"You have to be the most impolite person I have ever met," she said, still staring fixedly at the monsignor.

He was completely taken aback. He distanced himself from Miss Prudência in a quick step backward as if he had received an electric shock and said, "I rule this village. Don't forget that."

"And for that, you have to be rude?" she asked, getting up and taking a step toward the monsignor. Her teeth seemed to be even more prominent than before.

The monsignor took another step back. He was silent for a moment. Then he said, "I just want you to understand where the power is. Anything you need, you'll come to me."

"If I need anything, I'll go to the village council. My contract is with them, not with you. I came here as a courtesy to them—they had asked me to."

"I can send you back on your ass!" the monsignor yelled.

"I don't think so," Miss Prudência answered evenly. "I just signed a contract with the council. You send me home without a good reason and you'll have to pay me for the entire year."

The encounter invited comparison with an enraged rat threatening to attack a giant rabbit. The monsignor was shaking with rage, his fingers curling like claws and Miss Prudência slowly closing the space between the two of them, her face and ears getting hot and flushed.

"I'll find a reason!" he said fuming.

"And let me tell you something else, Monsignor. Since we are revealing who we are, I am an agnostic. So if you have nothing else to say that may be useful, I must go. Good day!" She turned and walked out into the rain, leaving the door open and the monsignor trembling with fury.

"Agnostic!" he yelled and looked upward for an encouraging sign from God, but all he could see was a water stain on the ceiling.

Miss Prudência strode through the village at a brisk pace. She didn't even notice the rain. She needed to collect her thoughts and recuperate from her interview with the priest. No wonder people became cagey when the monsignor was mentioned. She'd heard that he was difficult, but this was more than being difficult. This was being completely mad.

At the Department of Education, the superintendent had said, "That particular monsignor needs you." So they knew she was walking into a parody of fools and no one had forewarned her—not even that nice girl Angela. They were going to use her as the whip to punish their priest. That wasn't fair. She hadn't even met the other teacher, and she was already doubting the wisdom of her decision to come here. She wasn't sure that she wanted to stay in this remote village with such a brute for a leader.

When she entered the house, Angela was preparing lunch. She sat down next to the fire, dripping water on the floor.

Angela gave her a compassionate look. Poor woman, someone should have advised her about the monsignor.

Miss Prudência broke the silence. "Your monsignor is a madman, my dear," she said, "How can you deal with him?"

"The monsignor is hard to explain," Angela said. "After a while, you'll get used to him."

"I fear I may *not*!" she said with a lilt on the *not*.

"Here, have a cup of tea, and go change into dry clothes while I prepare lunch. Soon you'll meet Dona Mafalda. She is very nice and she doesn't like the monsignor either."

"Oh! That is indeed good news!" she rejoiced. "I like the woman already!" And she laughed that hearty laugh of someone self-assured about her place in the world.

Miss Prudência changed her clothes and came down to the kitchen to have a quiet cup of tea. She was in deep thought looking into the fire when Hercules came into the kitchen.

"What a handsome animal," she said, noticing the cat at the same time the cat noticed her.

Angela opened her mouth to warn her to stay away from Hercules, but the cat was already sniffing the new teacher's hand with a look of disdain. Then he butted his head on her hand, sniffed her for a little while longer, and walked away.

"You just made history," Angela said. "Hercules bites everybody."

"All cats want respect and some demand it," the new teacher declared as if she was reciting a basic life principle.

During the next few days, everyone wanted to meet Miss Prudência, and they brought the usual gifts—eggs, chickens, cake, fresh bread, cheese, sugar.

Miss Prudência was elated to have landed in such a friendly place. How could these nice hospitable people put up with that monsignor? There must be a reason. She would try to understand. *After all, everything could be done with understanding,* she thought.

Miss Prudência's congeniality was so contagious that in a few moments, one forgot about her homely features. What stayed in one's mind and heart was her laugh and willingness to get along and help others. If the monsignor wanted to create a hell for Dona Mafalda, he got the wrong teacher. Not only did they complement each other as gold on blue, but they became fast friends and allies against his tyranny.

When Miss Prudência saw Emanuel for the first time, he was sitting in the kitchen near the fire reading a report. She knew that there was another lodger, a police detective from the mainland assigned to investigate the problem of the Night Justice as well as the fate of the three young men who had disappeared. There was a general sense that he had failed in both probes. She had heard that Emanuel Santos da Cruz was one of those people who had been deployed to spy and been co-opted, like so many others. She had also heard that he had fallen in love with Angela—and cooptation couldn't take a better form than love.

When Miss Prudência came into the kitchen, she was struck by Emanuel's good looks. He had that stunning appearance of someone who didn't try to look good but did. He lifted his head from the report and looked at her, startled. He thought it was Hercules and he was already rolling up the report he was reading to strike the cat.

"Oh…" he said and stared.

Miss Prudência was stunned and also said, "Oh…"

He smiled and offered his hand for a handshake. Miss Prudência took it and vigorously pumped it up and down.

"I'm sorry, I didn't mean to startle you," he said. "I just arrived back from Europe and no one was home…"

"I am Prudência Piedade de Jesus or Miss Prudência, as they call me. You must be Detective Santos."

After the introductions, Emanuel learned that in his absence, the village had been assigned a new teacher who became a friend to all and an enemy of the monsignor—all in a few weeks. They sat near the fire drinking tea.

"The vote on who controls the Holy Ghost festivities is going to take place this evening," she said. "Such dissension within a village!" Miss Prudência declared derisively. "And with the blessing of your bishop! The monsignor is in for a surprise, I think..." She stood up. "Well, I must go, my dear detective!" she announced and left with a salute and a spring in her step.

The kitchen seemed oddly empty as if a multitude of people had left along with the new teacher. He heard her whistling down the garden and out of the gate.

Now he was alone in the house. He went up to his room and looked out the window. There he was, Hercules on the wall, on his usual spot, looking up at him.

Hey stupid! the cat said.

This was the moment. Emanuel had to put his plan in action before nightfall and while everyone was out. The whole village would be away and occupied for at least three, maybe four hours. He went down to the woodshop, got a sledgehammer, a pickaxe, and a shovel and went straight toward Hercules, who ran away with his hackles up.

While most of the old stone wall had a weather-worn patina that gave it a beautiful, timeless look, a section of the wall had evidently been repaired not long ago with new stone and cement—the very spot where Hercules would sit.

Emanuel had prepared for weeks for this moment. He wanted to complete his excavation project before anyone returned home. It took him an hour to break up the repaired section of the wall and clear away the stones and broken mortar from where he wanted to dig.

Hercules slowly approached the digging site and sat a few steps away from it—as if he was a supervisor overseeing the progress of an important archeological dig. The digging didn't take him long. Emanuel hit something hard, hollow-sounding, and sinister. He stooped to feel what he had discovered.

It was the wooden lid of a coffin.

Hercules looked at him and blinked, *Finally, stupid! Finally!*

At the Music Club House, the villagers were completely absorbed in the voting process. It was apparent from the outset that the Petticoats were in trouble. Those loyal to the bishop sat deflated on one side of the room, while the other side, the side opposing the bishop's attempted power grab, laughed and congratulated themselves for each Terrorist who went up to cast a ballot. The Terrorists were prepared to win and had bought fireworks for the occasion. No feast, either of a saint or of a pagan god, would see so much fanfare. The Petticoats were also poised for triumph. If they won, they would have held a mass and sung a new hymn composed for the occasion. The philharmonic and the choir had suffered quite a bit because those who identified as Terrorists refused to sing the hymn or play in the philharmonic or be part of anything that was going to celebrate the bishop and the stealing of the Holy Ghost.

António Dores, the village's poet and musician, frustrated deacon, horrible husband and father of two, was especially proud of the new hymn:

> *The victory of the saints*
> *Guided by God's face*
> *Who in the heavens He paints*
> *The promise of eternal grace*
>
> *Demonic disobedience*
> *Defeated today on a vote*
> *Instead of God's lamb*
> *They are the devil's goat*
>
> *This is the day of glory, glory alleluia*
> *And what does it mean to "youah?"*

At the monsignor's request, the priest from the neighboring village of Little Branch was also on hand to assist with the voting process. The monsignor had wanted backup clergy there to make sure that the sanctity of the voting process was respected.

Having avoided this fiasco in Little Branch, Father Benedito was mortified to be a party in promoting the schism within Two Brooks simply because his friend and fellow clergyman was too proud or too intolerant to make peace with his people. Father Benedito told the bishop that his village had refused to take a vote. It wasn't completely true, but if a vote was *never* proposed, it would never fester as a bone of contention. Sometimes courage came with a bit of cunning and humility, but Monsignor Inocente of Two Brooks was neither devious nor humble.

As the night wore on, the Petticoats shrank into a terrible sadness and simply waited for the *fait accompli* to be over and done with. The children had fallen asleep without having sung the hymn. Dona Mafalda and Miss Prudência were beaming while trying to look disappointed, as the results were announced.

Nascimento's adopted daughter, Manuela, was all prepared to sing a *paso doble* she had composed in anticipation of the Petticoats' victory. A song about a matador facing a bull in the bullring had nothing to do with the evening's agenda, but it was hard to resist Manuela's accordion. She played badly and sang even worse. Manuela fell asleep, drooling on her accordion, waiting for the time to rejoice and sing her *paso doble*:

> *Here comes the toreador with his cape*
> *It is red. No, it is yellow*
> *And the bull comes at it,*
> *Olé, Oléééé*

Finally, the last vote was counted. The Terrorists had won hands down. When Father Benedito declared that the Terrorists had triumphed, the crowd erupted in screams of joy so loud that the children woke up terrorized by the uproar.

Manuela lifted her face from the accordion and started to play, but the cheering was so loud that you could only hear her *Oléééé*. When Nascimento realized that Manuela was singing, she quickly silenced the child and the accordion—they were Petticoats and had nothing to celebrate. And Manuela thought that if she could have chosen, she would have been a Terrorist, and then she could have sung her *paso doble*.

The fireworks were lit off and for what seemed hours the night sky was ablaze with light and fire. Manuela had never seen such beauty so up close, so many lights and so much joy. And then she was told that she shouldn't feel happy because she was a Petticoat. She walked home holding her parents' hands, with Jaime carrying her accordion, Nascimento holding the Petromax light, and Manuela holding a secret—she was a Terrorist.

Father Benedito was offered a ride back to his village. He shook his head as the truck crawled through the sad procession of Petticoats illuminated by the firework display. He was tired and depressed about the evening's events. A divided village was a sad thing. *God forgive the monsignor and that damn bishop,* he thought.

As he approached his village of Little Branch, the screams of his own people were unmistakable. The entire village was massed around the church on their knees, wailing and begging God for forgiveness. His mother was at the top of the steps leading the weeping villagers in praying the Rosary. Sworn enemies made peace, brothers and sisters promised to be better to each other, husbands vowed to be better husbands, and even those who didn't believe in God were praying—just in case.

When Father Benedito ran up the steps of the church, his villagers redoubled their crying and praying. The sky was on fire and falling on them, just like the Bible said. Their sins were going to be punished with the end of the world.

It took Father Benedito no small effort to quiet them down. And just when he thought they were going to remain hushed, the racket from Two Brooks startled the Little Branch villagers into bawling and begging for God's mercy. Eventually, Father Benedito was able to explain what was happening in Two Brooks.

Those fools had voted as a divided village and in the process almost killed Little Branch with fright!

Everyone went home humiliated, embarrassed, revisiting the promises they'd made, furious with Two Brooks and cursing the bishop for pushing people into such discord.

Emanuel's whole body stiffened with anticipation and anxiety. The fireworks helpfully illuminated his excavation work. He cleared the dirt off the wood surface as much as he could and there it was, a coffin, buried only four feet deep under the section of the garden wall where Hercules sat every day.

It was time to set in motion the second phase of this investigation. He ran to use the post office telephone. When Dona Valquiria made the connection, Emanuel led with, "Come, it's true."

He waved Dona Valquiria away and resumed his conversation in a low inaudible voice. She threw him a long, hard look as if he had offended her. Usually she was able to eavesdrop on phone conversations and glean a bit more information. *Come, it's true.* What was true? And why should the police come? Was the bishop going to have those who voted against his wishes arrested?

Emanuel hurriedly left to look for Angela. Within a couple of hours, the police would be all over her garden and life would forever change. He found Angela with the other women quietly putting the chairs in neat rows. The Terrorists lingered in the street singing and dancing, while the Petticoats, defeated and dispirited, disappeared into the shadows and silently retreated into their homes.

Then she saw him. Alarmed by his disheveled, dirt-stained appearance, she cried out, "What's wrong?"

"Come with me," he said, took her hand to lead her out of the Music Club House. She followed and they pushed through people dancing in the street to get through to a quiet, out-of-the-way spot. The fireworks lit up her face. He hugged her for a long time and said in her ear, "I love you." He had convinced himself that her heart was no longer made of glass, given the blow he was about to deliver.

"I know," she answered, smiling up at him.

He lowered his head and kissed her on the mouth, savoring that last moment of peace and sweetness. "I've missed you so much," he said.

"I'm so happy that you're back," Angela said, frowning, aware that something was up.

He took a deep breath and said, "I found a coffin buried in your garden, under the wall where Hercules sits."

"What?" she asked perplexed.

But she had heard him well enough. Someone was buried in her garden. She felt her legs melting under her. She faltered and Emanuel caught her.

"I'm sorry, I'm so sorry," he said, with his mouth pressed against her head and her body against his. "The police will be here in a little while. Let's go home."

She felt completely numb. She swallowed. She needed to find her voice, but she was at a loss for words. They walked silently home. They entered through the front door, thereby avoiding the garden. They sat in the kitchen facing a dead fire.

"When did you get home?" she finally asked.

"A few hours ago," he said.

"And you didn't look for me?"

He was silent for a while and then said, "I needed to do this when no one was around. Today was the perfect day."

"Why didn't you tell me?" It sounded like an accusation.

"I'm sorry. This police business sometimes gets a bit dicey," he answered.

They were quiet, looking at nothing, lacking the courage to look at each other.

"Then you are not as harmless as we thought you were," she said.

"Harmless?" he asked confused.

"Yes, I thought you were happy with the events. No one went to prison because of the Night Justice, the three men went away, and we were together. But that wasn't enough for you."

Emanuel didn't know whether to be offended or not. "I never lied to you. It is my job to find out the truth. And, yes, I'm very happy that we're together, but that doesn't change the fact that I have a job to do."

"Who is in the coffin?" she asked, dismissing his explanation.

"I didn't open it. I have to wait for the forensic people."

16

If Only They Had Listened To Hercules

Angela woke with a start. Someone was at the door knocking. Emanuel entered the room. She looked at him expectantly. "Who was in the coffin?" she asked.

He held her gaze and said, "Manuel Barcos."

Angela felt the room spinning. She lay back onto the pillow and covered her eyes with her hand. "He boarded that ship to Brazil and he sent a letter to his parents," she said.

"We think that Saul took his place and that Pedro Matias, having been involved from the beginning, was behind the letter that Manuel's parents received... maybe from letters that he intercepted from Manuel to Madalena. It would have been easy for Lazarus to forge Manuel's handwriting and manner of expression and assist Pedro in this terrible scheme. The assumption now is that Saul and Pedro Matias murdered Manuel and Lazarus was witness to it all. We find no reason why Lazarus would have killed Manuel. Pedro Matias and Saul, however, had plenty of reasons. Saul left using Manuel's papers and later Lazarus fled because he couldn't live with the deception. Eventually he would have spilled the beans and implicated his father. There's no other plausible explanation, Angela. I'm sorry." Emanuel's voice was gentle but unflinching. "The police found one sabot in the grave—a woman's sabot, size five," he continued. "It's a brand-new sabot, just dropped inexplicably in the grave..."

"It's mine," Angela said. "Lazarus made me a pair, but misplaced one. I remember him telling me that he had never made just one sabot."

Angela looked at Emanuel as if he could rescue her from that terrible sorrow. She was feeling hurt for all—Manuel and Saul and their families. They were all doomed.

"It's Pedro's fault! I'm sure he killed Manuel, and Lazarus had to leave because he knew he wouldn't be able to keep their lies straight... or Pedro threatened him... maybe he threatened to hurt me, as he had done before and

Lazarus believed him… always. I bet he let poor Saul take the blame—led him to believe that it was his fault."

The Sacristy, Pedro and Amelia Matias, Joaquim and Maria Gomes, Dona Mafalda, Miss Prudência, Carlota Amora, the monsignor and the menagerie all waited silently for Angela and Emanuel to come down. They looked at each other, helplessly. The menagerie ran out the door and sat by Manuel's grave.

Angela scanned the room and fixed her gaze on Pedro Matias. He was pale and gaunt, looking small and defeated. Was this the same man who abused his family and caused so much hurt? He looked like a shadow of his malicious self. His head was pink from the burns and his hair had never grown back. He looked at Angela with shadowy eyes.

The monsignor said gravely, "It is time to be honest and decent. This village has been in the grips of malice and deceit and we no longer can survive such poison. Pedro, the most responsible for the sorrow and distress caused to the ones present, has something to say."

Everyone locked their eyes on him.

"I already confessed my sins to the monsignor," he said somberly. "I know that what I'm about to say is unforgivable, but I still beg you to forgive me." The silence was complete and then Pedro continued, "Manuel Barcos died. It was an accident. The night that he was going to leave for the city, to go to Brazil, he wanted to see Madalena again. He left his bags in the woodshop and wrote to Madalena to meet him at the windmill. Saul always found a way to intercept the letters. I found out that Manuel was going to see Madalena that night. I wanted Saul to give her a good beating, along with Manuel. I told Saul, but he already knew. He simply didn't believe that his wife would go meet Manuel. But she did." Pedro looked at his daughter and she lowered her eyes.

"When Madalena met Manuel, they said their goodbyes. Afterward Saul waited for Manuel and they fought. Manuel was furious because Madalena had told him that she loved her husband. Manuel picked up a rock and threw it at Saul. It hit Saul on the side of the head and he went down. It was like David and Goliath. Then Manuel attacked Saul, screaming like a madman, and grabbed him by the neck. Saul was dazed on the ground while being choked. I tried to pull Manuel off of Saul but he wasn't letting go. Then Saul punched Manuel. One punch sent the boy flying headfirst against the wall. There was so much blood and Manuel didn't move. Saul thought that he had killed him, panicked and ran away. He went directly to the woodshop where Lazarus was keeping Manuel's horse and luggage. He sent Lazarus down to where we were. Then Manuel came to—he wasn't dead after all. We tried to help him, and he said he wasn't feeling well. But before we were able to reach Lazarus' house, Manuel gave up the ghost. Maybe it was the blow to the head with everything else that killed him. We knew this time he was dead. Saul came back looking for us and found us in the garden with Manuel, dead, his eyes opened, as if looking up at the moonless sky. I told Saul that I... was going to blame him for Manuel's death and that Lazarus would stand by me. The three of us buried Manuel that night and Saul left in the wee hours of the morning. He took Manuel's luggage and horse and left like a possessed soul. He knew he would be the first suspect."

Angela was crying softly. Everyone was so quiet that even the menagerie didn't make a sound.

Pedro Matias continued, "Lazarus had always been a weak boy. He had no stomach for lies or intrigue. I knew it was only a matter of time that he would break and implicate everybody, including himself, for witnessing a murder. So I convinced him to leave and I made up the story about the limpets and the sea. I... may... have told him that I would find a way to hurt Angela if he didn't leave. If the monsignor hadn't got involved, no one would have questioned it." Pedro Matias looked at the monsignor and continued his story. "By then I had learned how to read. I didn't want to be swindled again by anybody so I secretly learned how to read and write—I went to the city to a special tutor. So, when Lazarus wrote, I knew how to contact him and tell him how things were going." Pedro Matias cleared his throat, "Then Lazarus, as I knew he would, messed the whole thing up." He sighed.

"Where is Lazarus?" Angela asked with eyes full of fire.

"I don't know. He didn't write after that letter to you, to the monsignor, and Dom Carlos. I think his heart was broken because of you and Dom Carlos. He told me that he would never write again. I don't know where he is now."

Angela got up as fast as a flash of light and punched, scratched and slapped Pedro Matias. He tried to protect himself by covering his face with his arms and hands. Angela attacked him with such fury that it took several people to pull her off of him. Emanuel restrained her in his arms.

"I want you dead, you bastard! I want you dead!" she raged. "You killed Manuel!"

"I'm sick. I don't have long to live," Pedro answered. "But for what it's worth, I'm sorry."

"You're a malicious, horrible man who has only caused pain and dissension. You deserve to burn in hell!" she yelled.

"Angela!" the monsignor said horrified.

She looked at the monsignor and said again, "Never! I will never forgive him."

Madalena was crying silently into her hands, sitting next to Saul's mother who was still as a statue.

Carlota Amora's eyes were more mournful than usual, and her face seemed to have lengthened in the last hour. The monsignor motioned for her to speak.

"I've known all along that Saul was alive and well because he wrote. To protect me, I suppose, he didn't tell me why he left. He was going to look for his father before he married Madalena. I knew something had happened for him to leave like that. I thought it had to do with his father because he went to Africa first. He's in Brazil now. We have old contacts there from a previous life. I know it in my heart that Saul didn't kill anyone. My son is a gentle soul and Pedro Matias is just trying to implicate him because Pedro is the one who killed Manuel," Carlota said accusingly.

Pedro opened his mouth to defend himself, but the monsignor put a hand on his arm to stop him.

Emanuel said, "We will know if Manuel died from a blow to the head. And if so, the Barcos family may bring charges against Saul, Pedro and Lazarus for murder or at least conspiracy."

A hush descended on the room. No one knew anything about these legal matters. Everything was strange and foreign. Not even the monsignor had a solution.

"These are matters that require thought and discussion," the monsignor said. "No one should rush into anything for now, until we know where we stand." The monsignor gave Pedro another look. There was more to come.

"I sent Lazarus the letters Manuel had sent to Madalena. I wanted him to make letters out of them for his family—to copy the handwriting and use the same terms or phrases. Lazarus did one and refused to do more, talking about not wanting to be involved in more deceit and lies..." Pedro said, bowing his head. "I wanted people to leave this case alone and at the same time give the Barcoses some peace, if they thought that Manuel was out there...alive."

The sun was rising. The dawn chorus of bird song ushered in the new day, and gradually the morning noises invaded the house.

Rosa, half asleep, made coffee for everyone. People were gathering at Angela's door. They knocked, called out and asked questions through windows and closed gates. The monsignor came out to tell the gathering that he would give an update later in church. Then he and Emanuel left to speak with the Barcos family.

Two Brooks was so silent that even the wind abated and seemed to be prepared for what happened next. Wrenching screams reverberated through the village. Men and women screamed as if their hearts were being ripped from their chests. Almost in unison, the villagers knelt in their kitchens, bedrooms, fields and gardens, hanging their heads, letting the tears run free down their faces. They cried all at once in their pain, sending a wave of grief so wide and deep that no one could do anything but mourn and obsess over the terrible wrong that had been done to Manuel.

At home, Angela silently prayed and wept. No. Even if the law let Lazarus and Saul off the hook, they could never, ever return. Some things were irreversible. It seemed that too much damage had been done for these families to reconcile. The Matiases, the Amoras and the Barcoses were irreparably wounded and forever estranged.

For the first time in her life, Angela felt the urge to leave the island and go to a place where there would be no reminders of these terrible wrongs. And then she understood what Lazarus and Saul must have felt and she began to forgive.

At six o'clock, the church was full, crowded with the parishioners from Two Brooks and the curious from nearby villages, eager to find out more about the scandalous goings-on in Two Brooks.

Monsignor Inocente, looking defeated and tired, addressed his people, now divided and resentful. He looked at his congregation and started, "Yesterday we had one of the most important days in our village—important because it will test the fabric of our souls and character, not to speak of our commitment to the principles of Christianity. Today we are in that unparalleled position to make decisions that will forever change who we are as people. Our worth as people hinges on the decisions we will make today."

Some people started to get uncomfortable with the fancy talking and some knew what the monsignor was saying, but the older folks were only guessing. They wanted the monsignor to get to the point as soon and clearly as possible.

The monsignor continued, "The village is divided into two camps—those who trusted the church leadership and those who didn't, and this schism will be costing us dearly in more ways than one. But I leave it up to you to make those decisions and consequently shoulder the consequences. If that was not enough of an injury, today we learned the fate of Manuel Barcos, Saul Amora and Lazarus Matias."

There was a murmur throughout the church and someone cried and fainted. The monsignor continued in a suffering tone, "I know that God is always with us, but there was a time in this village that a surge of something vile and malicious took over His presence. This shadow, this sadness, this absence of God, brought us here today to cry for three young men who in their own right were good, good sons, good husbands, but who are no longer with us."

The parishioners were crying openly—those who knew the whole story and those with story scraps and only a vague idea of what had happened.

"Manuel Barcos, who we all thought had immigrated to Brazil, has been buried for two years in, unbeknownst to her, Angela Matias' garden. His parents received one laconic letter that led them to believe that their beloved son was, after all, alive and well. This letter was a senseless act of deceit that hurt this poor family by giving them false hope. Manuel was not in Brazil, but buried in Angela's garden. Lazarus, Saul and Pedro Matias buried this poor boy on the night that he was supposed to depart for Brazil. The investigation and forensics will conclude Manuel died of natural causes. The men who buried him panicked because they thought they were the cause of his death."

The crying subsided. They all wanted to know what the monsignor was going to propose to the village.

"Manuel will have a Christian burial as soon as his body is released from the authorities. And then we must start the healing process of forgiving and letting go of anger and vengeance. If we don't, we will perish. We will lose our peace of mind, the fabric of all that is good. And as your moral guide, your servant, I beg of you to think about forgiveness, reparation, healing and life. We as a people need to forgive in order to heal."

But the congregation, red and swollen from crying, was not in the mood for fancy words and saintly appeals. What could they do when the Holy Ghost was now profaned, a young man had been murdered, and two men from the village had made a quick exit after burying someone in the garden? Fancy talking this time wouldn't do.

"Bullshit!" a woman shouted.

Everyone turned to the sound of that voice. It was Ema, Manuel's sister. The monsignor, unaccustomed to being challenged, especially on his pulpit, looked at Ema as if she had hurled a stone.

"Go home, Ema!" he roared.

But Ema didn't leave. The women around her took her hand and helped her settle down. The whole congregation was looking at the monsignor to see what he was going to do. The silence was complete.

"This service is over," the monsignor said, spewing rage. "Ema, come to the sacristy!"

But Ema, by now deep into disobedience, walked home with Miss Prudência.

Angela turned her back to the sea and saw Emanuel coming toward her. She tucked her hair behind her ears and crossed her arms, focusing on him. He was one step away from her. The sea breeze was strong, full of musky smells and salt. She hugged him and laid her head on his chest. "I want to leave this place," she said. "I can't stand this immense ocean always threatening to pounce."

"Remember when you asked me to marry you?" he murmured.

"Yes, you never gave me an answer," she said.

"Yes, I will marry you. We can go anywhere you want and you will never have to think of this wretched island again."

They looked at each other for a long time. Emanuel said, "But I need to tell you something very important."

Angela sat facing him, expectantly. He took her hands in his and softly said, "I have something to tell you about Dom Carlos."

She paled but held his gaze.

"He is very sick," he said.

Emanuel was looking at her precious face full of anguish for another man. "Shortly after he arrived in France, he was involved in a terrible car accident and was in a coma for a long while. Only now is he regaining his health. But he's still very weak."

Emanuel paused, waiting for her to ask questions. She was like a statue.

"His wife, Vivienne, took care of him and made all the decisions, being the next of kin. He was, and still is, completely dependent on her." Emanuel squeezed her hands tightly before saying, "You see, he didn't write that letter. He couldn't write and still can't."

"I knew it in my heart. I knew it," she murmured.

They were staring at each other.

"How did you find out?" she asked.

"The monsignor asked me to go to France. That's where I've been for the last three weeks, investigating… not on the mainland."

She felt disoriented.

"After all, Dom Carlos is his son and he too didn't believe that he could just write you off. The monsignor was worried about Dom Carlos. I guess the man cares, after all."

"Did you talk to him? Did you see him?" she asked anxiously.

"Yes. He's in a body cast. He injured his larynx seriously enough so that he hasn't been able to speak. I also talked to his attorney. He told me that Vivienne has the authority to make decisions for him, including keeping out anybody who tries to visit. I had a heck of a time trying to see him. He can communicate by blinking." Emanuel sighed deeply and said, "Even his blinking annoyed me!"

Angela put her hand over her mouth to suppress a sob.

Emanuel continued, "His attorney refused to terminate his business in Two Brooks. Vivienne wanted to give you everything to completely sever your contact with him, but the attorney found a loophole that didn't allow her to do that. Before the car accident, Dom Carlos told his attorney that he wanted a divorce and then return to Hawk Island. The attorney knew his client's wishes and that gave him pause…"

"Who has the right to intervene then?" Angela asked, "She could harm him…"

"According to the attorney, she isn't malicious. She is a woman who realized she'd made a serious mistake and is trying to rectify it. The attorney doesn't believe that she would harm him that way. They have had a long history together. They've known each other since they were children… just like you and Lazarus," Emanuel said gently.

"Does the monsignor know?" she asked.

"Yes. As soon as I told him, he went to France. It was as if his heart suddenly emerged from a long coma. He asked Father Benedito to take care of the parish and left in the middle of the night." Emanuel rested his lips on her brow.

He paused and added, "I told Dom Carlos the truth about everything, including us. But he already knew it. I guess Vivienne had sent a private investigator and he took pictures of us… holding hands, kissing… I told him about the mountain of letters you wrote and about the letters you received… dismissing you."

A moment of panic gripped her before she picked the spy out of a mental line-up she hastily assembled: *Who was the private investigator? Ah! It must have been the mainlander selling needles. Of course. She hadn't liked him from the very beginning. Selling needles and taking pictures of the landscape didn't go together. And those beady eyes always fastened on her…*

Emanuel continued, "The attorney told me that Dom Carlos received a letter from you terminating your relationship, and after that letter Dom Carlos agreed to work on his marriage. So, it was partly true when Vivienne said that they were working on putting their marriage back together. I guess she covered all the bases."

There was a long pause.

"Yes," she said. "The answer is yes, we will marry," Angela said, taking his face in her hands. "Oh Emanuel, this doesn't change anything about us. I love you."

"I want us to get married," he said quietly. "But before we do, I have to go away and let you make up your mind, away from me."

"You promised you would never leave me," she said with alarm.

"I'm giving you the space for you to choose."

"I do choose! I chose you," she said, holding his hands in hers. "Dom Carlos accepted all too readily that I had changed my heart about him!" She said in disbelief, "How could he?"

"You got me by default. I have to do this," he said hugging her head to his chest. "Let me do this. Do it for me. I'm a foolish, proud prick."

"Yes, indeed you are a prick! Why do men do these stupid things?" She turned around, moving away from him but stopping after a few steps. She asked with her back to him, "When will you leave?"

"There is no hurry... in a few days."

Dona Mafalda couldn't accept that she was going to lose her best friend, her kindest fan, her beautiful gypsy. She slipped into Emanuel's room at midnight with rollers in her hair to plead with him to stay.

"Please stay," she said, with tears blurring her vision. "Two Brooks won't be the same without you."

"It's too confusing," he said.

They were quiet. "Did Angela destroy your life?" she asked.

He pressed his lips together as if to repress a grimace. Then after a while he said, "Angela gave me one of the most precious things I have ever had—a home. She gave me love and a home. How could that ever destroy a man?"

"I want to be loved like that," Dona Mafalda said wistfully.

Love. What a dangerous thing. He wished he could tell Dona Mafalda that she was lucky for not being a prisoner of such cruel master. But who could speak of love and anguish and be believed? So he quoted:

I have never loved too much,
But if I had
In you, that love I would find…

"A police detective who quotes poetry," Dona Mafalda said with a smile. "How can we not love you?"

"Angela wants to marry me. She doesn't want me to leave."

Nonplussed by his statement, Dona Mafalda asked "Then why are you fighting against your happiness?"

"Because I would always wonder if she could have Dom Carlos… would she choose me?" he said.

"I didn't think you were the type for big, romantic, stupid gestures!" Dona Mafalda said impatiently.

"I'm not. But my pride got the best of me," he said.

They were silent for a while. Then he cleared his throat as if preparing to speak, but said nothing. He cleared his throat and tried again, "I will come back if she calls me. And if she does, this time it will be on my terms. We will get married and live in this godforsaken place until the end of our days. As you see, I am doing this for myself. I can't bear the thought that she married me because I'm under her nose, like a misplaced item, because I happen to be in her line of vision."

My Angel,

My father wrote to me a few weeks ago. I know that he is sick and, in an effort to redeem himself, he confessed to the authorities everything that had happened. I am willing to take responsibility for my cowardice and go back to be with you. I am not afraid anymore. In the last two years, I learned that fear and cowardice are the undoing of a man. And I am a man, Angel—the person you loved was a boy. The person who fled was nothing but a frightened boy.

I also suspect that my father lied about you and Dom Carlos to keep me away. Even if that was the truth, I want you back. You are my wife and the love of my life. You could have had a thousand lovers since I left—I don't care.

I am in America, in New England, in a place called Newport. I am making good money restoring antique furniture for rich people. It is easy to make money in America if you are willing to work hard. I am going to school at night. My limited English saved my life. I can't thank the monsignor enough for paying for my education.

How is the monsignor, that ill-humored man? The more people I meet, the more I appreciate those I knew back home.

Above all, my Angel, I appreciate you. I miss your easy laughing, your generous loving and your willingness to take everyone into your heart.

Please come back to me. Come to my new life or allow me back into our home.

Of all the things I can't live with, is your absence.

Love always,
Lazarus

Hawk,

There is so much I want to tell you, but for now I just need to say that I love you. I am so sorry that Vivienne wrote you and misled you to believe that I had changed my mind about you. Emanuel and later the monsignor came to see me and would not take no for an answer until they were allowed in. I am forever grateful that they did. The divorce is almost final. Vivienne consented to give me the divorce or go to jail for fraud by forging various documents (including letters to you).

I know about Emanuel and the relationship that developed between the two of you after I left. The circumstances seemed to plot against me, but now nothing matters.

I believe that I will be as good as new. I just need a bit more time. But I want you back, Hawk. I want you in my life. I want you to be my wife.

I love you.
Dom Carlos

My Joan of Arc,

Here I am in my apartment, three thousand miles away from you, thinking of my foolish courage. I wanted so much to be brave and fair, to give you the space that I thought you needed. I was also selfish and insecure—I wanted you to love me and me alone. Every day since I left, I think that I acted like a fool. I should have stayed with you.

I miss you so much that it hurts. I will wait for your decision. But even if you decide not to be with me, I will always cherish the greatest love of my life. I have never been as happy as I was living with you on that crazy island of yours. For the first time, I felt that I had a home. And you, Angela, you are my home, the place where I found a glimmer of peace, the place where my love is.

I will love you always.
Emanuel

Two Brooks was at the Easter show. Everyone was there to celebrate spring. This was time for rebirth to all, including Pedro Matias and António Dores and all others who felt they were lost and forgotten. The village had been pushed to the edge of a precipice with its wickedness and the villagers realized that they were teetering—one gust of wind and they would fall.

The monsignor would soon return from France to a village that, much to his surprise, was no longer divided. The Petticoats had shelved their plans for their club, and the funds being raised to buy a brand-new philharmonic were put toward the monsignor's scholarships for the children to go to college. To the monsignor's chagrin, the transformation from disunity to peace had happened without him.

Father Benedito couldn't wait to go home. He couldn't wait for the return of the monsignor who scared him half to death, with all that honor and all that courage that invariably ended up in a big fat mess. Father Benedito opened the window and sat on the windowsill. He took his harmonica from the pocket of his cassock and played. He counted his blessings and prayed that the monsignor, with his tumultuous heart, would not delay in coming home.

The women sat near the fire drinking tea and eating sweet bread. The Sacristy had got together to talk and celebrate—on this occasion to welcome Dona Mafalda and Miss Prudência as members of the core Sacristy.

There were no men in the house. The absence of men was unfamiliar, but at the same time peaceful. There is always a hidden gift in everything that hurts. Angela had always lived with a man—her loving and kind father, but who couldn't understand her thinking. Then her loving and kind husband, but who needed her courage. Dom Carlos who protected her, but needed her passion. And finally, Emanuel, who loved her with an intensity that left her breathless and who needed her to love him and him alone.

Lazarus had disappeared two years ago, Angela remembered with a shiver. And that had been the beginning of her journey learning about loss.

Dona Mafalda had become a different person in the last two years. She lost thirty pounds with her grief diet for losing Dom Carlos and Lucas. When Emanuel left, there was nothing else to lose. She had resented Angela because love was always so eager to find that intense and skinny girl: Lazarus and his eternal love that everyone still talked about after so long; Dom Carlos, renouncing civility to bury himself in a cave of savages just to be with Angela; Emanuel, the roaming gypsy with endless appetites who found home in Two Brooks, broken and at the same time enlivened by Angela's love. But she too was here without being able to explain why. She was quietly hoping for Dom Carlos and Emanuel to come back and for things to be as they were before everything went wrong. She had gained a few lines around her eyes and mouth, her gayety dimmed a little and she was vigilant in shunning the uncouth ways of Two Brooks—petrified that she would become one of them.

Maria Gomes, Carlota and Regina continued to strengthen their friendship. No one could understand the bond between them. They would sit drinking tea or moonshine and talk about their childhood days, about the village, about Regina's tawdry lifestyle and they laughed as old friends do.

Lucas was waiting for the summer to be claimed by his American girl and transported to a new world. And when Dona Mafalda walked by the garage, Lucas' eyes followed her until she disappeared. He too had loved and lost. Lucas would always ache for Dona Mafalda, but he felt a sense of freedom, of relief that he didn't have to walk on egg shells—didn't have to always be concerned about his grammar, his vocabulary, his table manners, how he dressed. He hadn't realized that loving Dona Mafalda had been so exhausting and when their relationship ended, he felt that a door had been unlocked and he was released from being Dona Mafalda's project to make him a kind of Renaissance man. He hung in the balance of longing for her and relief to finally be rid of her and be able to be himself again.

Ascendida was still waiting for her miracle—to right all the things where she had been wronged. She grew ever more distant from her husband, Aldo, and blamed him for all her ills because he drank. She loved her six children, while pitying them for having been born into a world of random cruelty and wanton neglect. Sometimes she tried to see in her husband a picture of Mario, the man she would always love. And at other times, she would feel so remorseful about her shabby, dismissive treatment of Aldo that she would run to confession and cry at the monsignor's feet. Her penitence was always the same—be kind to him, be kind.

Aldo was often brought to his parents instead of his home when he was drunk. Most of the time, he passed out in bed without a whimper, but sometimes he would want to go home to make love to Ascendida. His parents, knowing the perils he faced at home, locked him in his room as they did when he was a little boy who refused to be sick. And Rosa would come and see him, tend to her loving father, go home and lie to Ascendida that Aldo was taking care of his father who had diarrhea, hemorrhoids, ingrown toenails, or any other malady that Ascendida would recoil from treating.

Rosa's endless need to serve others seemed to widen her world of care each passing day. But her overriding responsibility was her father, Aldo, and her mother, Ascendida. Her job was to protect Aldo from Ascendida until he quit drinking. Nothing in the world could displace that preoccupation in her mind and heart. Not even her drowned family—they were now such a distant memory, but a reminder nevertheless that life could turn in a second if you weren't watchful.

Angela's house was Rosa's domain and now she had a say in whether they should or shouldn't take in a lodger. This little bit of power over unsuspecting strangers reinforced her conviction that the world needed her to maintain peace and prosper. And if a misguided businessman dismissed her as only the maid, they did so at their peril of being told there was "no room at the inn."

Nascimento continued to fight her addiction to voyeurism. She was a dedicated wife and mother and when she thought she had turned the bend, she fell again, like a drunkard into a vat of wine. She was most concerned about the perils of going beyond Two Brooks. In the city, she had found a perch from which she could peer down at an apartment, the curtains pushed to the side, its inhabitants loving and laughing, oblivious of being watched by a voyeur.

Nascimento, especially at night, would obsess about getting up and going to the city, on foot, to peep down at that apartment.

Madalena spent hours looking down the road, as if expecting someone returning from a long journey. Saul would be returning soon. If only he had stayed a few more days, maybe she would have been a mother by now and Saul would have a son to hold him back. Carlota was not sharing her letters, but was smiling more often and repeated like a mantra, "He is almost here, I feel it."

At times, Madalena had vivid dreams of Saul picking her up, high up in his arms, like an offering to the heavens. She felt cursed. Not even in her dreams could she find reprieve from the evil eye. She asked the Barcos family to forgive the hurt she and Saul had caused them, albeit unintentionally. Maybe it was the hurt of others, weighing on her soul that kept Saul away as a punishment.

Miss Prudência became such an integral part of the village that people couldn't imagine ever being without her. The monsignor had shifted the protagonist of his cautionary warnings, from Dom Carlos to Miss Prudência. She was now his new foe. Once in a while, she would visit him just to engage in a battle of wills and would leave his house smiling, satisfied with the debacle, thinking of still other ways to get under his skin.

The monsignor, much to his chagrin, looked forward to their contests and would emerge more exhilarated than exhausted. They both kept mental ledgers of who had won each clash of wills—more shouting matches than reasoned debates. Recognizing her sharp knock on the door, he would, with a grimace, tell Catarina, "That woman is here again. I'm going to pulverize her today! Boil some tea!" In his running battle with Miss Prudência, he was most tested when she attacked the bishop. While the monsignor and Miss Prudência without fail took opposite sides in their battle of wits, it was mighty hard for him to mount a credible defense of the bishop. The monsignor had had many enemies, but none like the bishop. His concerted effort to please the bishop had been a losing battle and he was growing tired and resentful. Sometimes he found himself fantasizing punching the bishop right in the nose, just like Dona Mafalda had done to him.

The women of the village were hurting without Lazarus, Emanuel and Dom Carlos. Silently, they resented Angela for chasing them away. They gave her sour looks and the evil eye—"You will never again be loved!" they murmured when Angela went by.

Maria Gomes had asked the women in the village, "Have you cursed my daughter?"

The women denied hate, but confessed to being upset with Angela—that girl was greedy, she consumed three beautiful men. Those men belonged to all of them, not just to Angela, but Angela had driven them away. Yes, they did resent her.

Regina, Maria Gomes and Rosa burned sage in the garden every week to scare off evil spirits that were keeping those three precious men away. Maria Gomes went to spiritualists in the city to lift the evil eye from her daughter. Angela was always finding garlic and other evil cleansing herbs in the pockets of her clothes.

"There's no such thing as an evil eye!" Angela said full of frustration as she patted herself down for bundles of strange-smelling herbs.

"Of course, there is!" Rosa refuted. "You, Dona Mafalda and Miss Prudência, with your fancy ways, call it something else."

"Karma," Angela said.

When Angela's fig tree died for no apparent reason, when her grapes shriveled and fell off the vine with mold or mildew, when Dalia lost all her feathers and couldn't eat or drink for days, when Nixon had a terrible case of pink eye, the villagers exchanged knowing looks—evil eye. Even those who got too close to Angela were ensnarled by the black cloud of evil eye. The typewriter salesman too had fallen in love with the strange widow, and one evening he fell off his legs, as if shot, and broke his foot—just like that.

"I told you that you were going to get hurt," Rosa admonished. "Who knows, you may very well die the next time you look at Angela."

Even the almighty Hercules ate a poisoned mouse and could hardly walk. He hid in the chimney room, away from all eyes because he could hardly bite anybody and he had a reputation to uphold. His greatest humiliation was when a new lodger came to the house and he was about to bite his ankle when he threw up a hair ball in the middle of the kitchen, then fell on his face exhausted. No amount of sage burning was going to help with the evil eye.

Every day those who knew Angela searched for signs of transformation brought about by a difficult decision—but to no avail. Angela didn't know what to do about the men she loved, and so she waited.

She waited quietly at night for her soul to whisper an answer. She waited in the empty church during the day, when everyone else was engaged in their daily chores. She stared at Jesus crucified, who seemed indifferent to her confusion and cared only about the glory of His suffering.

"Please, Jesus, do something useful!" she said with despair, "Tell me what I should do!"

She waited for signs in everything and even made bets with herself: "If we have sun for three days in a row, it's a sign that I must..."

Often she accused God for giving her such a mercenary heart. "If I love three men, why do I have to choose only one? It's your fault! You, who claim to be infallible, you failed when you created the human heart!"

Certainty came to her one night while lying in bed with moonlight streaming in.

She knew.

She knew that her love for Lazarus, Dom Carlos and Emanuel was special. She knew that she'd been blessed with their love and her heart burst with gratitude.

And it was clear.

She got up, lit a lamp, took out the paper and the inkwell and started to write the most important letter of her life.

Oh my beloved...

CPSIA information can be obtained
at www.ICGtesting.com
Printed in the USA
LVHW041155171120
671900LV00005B/292